ADY 2

D0389604

FROGSKIN
AND
MUTTONFAT

A Mystery
by
Carol Caverly

A Write Way Publishing Book

Prologue

Sheila Rides Horse lay on the cot in her small room at the back of the house, her head propped up with three thin, lumpy bed pillows, the tattered quilt scrunched down around her ankles where she had pushed it to avoid the heat. She wasn't asleep. She was sure she wasn't asleep, but the walls of her narrow room were disappearing. She was outside, sitting on a rock. She could feel the hard ridges and uneven protuberances digging into her soft buttocks. Her large bare feet splayed firmly on the ground in front of her.

Her thoughts stretched out into gossamer threads that sucked up the night scents, tangled with the sharp breeze, and searched for the unusual. A meaning. A message. She wasn't frightened. She had done this before, knew how to hang on to that one piece of reality that would keep her safe.

She focused on something between her feet. A plant? A rock? Her eyes caressed the odd shape, trying to know it, but she was puzzled. The thing had a peachy glow that spoke of succulence, yet its branches ... Yes, branches. A bush, a shrub of some kind. She clung to her thoughts, gripping their solidity to ward off the sweet, fuzzy haze that shredded reason.

Then the bush began to move. Pulsing with life, the branches writhed, swayed and began to reach for her. Flesh-colored, but hard as stone, the tendrils brushed her legs, curled around her arms, stretched to her neck, twining, squeezing.

She grabbed frantically for cognition. "Fin ... fingers ..." but mind and breath began to swirl away. The cold, reaching fingers tore at her mouth and reached for eye sockets. With a final burst of terror, she threw her head back and caught a pinprick of light. Clinging to the glow, she willed it closer and closer until it burst into shape. A light bulb hanging from a chain. Her room. Her bed.

"Holy shit!" Sweat poured down her face and neck and between her heavy breasts. She wiped it off with the tail of the ragged T-shirt she wore as a nightgown, then stared at the shirt, surprised to find it soaked through. Impatient, she yanked the clammy shirt over her head and dropped it on the floor, then stood up on rubbery legs.

"What in hell was that all about?" she said, comforted by the sound of her voice. She had had her share of visions, but nothing with that kind of power.

The cards, she thought. I gotta get the cards. Naked, she padded to the sink on the far wall and took down a packet wrapped in a blue velvet cloth from the shelf above.

The cloth dropped to the floor unnoticed and with trembling fingers she began to shuffle the deck. The cards, worn to a limp softness by years of use, calmed her. Holding the deck in both hands, she touched the shuffled pack to her forehead and her heart, then sat on the edge of the bed. Fanning the cards face down on the sheet, she pressed them briefly into the dampness to soak up the fear. Quickly, she gathered them up again and began her spread.

She flicked the cards into patterns with the speed of familiarity, but no matter how she varied the spread the message remained the same: Danger, the Tarot symbols warned her, Anguish, Foolish Decisions, Deception and Sorrow. Always the suit of swords dominated, with its reigning king present.

So all right, she thought, wiping her hand across her face, a man is involved. The King of Swords, a dark-haired man, a man to be feared, avoided, a man who wasn't what he seemed to be.

She gathered the cards and shuffled them again, thoughtfully. Always enigmatic, the cards had their own ways of signaling urgency, demanding attention. Repetition was one of them, reinforcing the message of her vision and that awful clawing bush. Forces were swirling around her. Danger poised, ready to pounce. But from where? What was the meaning of a twining, grasping bush? Danger from the earth? She shook her head, bewildered. She only knew that to ignore the warning would be to her peril.

Heart racing, Sheila did a final three-card cut. Influences. Past, present, future.

There the bastard was again. In the middle, controlling the present, the King of Swords sat on his throne brandishing crossed sabers. No use denying it: he's here now. *Somewhere. A dark-haired man.*

The King was the force. He would cause the chaos indicated by the card to his right, The Tower. Crumbled by a bolt of lightning that threw a man and woman helplessly from the parapet, The Tower was a harbinger of violent, cataclysmic change. Her fingers traced over the lurid pictures on the cards, absorbing the symbols, searching for connections, then moved to the third. The Hanged Man.

He hung upside down by one ankle, the free leg crossing the other at a right angle to form a cross. The hands were hidden behind the back. Helpless. The ancient symbol could mean many things, she knew, but it was always the surrendered one. A life surrendered to habits perhaps, to patterns. Patterns repeated over and over again. But whose life? The king's? Hers? Until she knew more she would have to be vigilant.

The king was the key. She had to find the dark-haired man.

Chapter One

I stood on the crumbling sidewalk in front of the old house and looked around with a wry sense of *deja vu*. Another whorehouse. I was developing a reputation: Thea Barlow, Whorehouse Connoisseur. I lifted my heavy hair off my neck to let the hot breeze dry the perspiration clinging to my skin. I should have worn shorts on the plane, rather than slacks.

Picking up my suitcase, I headed up the stairs of the renovated bordello, or, as the garish sign posted outside the house said:

RAWHIDE WYOMING'S OWN
RACY LADIES BED AND BREAKFAST

Fourth of July bunting draped the fanlit front door. Inside was a small vestibule; an oak table blocked off a narrow hallway beside the staircase and appeared to be used as a registration desk of sorts.

Nobody was around. I let my suitcase drop with a thunk,

hoping to rouse someone. I could hear a low mumble of voices coming from a back room somewhere.

I glanced around. To the right was a good-sized dining room with more seating than I would have expected for a bed and breakfast. Across the hall from the dining area was a sitting room with old, but comfortable-looking furnishings, and softly colored Navaho rugs on the floor.

Racy Ladies might be interesting, but I hadn't come to Rawhide, Wyoming, to write about another whorehouse. I was after bigger quarry this time: Kid Corcoran, Last of the Western Bandits. Web Corcoran had earned his fame in the 'thirties with a series of inept, but nevertheless successful, bank and train robberies throughout Colorado, Utah and Wyoming. The western press, hungry for entertainment during the desperate days of broken banks and dust bowls, launched the small-time criminal into something of a myth. I was eager to interview him. It was going to be a great story.

Then, of course, there was Max. To be honest, Max Holman was the real reason I was in Wyoming again, even though both of us had cloaked the visit with the safe premise of work to be done.

But right now all I wanted was to get into my room. It was ten o'clock in the morning on a blasting hot July day and I had been up since the beginning of time. My patience was at a low ebb.

Placed out of reach on a shelf behind the registration table was one of those round bells you bang for attention. Impatiently, I stretched across the desk. As my fingers grazed the bell a voice bellowed out.

"Bring me some goddamned coffee, I said! Where in hell are you?"

The bell clattered to the floor, but the sound was drowned out by the man's continued roar.

"Get your stupid butt in here, Florie. I—" The words were cut off by one of those raspy, phlegmy coughs that seem as if they will end in death by strangulation.

Steps clattered in response to his noise. I crawled under the table to get the bell.

"Shut up, Grandpa. You're a hateful old man." The woman's voice was low and venomous, but I could hear her plainly. The old man's room had to be on the other side of the hall. "If you think your life is so miserable here, just wait until I ship you out to the nursing home. You'll be sorry you ever came back to this town."

The threat outraged me. He might be an irascible old man, but no one deserved to be spoken to in that manner. I grabbed the bell. As I emerged rear first from under the table, the front door opened and someone came in. From my awkward position I saw two sets of legs, male and female.

But the angry voices coming from the other room held my attention. "Just try, you bitch."

Good for you, I thought, cheering him on. *Fight for yourself.*

More phlegmy coughs. "Some way to treat your own flesh and blood," he whimpered, echoing my sentiments exactly.

I scooted out from under the table and stood, bell in hand. The male half of the newly arrived couple looked at me with a raised eyebrow. He had a gorgeous tan, the kind that had to be worked at, a Ralph Lauren polo shirt, designer jeans, and a rather smarmy look to his handsomeness. I shrugged, put the bell on the table and banged it. The ring was puny, and didn't stand a chance against the argument blasting through the wall.

"I never wanted you in my life," the unseen woman's voice went on. "Why didn't you stay in California? I'm trying to run a business here and you're ruining everything." Her voice broke on what might have been a sob. At least it dropped to a lower register and became a mumble to our ears.

The male newcomer stepped closer to the desk, his eyes bright and avid with interest in the conversation. Snoop, I thought righteously, as if I hadn't been taking it all in myself. The man's wife, or whatever she was (she looked more like a whatever), stood in the middle of the sitting room, eyeing everything with a pinched look of distaste.

"Come on, Gar," she said, petulantly, "let's get out of here. I'm not staying in this dump. We'd be better off at the Best Western."

She was petite and quite pretty, with lovely, soft reddish hair that skimmed her shoulders, but there was a look of rest-less discontent about her, as if nothing ever satisfied her for long. She wore a green silk shorts outfit with a loose tunic and gold accessories that reeked of money. I couldn't imagine that she'd feel any more at home in the Best Western than she did in this rustic place. But then, I was having an attitude problem: I'd taken an instant, if unfair, dislike to both of them. Her whiny bitchiness wasn't making it any better. Nor was his slow, deliberate appraisal of my body, with its accompanying smile indicating I should be all aflutter at his approval. Jerk.

The unseen man's bellow rose again, startling us. "Get me out to the old place, Florie, and I'll leave you alone. Gimme a break—I'm an old man; I want to see the old place again."

"I can't," she said, her voice barely audible.

"Then find someone who can, damn it. What's wrong with that worthless husband of yours? You'll be sorry, girl. I'll make you sorry as hell. All you do is snivel ..."

I'd had enough. When I raised my hand to bang the bell

again, my eavesdropping companion made a move as if to stop me, then, with an unctuous smile, dropped his hand to his side. I gave him a dirty look, hit the clapper repeatedly, and yelled out for good measure. "Anybody home? You've got customers out here."

The argument in the other room stopped abruptly. Silence. Then unintelligible whispering. Finally, a door slammed and footsteps came our way.

I guess I had expected some kind of out-sized virago, possibly with whip in hand, but the woman who appeared was tall and painfully thin with a pathetic caved-in appearance. Thirty something, with only a cute hairdo of bouncy blondish natural curls to save her from looking like a limp, worn-out dishrag.

"Sorry about that, folks," she said with a forced smile. "I didn't realize anyone was here. What can I do for you?"

I held out my hand. "Florie Dunn?" I asked. "I'm Thea Barlow. I have a room reservation."

"Oh, yes." She reached for the reservation book and opened it in front of her. Her facade of chirpy politeness slipped away, and I saw her hand tremble as she thumbed through the pages. Lines of worry creased her forehead and compressed the corners of her eyes. My feelings softened a bit. I knew only too well that old people could be a trial and sometimes a burden, but that was no excuse for threats or abuse.

"Yes, here it is." She straightened with a weary effort, but the smile she gave me was genuine. "For a week. We're so pleased to have you."

"I also spoke to you on the phone, Mrs. Dunn—"

"Florie. Please call me Florie."

"Okay," I said, "Florie it is. I spoke to you about wanting an interview with ..." I let the sentence dwindle off, deciding I didn't want to go into this now with the couple hanging over my shoulder.

Florie looked blank for a minute, then said with a heavy sigh, "Oh, yes. I don't know, now. He ..."

"That's all right, we can talk about it later. Why don't you help these people?"

She handed me a registration form to fill out, then turned to the other couple.

"I'm not staying here, Gar," the redhead said under her breath.

He ignored her. "We'd like a double for at least two nights. Understand you've got great fishing around here."

"We sure do," Florie said, patently eager for another customer. "I'll be glad to get—"

"Where's that goddammed Indian?" The raspy disembodied voice bellowed through the wall again, making us all jump. Thumps sounded, and another roar: "Tell her to bring me some coffee, or I'll get the goddammed stuff myself."

"He's getting up," Florie said. "He shouldn't get up."

The man beside me made an exasperated sound and shoved his half-filled-out form across the desk. "Sorry." He shook his head with a rueful smile. "I think we'll go somewhere else after all. Come on, Trish."

"Look, I'm sorry," Florie said. "It's my grandfather. He's usually not this bad. We're very quiet here. Really."

Despite her pleas, the couple walked out with what I thought was undue haste. Headed for the Best Western, no doubt.

"Shit," Florie said under her breath. "I'll kill that old fart."

She looked up, gave me a phony smile and hurried through her spiel. "Here's your key. You're up the first flight. There are four bedrooms there, all named after the girls who used to ply their trade here. You're in Mavis, to the left of the stairs." The thumping behind the wall began again. "Here's a pamphlet that ex—"

A huge crash followed by a bellow of rage reverberated through the hall. Florie Dunn jerked around with a stricken look. "Oh, God." She turned and ran through the door at the end of the hall.

I hesitated a moment, then ducked under the table and ran after her. The door led to another hallway. I followed Florie into a small bedroom, expecting the worst.

We came to an abrupt halt inside the doorway. An old man sat calmly on the edge of the bed, glaring at us out of angry eyes. A spindly-legged bedside table lay on its side with a lamp, clock radio, ash tray, box of tissues and a variety of other things strewn in a mess across the floor.

"You did that on purpose," Florie said in disgust.

He continued to glare. Florie whirled and left the room.

The old man turned his gaze to me. His blue eyes were small and had the washed-out filmy appearance that comes with age. Even so, there was a shrewdness to them, and I guessed he didn't miss much.

"Who in hell are you?"

"A guest." I said. His khaki trousers and well-worn blue plaid flannel shirt covered a solid, but wiry-looking small frame. No more than five-eight or nine, I guessed. He had one of those round boyish-looking faces that was probably just now showing his real age. A plastic oxygen hose connected to a portable carrier beside the bed dangled around his neck, rather than from his nose.

"Well, don't just stand there, get me my shoes." He unhooked a cane from the headboard and pointed it at a pair of off-brand athletic shoes against the wall, then glared at me again.

I was used to crusty old men, and held back a grin, more

amused than irritated by his over-the-top rudeness. He reminded me of Gramps, or I thought sadly, of the man Gramps had once been.

"Say please," I said.

His mouth twitched a bit, and a gleam of humor flashed briefly behind his eyes. "Service ain't much around here," he mumbled, as if in explanation, or maybe even apology. "Shoes?" he asked sarcastically, pointing at them again. "I got to get a smoke."

The hint of inquiry in his tone was probably as close as he ever came to "please." I relented. Of course, I was also pretty sure I knew who the old guy was.

Web Corcoran, a.k.a. Kid Corcoran, sometimes known as the Nickel Kid. Last of the Western Banditos.

"I have you at a bit of a disadvantage, Mr. Corcoran," I said, as I crossed the room to get his shoes. "I do know who you are. I'm Thea Barlow, an editor for *Western True Adventures* magazine. I called your granddaughter several weeks ago and she said you'd be willing to talk to me. I hope you were a party to that decision, because I think our readers will be really interested in hearing about you. Your exploits brightened a lot of lives back in the depression."

The old newspaper stories were wonderful. One of my favorites involved a bank heist, followed by a Keystone Cop-ish car chase through the streets of a small Utah town. Finally the Kid ditched his car for a saddled horse he snatched from somebody's corral and fled cross-country where the Pinkerton cars couldn't follow, juggling his bags of loot. In the process he—either accidentally or intentionally—tossed one of the bags to a group of boys who'd been following the chase on foot. As it turned out, that bag contained most of the money and the Kid ended up with a haul of not much more than a hundred dollars.

I asked, "Are you familiar with the magazine?"

It was a loaded question. I could see a copy of the latest issue on a stack beside the bed. He harrumphed a bit, but appeared more concerned about pulling one of the objects that littered the floor closer to him. He poked at it with the head of his cane, trying to draw it forward.

"Here. Let me," I said, and picked it up by its handle. It was a knife of some kind, handmade, the long, narrow blade covered by a leather sheath wrapped tightly at the haft with a rawhide strand. I felt sure it would be referred to as a "pig-sticker." A jailhouse remnant? I handed it to him wordlessly.

With a penetrating look, he took the knife and placed it on the bed beside him, then stuffed his feet into his shoes. But when Florie Dunn came back in the room with a mug and carafe of coffee I caught the swift movement of his hand as he shoved the weapon out of sight under his pillow.

Florie didn't notice, her eyes were on the shoes. "What are you doing?" she asked, watching him lace up.

"Getting out of this damned bed for awhile."

"The doctor said no. Not for another day, at least."

"This young lady here is going to take me out on the porch so's I can get a smoke."

Florie's jaw firmed up again and she shot me one of those and-what-business-is-this-of-yours looks. I didn't want to become a part of this battle, or any other between the two of them until I knew more about what was going on.

I raised my hands and grinned at him. "Sorry," I said. "This young lady is not going to do any such thing. I just got here. I'm going up to my room and get unpacked. I'll see you later." I nodded to both of them, and got the hell out of there.

Chapter Two

I lugged my suitcase up the staircase, stopping to catch my breath on the first landing. The thing weighed a ton. I was pooped. All I wanted was to get settled in my room and relax a bit. The flight from Chicago to Casper, Wyoming, had left during the wee hours of the morning. From Casper I'd caught a puddle-jumper, laughably called the Antelope Airlines, piloted by a man—a kid, it seemed—wearing jeans and a John Deere cap.

On the ground in Rawhide, the pilot became a *gratis* taxi driver and brought me into town in a twenty-year-old pickup truck with a loose steering wheel and a hole in the gas tank. We only had to stop once while he raced around and filled the tank from a gas can he carried in the back. I soon learned his name was Kendall. He was twenty-five, not the fourteen he looked, and he sure as hell hoped that I was going to the rodeo that night 'cause he was all set to ride a saddle bronc and if he won top money he might put it into this here truck, but probably wouldn't 'cause he much preferred to fly any-how. Sweet as he was, neither of the rides I'd had with Kendall were my most favorite things in the world. I felt fortunate to be let off at Racy Ladies in one piece.

I struggled up the rest of the stairs and looked around. Each of the four rooms had a name scrolled on the door enlivened with a fancy gilt border. I found mine, Mavis, but was a bit envious of the room opposite, named Hard-Nosed Lu. She sounded much more venturesome. Lucky was next to me on the right and Jenny Frisco on the left. I hoped we didn't all share the bathroom that was situated between Jenny and the unfortunate Lu.

A large bulletin board with stuff tacked on it hung on the wall next to the bathroom, and tucked around the corner from the stairwell was an archway with another flight of stairs to either more rooms above, or storage space. Worth investigating at another time, perhaps.

My bedroom was fine, even though the air conditioner turned out to be one of those cheap rattly things stuck in a window. I turned it on, hoping for the best as it wheezed to life.

I tossed the key and brochures I'd been given onto the dresser and inspected an old photograph hanging on the wall beside the mirror. The woman pictured wore a long dress with tight sleeves and held a parasol demurely over her shoulder. She looked prim and crabby, but maybe it was just the tight corsets getting to her. *Mavis Perkins*, the placard underneath said, *came to Rawhide with the railroads*. Looked like a pretty tough cookie to me.

To my delight, I didn't have to share the bath down the hall. I had my own. No shower, but a wonderful old enamel tub with feet.

I put my suitcase on the bed and unzipped it. I had a couple of hours before Max was supposed to meet me here.

An independent oilman and geologist, he was off sitting a well somewhere in the boonies.

"The West goes wild on the Fourth of July!" Max's fax had said. "Steers, sheep, pigs and cowboys, including yours truly, cavort at Wild West Days in Rawhide, Wyoming. Will you come?" He had followed up that message with a phone call and a kicker: The town's most notorious son, Web Corcoran, a.k.a. Kid Corcoran, or the Nickel Kid, had returned to Rawhide after a long stay in a California penitentiary. Max knew his story would be prime fodder for *Western True Adventures* and of great interest to me.

He was right. I was always on the lookout for interesting material. There's not much new to be said about the Old West. *Western True Adventures* is a pulp magazine aimed at a small but faithful audience interested in all the minutia of history to be gleaned about the old, and not so old, Wild West. Max knew the presence of Web Corcoran, and even the Racy Ladies brothel turned bed-and-breakfast, another possible story, would be enticements.

Of course, all of this was totally immaterial and came under the heading of obfuscation. Both Max and I knew that the real reason for this visit was to decide, once and for all, if there was a spark worth fanning in what had once been a hot and steamy relationship.

I'd met Max on my first trip to Wyoming. It seemed like a hundred years ago. In fact, it was only three. I had just been hired at the magazine and was working on my first project, the history of an old whorehouse called Halfway Halt. At that time I was quite desperate to prove myself a success at something, anything, so the new job took precedence over everything else. When the project was finished I went back to Chicago.

Max and I maintained our relationship pretty well for over a year. At that time his business brought him closer to Chicago and frequent visits were possible. But when his oil prospecting turned back to Wyoming and California, things became more difficult. A blaze like that which roared between Max and me is hard to tend long distance. A few smoldering embers was all that remained at this point, and we had both started seeing other people, though we didn't talk about it much. We hadn't seen each other for close to eight months. The time had come to decide whether we needed a bellows for fanning, or a bucket of water.

On one hand, I was looking forward to seeing Max again, on the other, I thought it pretty pathetic, or perhaps prophetic, that I couldn't quite remember what he looked like. Something that would soon be remedied.

In the meantime, I was dying of thirst. I remembered seeing some kind of a shop across the street. If they didn't have a cold drink, surely it wouldn't be difficult to find one somewhere else.

I unpacked a few things and put them in the odd little closets tucked in corners and under the eaves, then went out into the hallway. A girl loaded down with baggage trudged up the stairs. I waited at the top while she maneuvered up the last few steps.

She wore spike-heeled granny boots laced up her ankles, a teeny-tiny, dark flowered chiffon skirt that just flirted with the idea of covering her butt, and a sleeveless low-cut latex top that pushed her boobs into alarming prominence. A fat rose pinned back the brim of a squishy hat pulled low on her forehead.

"Jeez," she said, hitching the strap of an over-large duffel bag back in place on her shoulder. "You'd think they'd have a bellboy or something."

She let an enormous camera bag that hung from her other shoulder slide to the floor and juggled the purse, newspapers, tote and briefcase as she looked around.

"Whoa!" she said with delight. "The rooms really are named. Where's Hard-Nosed Lu? That's me. Who're you?"

She had a pixie face with astonishing blue eyes and a wide smile. Tiny, twenty and adorable, I thought, with the wistful twinge of a thirty-two-year old.

"I'm Mavis," I said, gesturing at the label on my door. "Otherwise known as Thea Barlow. I think you've got the best of it; Mavis sounds kind of prim and mousy to me."

"Anybody in these other rooms?"

"I don't know, I just got here."

"Well, I can't imagine there're waiting lines for anything in a jerky town like this. God, talk about nowhere." She eyed my linen slacks and silk shirt. "What are you doing here?" she asked bluntly. "You don't look like your regular Joe Blow tourist to me." She tried to slide the camera bag towards her door with her foot, then the notebook and newspapers slid, and the juggling began again.

"Here, let me help." I picked up the heavy camera bag. "You a photographer?" I asked, and set it down in front of her door.

"Yeah, kind of. At least I'm heading that way. I'm a reporter, here for a story." Her face lit up with pride.

"Oh, really? What about?"

Maybe my birds-of-a-feather interest came across too aggressively for her. The big blue eyes narrowed, flitted around the hallway and brushed over the bulletin board hanging by the bathroom door. A poster featuring a bucking bronco announced in big letters a weekend of rodeo events, craft exhibits and a free buffalo barbecue.

"Small town rodeos and celebrations," she said, obviously plucking the idea from the poster. "What about you?"

She was so patently suspicious of me and my motives that I wanted to laugh. Lois Lane, hot on the trail of a fast-breaking story. There couldn't be more than one big news item in a town the size of Rawhide; she had to be after Web Corcoran, too. But why she was afraid someone might scoop her was beyond me. Kid Corcoran's seedy past wasn't a hot item. A few of my competitors would be interested in his story, but we were used to rehashing the same material. If she wanted to sell to them, or anyone else for that matter, it wouldn't bother me.

Unfortunately, I can never resist a good toss in the game of one-upmanship. "Small world," I said as ingenuously as she. "I'm here for a story, too. Ever heard of Kid Corcoran? He was one of the last of the old-time bank and train robbers. He might make a more interesting article than small town rodeos. I could probably arrange an interview for you if you're interested."

Her look of dropped-mouth surprise changed quickly to suspicion and anger. Before she had a chance to reply, I gave her a lofty wave, batted my baby browns, and trotted down the stairs, hot on the trail of some iced tea. But I must admit, my curiosity was piqued. I had done my homework. Kid Corcoran was no Butch Cassidy, or even a Bill Carlyle, more truly designated Last of the Train Robbers. Kid Corcoran was a very, very small blip on the edge of Western history. None of the newspapers or magazines that might be interested in him, including ours, paid writers enough money to be worth a plane ticket from very far away. And young Lois Lane certainly didn't look like she was from around here.

Had I missed something? Was there more to the mildly infamous Kid than I was aware of?

***

Outside, I took a quick look at some For Sale items on the porch. A wicker chair and potted geranium sat on one side of the front door. On the other, a screened-in porch ran the length of the house. At its far end was one of those fabulous-to-look-at but perilous-to-sit-on peacock chairs. Craft items were scattered artistically on and around a bench and two small tables close beside it. Too much country charm for me.

I went down the front steps. The ever-present Wyoming wind did nothing to cool the heat, but did manage to throw copious amounts of dirt and debris through the air, depositing a fine coat of dust on everything in sight, including an open Jeep badly parked at the curb. I resisted the urge to write something rude on the fender and crossed the street, picking my way around raised ribbons of tar bubbles.

I had my eye on a small park-like area about half a block down and across from Racy Ladies. An old depot building, now painted bright blue and turned into a gift shop, sat on a patch of green grass shaded by two huge cottonwood trees. Tubs of slightly parched, but still brilliant petunias flanked the front door. Off to one side was some kind of a restored train engine on display. A veritable oasis on a street otherwise filled with drab remnants of unrenovated history.

A sign above the store's entrance said Wyoming Jade, then in smaller print underneath: Rocks, Minerals, Gifts, Refreshments. A bell jangled when I opened the door. The inside was bright and airy, not overcrowded with tourist junk. A woman with a frizzy, graying perm and a bright smile sat on a high stool behind a counter at the far end of the store.

"Hello, there," she said. "What can I do for you?"

"Iced tea would be wonderful if you have some."

"Of course I do, honey." She jumped down and bustled around getting a large paper cup and ice. I could see why she liked a high stool. She was short, five-one or -two at the most, but filled with energy and good-natured chatter.

"Sure is hot out there. Where you from?"

"Chicago."

She chuckled. "You're a long ways from home." She poured tea from a glass jug into the cup and handed it to me. "Fresh sun tea. I make gallons of it every day. Sell more of it than that nasty old soda pop, but don't tell Pepsi I said so." The words burbled out of her like a warm spring. "You just going through town, or staying awhile?"

The bell over the door jangled again. An elderly couple festooned with cameras strolled in. Sipping my tea, I wandered off to look at the merchandise while the newcomers received the big greeting.

"Hello, there. Where you folks from? What can I do for you?" Tourism was alive and well in Wyoming.

The shelves held the usual tourist gimcracks, as well as some quite nice gift items, but I was drawn to the opposite end of the shop where there were trays of polished agates, rough hunks of turquoise, and rows of mineral specimens.

A locked glass case sat against the wall and obviously contained the more expensive items. A hand-lettered sign on the top shelf said Wyoming Jade, but an exquisite set of four widely flared wine glasses on the second shelf immediately caught my eye. Each was a different color: pink lightly veined with threads of green; white; pale green; and a dense shimmering black. The bowls were translucent with the delicacy of the finest porcelain.

"Nice, aren't they?" the bouncy little woman said, appearing magically beside me.

"Gorgeous. What are they made of?"

"Jade," she said, mildly incredulous, as if I should have known. "Everything in the case is jade, honey. Wyoming jade."

"Wyoming? What do you mean?"

"Why, that it was found here."

"But surely—" I said, gesturing at an intricately carved vase on another shelf and a grouping of kimono clad figurines. "Surely those are Chinese."

"They were carved in China, but the jade was found right here, by my daddy, in fact. Just about fifty miles up on Soda Creek."

"Is it *real* jade?"

She gave a little snort. "You bet your life it is."

"I'm sorry," I apologized, "I didn't mean to refute you; I'm just amazed, is all. I've always associated jade with the orient, and museums, and stuffy old mansions, not—"

"Wyoming? Well, honey, some of the finest jade in the world is, or was, found in Wyoming. All of this, of course, is top gem quality," she said, indicating everything in the case. "And Wyoming's the only place where you find the real black jade." She took a full ring of keys from her pocket. "Here, let me show you."

She unlocked the case, took out the black goblet and handed it to me. The bowl was eggshell thin.

She said, "Hold it up to the light. Thin as it is you can't see a trace of green. Russia's got some jade they call black, but it's really a dark, dark green. You only find this quality here in Wyoming. It's prized all over the world."

I checked the price on the bottom and gasped. "Is that for the set?"

"No, honey," she said with a broad grin. "That's just for that black beauty. They're each priced separately. A man from

Gumps was here a while back and offered me a pretty penny for the set, but I'm not quite ready to give them up yet."

She put the goblet back with its mates and took out a strand of apple green beads. She placed them against my cheek. They felt like drops of ice on my overheated skin. "You can wear jade beads on your bare skin all day and they'll still feel cool. Don't absorb body heat like other things might."

She returned the beads to the case, and I picked up a hunk of rock from the top shelf and examined it with curiosity. There was nothing pretty about it.

"That's a piece of rough, honey. That's how it's found in the wild."

"But how would you know it's jade?"

"You soon get the feel for it. It all has this ugly rind on it, unless it's been weathered away by water. But out in the field it usually doesn't look like nothing. You have to knock a piece off and see what's inside, or touch it to a grindstone." She took the rock from my hand and turned it over. On the bottom was a bright green polished spot. "That's a good forest green, top quality. Worth two, three hundred dollars."

"And you can just go pick this stuff up?"

"No, no." She chuckled. Her small blue eyes disappeared when she laughed, pushed shut by her plump, rosy cheeks. "Not anymore. It's pretty much picked over. Back when I was a kid we used to go jade hunting every weekend. The whole family. We'd take a pickup truck and a couple of tents. Everybody in town'd be out in the fields looking for the best spot, staking claims, you name it. Jade fever. You could find boulders then, fifteen hundred pounds or more. Trying to get them home was something else." She slapped her knee, laughing brightly at the memory. "Once found, you ran the risk of having someone steal it out from under your nose, particularly if you had to leave to get equipment to move a big piece. Worth a fortune. All kinds of skullduggery went on. But it was sure exciting."

"This is fascinating. I had no idea ..."

"This is only a small portion of Daddy's jade. I've got the best stuff put away, and quite a bit of my own, too."

"I'd love to see more. I'm kind of pressed for time right now, but I'd love to come back."

"You're staying in town then?"

"Yes. As a matter of fact, I'm right across the street at Racy Ladies."

"You're staying *there?*" Her boundless good humor disappeared and she gave me a hard look.

"Is there something wrong with the Racy Ladies?"

She gave a snort of disgust. "Well, Rocky Dunn's all right I guess, but Florie, I'd sure like to know where she got the money to buy that place. And don't turn your back on that kid. He'd slit his mother's throat if he had a chance."

"What kid?" I asked uncertainly.

"Web Corcoran."

The eighty-year-old kid. "Kid Corcoran?"

"Who else? He—"

The bell jangled again and a voice boomed through the store. "Hey, Hildy. What's up? I got news." A big beefy man burst through the door, spotted us, and charged forward.

"Watch that shelf, Buster, you old fool."

Everything about the man was oversized. Tall, with ham hands, a large bulbous nose and a huge belly that preceded him like the prow of a ship. He swept off an enormous cowboy hat, revealing a bald head with a fringe of gray hair that traveled from ear to ear at the base of his skull. His elbow hit a rack of postcards and set the stand rocking.

"Watch out," Hildy yelped, steadying the rack. "For God's sake, Buster, you're worse than a bull in a china shop."

"Sorry, but I only got a minute. Finally caught up with Deefy out to Jeffrey City. Could have saved me some lookin' time, though; he's in town this weekend. Doing his mountain man bit at the fairgrounds. Anyways, by God, you were right, Hildy. He said that piece of mutton fat was—"

"I was just showing this young lady Daddy's jade," Hildy cut him off mid-sentence. "She's real interested. She's staying over to Racy Ladies." Obviously, she didn't want his earth-shattering news about mutton fat blurted out in front of a stranger. I held back a grin.

He swung his great bald dome around to look at me. I could practically see his mind—hell-bent on forward action—attempting to shift gears, trying painfully to backtrack.

"This clumsy galoot is Buster Brocheck," Hildy said, by way of introduction, then realized she didn't know my name. She was quicker on her feet than her friend, though, and switched tack nicely. "Buster here knows his jade, too, and has some dandy specimens."

Buster was having problems keeping up. He stared blankly from me to Hildy and back again. He nodded, as if to acknowledge the introduction that hadn't been made, but evidently decided to give up on the rest of it. With a bewildered, shy smile, he ran a hand over his bald pate, and started to back away down the aisle.

"Watch out for those pots, Buster! They cost me a fortune."

He nodded to me again and pointed a finger at Hildy, saying, "I gotta talk to you big time. Okay?"

About *mutton fat*? I thought, this time unable to suppress a smile.

"I'll see you tonight," Hildy answered. "Don't worry."

He went out the door. Wordlessly, she locked up the display case. Evidently my lesson was over.

"So," she said, finally. "I take it you've already run into the Kid. That old bastard's a murdering thief. Why they let him back in this town I'll never know. Some of those snot-nosed kids running the Chamber of Commerce even wanted him to ride in the parade this morning. 'Give our Wild West Days a touch of authenticity,' they said. But not all of us 'round here've got short memories."

"And you're talking about Web Corcoran? Kid Corcoran?"

"You better believe it."

"A murderer?" I asked with some disbelief. "I thought he was just a small-time crook."

She made a disparaging sound. "You must have been reading those old papers. All that newspaper crap was just a bunch of cow pucky. We knew Kid Corcoran around here for what he really was a long time afore the press got hold of him. If you have business with him, you better get it done fast."

"Is he *that* ill?" I said, surprised.

She gave another inelegant snort. "Are you kidding?" she said, her voice filled with bitterness. "Sick or not, that's one man who's not going to die a natural death."

Chapter Three

A sudden spate of customers stopped our conversation, but I definitely wanted to hear more. Were her murderous accusations simply a manner of speaking, or was there something more to them? I hung around the store awhile, purchased a small secondhand book on jade, but the tourists were persistent lookie-Lous. I finally left, figuring I could catch Hildy later in the afternoon.

I knew there were no murders connected to the thefts, robberies and con activities that Corcoran had finally been caught and sent to prison for. Besides, those crimes had all been committed in California. He'd been long gone from his outlaw beginnings in Rawhide by then.

Even so, Hildy's ranting seemed more personal than simple complaints of a morally indignant citizen against an ex-con moving back into the neighborhood. Corcoran, released a year and a half ago, had been in the pen for forty years. How long had he lived in California before that? Whatever Hildy had been so indignant about had to have happened in The Kid's early, myth-making days here in Wyoming. Hildy wasn't old enough herself—somewhere in her sixties, I figured—to have been directly involved with him in the earlier days. She couldn't have been much more than a toddler at the time. Others in her family could have been involved, though, and the tales passed down.

It was senseless to speculate when I could ask some direct questions later. I might even talk to the Kid first. See what he had to say for himself.

I hurried back to Racy Ladies. I didn't want to miss Max. A note stuck on my door said Max Holman had called twice. I was to call him at the number included and could use the phone downstairs in the sitting room.

When I dialed the number some cretin answered whom I could barely understand, but I kept yelling for Max until he finally showed up on the other end of the line. The connection was lousy and kept cutting in and out.

"Thea? Is that you? Where in hell have you been? I've been trying to call you."

I smiled. Yes, this was the Max I remembered. Max could face any adversity life might throw at him—and he'd caught his share—with grit and aplomb, but minor inconveniences irritated the hell out of him.

"Well, hello, yourself. I was out. Where are you?"

"I'm still at the damn rig, and I'm not going to be able to get in for a while. The drilling's going faster than I expected. We're close to a primary zone, and I've got to be here to look at the samples. Are you okay?"

"Yes, I'm fine," I said, trying to ignore a rush of disappointment so strong it took me by surprise.

We spoke a bit longer, hampered by the static and cutting-outs. I told him not to worry, there was plenty for me to do.

I'd take in the rodeo and barbecue, and he said something about getting a car for me and that he'd be here as soon as possible.

"I'm sorry as hell, sweetheart. I'll make it up to you, okay?" he repeated for the third time before we finally hung up.

Ah, true love. Is this a test? Well, I wasn't about to sit around and mope or, for that matter, twiddle my thumbs waiting for Max.

I finished unpacking, and changed into a T-shirt, shorts and Keds. It was one o'clock and I was starving. I locked the door and put the key in my pocket. The locks were the old-fashioned kind with big brass plates on the door and didn't lock automatically when the door was closed, something I'd have to remember.

The house echoed with my footsteps as I trod down the well-worn stairs. As usual, nobody was around downstairs, which heightened the eerie sense of desertion that hung around the old house. I thought momentarily about looking up the Kid for an interview, but my stomach said barbecue was more important. I'd never had buffalo before, and man, was I ready. One humpburger to go! I headed out the front door, then a second thought sent me back inside to the telephone in the sitting room.

Max had said something about a car for me. The details were lost among all the apologies and the bad connection, but a car would be convenient. I wondered what he had in mind. I dialed the number for Max again.

After innumerable rings the phone was answered by the same gracious receptionist I'd had before.

"Yeah?" The line crackled with static.

"Max!" I hollered. "May I speak to Max Holman?"

"Not available. Whaddaya want?"

"What?" I asked, thinking I'd misheard.

"He's fishin'."

"Fishing?" I yelped. "He's gone fishing?"

"That's what I said, lady. You got a message?"

"No." I slammed down the phone. Fishing! I couldn't believe it. Here *I* had traveled hundreds of miles on a stupid little plane, at *his* invitation, and he was too busy to meet me as planned, but had plenty of time to go fishing!

I stomped out of the house, and ate up the few blocks to the main business district at close to a jog. Viewing the small town hoopla with a jaundiced eye, I flew by the sidewalk sale tables and the clerks garbed in various takes on Jesse James or dance hall girls. Banners flapped in the wind. I ignored it all, too busy devising various scenarios by which I'd reduce Max Holman to a sorry piece of repentant manhood.

Having passed the fairgrounds on the way into town from the airport I knew the general direction, and headed for the edge of town. An easy walking distance, or at least a therapeutic one. I gave in to the heat and slowed my pace. By the time I caught up with the crowds who had parked their cars and were headed in the same direction, I actually found myself nodding and smiling at all the friendly people who spoke, thinking they should know me, uncertain why they didn't, but willing to take the blame. I was enormously pleased to be taken as one of them, not the obvious tourist.

A steady stream of cars and trucks, most with horse trailers attached, drove slowly through the fairground entrance. I pushed through the pedestrian gate with my fellow walkers, deftly dodging a very small boy on a very fat pony. Children of all ages and sizes were everywhere, all of them running and screeching with excitement. The adults strolled more casually, one eye on their kids, evidently reveling in the thought of a relaxing day away from the usual chores and a chance to visit with friends. I paused to let a battered old flat-bed truck carrying a country band move slowly through the crowd. STUCKEY BROS. COWBOY RHYTHMS read the banner hanging from the truck's bed. Another announced in bold letters they were STRUMMIN' FOR JESUS. I hoped He wasn't too critical.

I moved on. No one else but me seemed alarmed by all the horseback riders prancing around among everyone else. I headed for the grassy picnic spot where the cooking was taking place, keeping a wary eye out for flying hoofs.

Odors of barbecue and frying potatoes vied wondrously with that of horse and cow. I took a place at the end of the long line, then saw the couple I'd met earlier at Racy Ladies, or at least the male part of the couple, waving at me.

"We saved you a place," the George Hamilton wannabe called with a wide smile. I popped in line with them and eagerly grabbed a plate.

"We meet again," the man said with a chuckle. "I'm Garland Caldwell and this is my wife, Trish."

"Thea Barlow. Thanks for letting me in. I'm starving."

We smiled at each other with the self-consciousness of strangers searching for common conversational ground. I filled the awkward pause with, "Did you get settled in another room all right?"

"Yes. We're at the Cattleman's Inn. Nice rooms."

"With *good* air conditioning," Trish added.

I laughed. "I'll probably envy you in a couple of days. All I've got is one of those window jobs which sounds like it has asthma." They shook their heads pleasantly, as if amazed at my wanting to stay in such a place as Racy Ladies.

"We usually go the bed-and-breakfast route, but that place

didn't seem up to snuff," he said. "You really think you can hack it with that old man?"

"I doubt he'll be a problem. I think we just got there at a bad time."

"I understand he's some kind of ex-con. Have you heard anything about him, or met him yet?"

Again I noticed that eagerness about him, an avid gleam in the eye that implied much more interest than he indicated. Men are indeed bigger gossips than women.

"No," I lied. "I haven't."

"Well," he said, laughing, "I'd watch my back if I were you. You can't be too careful these days. And if it gets too scary over there, I suggest you try the Cattleman's."

"I'll do that," I said. Fat chance.

"Where are you from?" I asked—Trish—I remembered. She looked like a Trish, still flawless and cool-looking in her green silk, while I could feel my hair, dampened with sweat, spronging around doing its own thing.

"Cal—" she began, only to be cut off by her husband.

"Caldonia, Oregon," he finished for her, obviously one of those men who felt he had to control every conversation. "This is our first trip to Wyoming. I understand the fishing and hiking are outstanding."

I nodded noncommittally. He didn't want to know what I thought about fishing at this point.

"We've already got a date with some brown trout set up for tomorrow," Garland Caldwell said. He motioned Trish and me ahead as a server held out sandwiches dripping with rich sauce. I took one on a limp plate and passed on the beans and potato salad.

"*I'm* not going fishing," Trish announced, emphatically plopping a glob of the salad next to her sandwich.

Garland's face darkened with anger. He began to say something, then shut his lips grimly and filled his plate. This had the feel of an old argument, I thought.

"I," Trish said cheerily, fully aware of the effect she was having on her husband, "will go shopping instead." She gave him a taunting smile and licked her fork.

His ill-contained fury seemed excessive to me, as did her delight in provoking it. There was a glitter about her that made me think she enjoyed probing the edges of danger. And where in hell she thought she'd go shopping in Rawhide was beyond me.

We moved out of the line. All the picnic tables were occupied, so we wandered, looking for a place to perch, eating as we went.

A motley group of trucks and trailers sporting huge water tanks filled the open area in front of the large quonset exhibit building. Garland and I sat on a bumper and leaned over our plates. Trish eyed the dusty truck and chose to stand instead.

"Why on earth would they display old stuff like this?" she asked, wrinkling her nose.

Garland looked around. The food had diffused his anger, at least for the moment. He smiled at me and rolled his eyes. "Read the sign," he said with just the slightest amount of sarcasm. Then, to satisfy his own curiosity, he strolled over to the huge poster propped on an easel. "County fire fighting equipment," he said, pointing his fork at the sign. "Shows all the ranches where this stuff is stored."

The buffalo was surprisingly delicious, tender and flavorful. I gobbled up the last bit and dropped the plate into a garbage barrel. Spending an afternoon with this couple wasn't on my agenda. I had enough troubles of my own without witnessing firsthand all the worst things that could happen in a marriage. Thanking them again, I excused myself and entered the cool interior of the exhibit building.

Bake sale tables sat cheek to jowl with those offering craft items, horse equipment, T-shirts, balloons and even a cappuccino cart. I strolled the aisles with enjoyment; I hadn't been to anything like this since I was a kid.

At the end of the second aisle, tacked on the wall above a card table covered with a royal blue velvet cloth, was a sign that said *FORTUNES TOLD; TAROT READINGS $7.00.* The sign featured the regulation picture of a gypsy with a crystal ball, but beneath it sat an Indian woman, thoughtfully shuffling the cards and watching the crowd. I smiled. A North American Indian reading Tarot cards. It struck me as delightfully incongruous.

She was a large, big-boned woman. Heavyset rather than overweight, with beautiful, golden-bronze skin stretched smoothly over the flat planes of her homely face. She wore a traditional fringed, deerskin dress with a headband and eagle feather. Beneath the table I could see well-worn running shoes on her feet. She could have been anywhere from thirty to sixty as far as I could tell.

As I watched, two giggling school girls ran up to her table.

"Sheila, Sheila," one of them squealed. "You've gotta tell us if Tiny Butler's going to ask one of us to the dance. Can you read us both together? Please, please?"

With a jerk of her head, the woman motioned them to the chair. The girls fished wadded up bills from their jeans pockets, then with another burst of giggles precariously shared the metal folding chair.

I moved to an adjacent booth, pretending to be interested in the belts, buckles, hatbands, and everything else made out of rattlesnake skin. Yuck.

I couldn't hear the reading, but it seemed to delight the girls, who greeted each statement with more squeals of excitement. Nor was I standing close enough to be considered a kibitzer, but at one point the Indian woman caught my gaze and held it for an uncomfortable moment. She didn't return my automatic smile. Not that her look was unfriendly, just expressionless. The stereotypical taciturn Indian, I thought happily, still tickled by the idea of an Indian reading Tarot, that most ancient of medieval European necromancy. And why not?

I'd never had a reading before. What a hoot it would be to get one from this woman, I thought. But I'd missed my chance. Three other women were now waiting in line. So when the girls jumped up and ran off, I turned away, thinking I'd check the line later.

"You!"

I looked over my shoulder. The Indian woman jerked her head at the chair in front of her table. "You wanted a reading?"

"Well, yes," I said, glancing at those waiting. I'd already butted into one line today.

She motioned at the chair, throwing, "She was next," at the others.

So who was I to complain? I sat.

She shuffled the cards loosely and looked me over, seemingly taking in every pore of my face. "I saw you watching."

If I had any thoughts of political correctness, I forgot them. "An Indian reading Tarot cards intrigued me."

"What did you expect? Burnt eagle feathers?"

I laughed. "No."

"You pay your money, I'll read anything you want. Tea leaves, handwriting, horse droppings, you name it. But Tarot is mine."

"The cards are fine, they just didn't seem to go with your ... uh ..." I wasn't sure whether to call it a dress or a costume. Whatever it was, the soft skins and fancy beadwork were beautiful, and I told her so.

A small smile of pleasure twitched her mouth. "It's not real."

"What?"

"Not authentic. I made it myself." She shrugged. "It's good for business; the tourists expect it."

"I like it, anyway," I said. "How long have you been reading the cards?"

"Thirty years. I know them well."

"Who taught you?" It still seemed amazing to me.

Her answer—"A nun taught me at school"—left me finally speechless.

"What's your question?" she asked. "What do you want to know? Remember I'm not a doctor or a shrink." She did a quick three-card layout, but she was looking at me again, my face, not the cards. There was a stillness about her, her eyes a bit out of focus as they plumbed mine. I suddenly felt exposed and vulnerable.

"No special question," I said nervously. "Umm ... Just what do you see ahead for me, I guess. That kind of thing." But she wasn't listening. Her gaze had dropped to the three cards in front of her. A frown creased her smooth brow.

Though I know a little about Tarot, I'm certainly not familiar with all the cards and their symbolism. But of the three cards face up in front of her—a brick tower ripped apart by a lightning bolt; a man on a throne—the third card was recognizable by anyone. A grinning skeleton sweeping the earth with a scythe. The Grim Reaper. Death.

Chapter Four

A quiver of fear raced up my spine. *Gramps*! I thought, so suffused with a rush of sorrow that I almost missed the startled glance given to me by the Indian woman. She gathered the cards quickly, shuffled, laid out three more, gathered them again and repeated the process with a more complicated spread. Her fingers worked so quickly I couldn't follow what she was doing, or what cards were turning up. Clearly, she had forgotten me and was lost in her work.

"What is it?" I asked. "What do you see? Wasn't that the Death card?"

She shuffled again, thoroughly, deliberately, but didn't answer my question.

When she looked at me again, her face was as emotionless as before, but tiny beads of sweat hovered above her lips. She touched the pack to my forehead, then handed the cards to me.

She said, "You shuffle."

I did.

"The Death card can mean many things," she said dismissively. "Cut the pack three times to the left." Then, "Pick them up right to left. Cut them again into three."

She directed me to put the three sections in front of her in a vertical row. Only then did she touch them. With a quick move of her hand she spread each pile into a row. Only the edges of the cards were visible, yet she seemed able to read them this way as well. She studied them, shook her head, and muttered under her breath.

"What is it?" I asked impatiently.

She seemed surprised that I was still there. Forcing her face into a stiff smile, she said, "This is the past, the present, the future," gesturing at each row, top to bottom.

She began to point to different cards and delivered the blandest of interpretations, even at one point throwing in that old saw "I see you taking a trip over water." I knew she was making it all up, that it had nothing to do with what she really saw in the cards.

"Please," I said, "tell me about the Death card. What does it mean?" All I could think about was Gramps, the light of my life. While Mom and Dad earned a living Gramps saw that my brother and I got to all the fun things in life. Carnivals, zoos, swimming pools and ice cream parlors. I knew death was inevitable, but I couldn't bear watching the death of his spirit. I wanted a miracle, to see him whole again, grumping around like Web Corcoran, irascible, but alive and fighting. I couldn't bear to give him up.

"Tarot speaks in symbols. The Death card talks of transitions, sometimes physical, most often not." She paused briefly, then said, "I haven't seen you around before. You new in town?"

"Yes," I answered warily.

"Tourist?"

"Not exactly."

She looked at me expectantly, obviously wanting more details.

"I'm visiting friends."

"Who?"

I began to wonder if this were some kind of act, a con man's lure, leading me into more readings, or more money. I wasn't getting much for my money.

"Look," I said impatiently, "aren't you supposed to be telling me things like I'll meet a tall dark stranger?"

Her head jerked back in surprise. Her eyes bored into mine. She leaned forward and tapped the last card in the middle row. "This," she said with startling intensity, "is the card to worry about. The King of Swords. A man with dark hair. Up to no good. Who did you come here to see?"

"Max Holman," I answered, caught up in her urgency.

"Oh."

"You know him?"

She said, "I know who he is. Where are you staying?"

"Racy Ladies."

The look of alarm that flashed across her face frightened me. I jumped on it.

"Why does that bother you? What's wrong with Racy Ladies?"

"I don't know." She gathered up the cards.

"Wait a minute. You haven't told me anything yet. Don't I get a reading?"

She shook her head. "Can't tell if it's you or me influencing the cards. Just listen to me; pay attention. This"—she gestured to the table top where the cards had been spread—"this is not about your grandfather. Be watchful."

"About what?" A tiny *frisson* tightened the skin on the back of my neck.

She shrugged. "No charge. See me tomorrow; I'll try again."

"Where will I find you? What's your name?"

I caught the first name, Sheila, but the rest was a muddle. I asked for a repeat. It sounded like Rishearse.

"I'm sorry, would you spell the last name?" I wanted to be sure I could find her again.

She raised an eyebrow, then spoke very slowly, as if to an idiot. "Rides Horse. R-I-D-E-S and you know how to spell horse."

She was right, I felt like an idiot. And dismissed. Another woman had been motioned into the chair. I stood there a moment, as if paralyzed. A part of me wanted to stay and see if this next person got a successful reading, but only a very small part. I forced myself to turn and walk away. Her words seemed to follow me, floating in the air, whispering in my ears: "Watchful. Be watchful."

Stepping back out into the sun and heat, I shivered. With relief, I thought, trying to shake off the foreboding sense of unease the Tarot reading had given me. She's a charlatan, I told myself sternly, and I had allowed her to play me like the greenest of greenhorns. Angry at myself, and a bit humiliated, I put the Indian woman out of my mind.

A voice droned over the loudspeaker. *"This will be the last group of calf-ropers, folks, before the main show begins. Let's give these hardworking cowpokes a big hand."*

I stopped a moment to watch three young boys gathered around a man on a big chestnut-colored horse. He wore deer-skins, dark with use, and a coonskin hat. A pet fox lounged across his lap, indifferently letting the boys scratch his ears. I couldn't resist; I joined them and reached out my hand, as well. The fox lifted his head and eyed me brightly, maneuvering a bit so my fingers landed on what must have been a particularly itchy spot behind his right ear.

"How old is he?" I asked, delighted.

"'Bout four years, I reckon," the man said with a grin that revealed brown broken teeth and lots of gaps where others should have been. "Got him as a pup." Greasy gray hair straggled from beneath the cap and an unpleasant odor that couldn't all be blamed on the fox hung around him.

The horse shifted restlessly. I backed cautiously away, gave the man a smile of appreciation, and joined the milling crowd drifting towards the rodeo arena.

A gap opened ahead of me and I glimpsed the small figure of a man standing by the fence in front of the grandstand. He held something in his right hand. The gap closed before the image actually registered in my brain: Web Corcoran carrying his oxygen unit. I'd bet my life on it.

Quickening my step, I dodged around the large family group blocking my way. A casual chat with the Kid might be much more revealing than a formal interview with a tape recorder and notebook.

"Hey there," a voice called and a hand gripped my shoulder.

I didn't recognize him at first, probably because of the hat. The brim of the straw cowboy hat was folded tight to the crown on both sides, and sharply down fore and aft. It looked to be at least ten years old.

"Remember me?" he said. "Kendall Hauser. I flew you in that little screamer from Casper this morning."

The pilot. "Well, hi, Kendall," I said. "Who's your friend?" A creamy, golden-colored unsaddled horse with spots on his rear trailed behind him, nose bent to the ground, rather stupidly looking for something to eat in the loose dirt.

"This is Clover."

"Clover? Sounds more like a cow."

He grinned and jerked at the rein held loosely in his hand. "Look up here, Clover, and say hello to the lady." The horse obediently raised his head and shook his beautiful white mane. We eyed each other warily. "Best ropin' horse in the county," he said. Then with the engaging grin that was banishing my blues, "Where's the boyfriend?"

I'd told him about coming to see Max Holman when we were flying up here.

"I guess he's sitting an oil well that's about to burst, or some fool thing. He'll be in later tonight, or in the morning."

"Well, come on then. Join me. I've got the best seat in the house. You don't want to sit in the stands anyway, that's for weenies. And I need a hot-looking woman to cheer me on."

He threw the reins over Clover's neck and in a sleek movement was up on the horse's bare back. He bent over, slid his hand under and around my left arm and grabbed my wrist.

"Step on my foot," he said.

"No, really," I began, "I can't—"

With amazing strength, he lifted me off the ground. I grabbed for his shirt, one of my flailing feet stepped on his braced foot and I landed with a thud right where he wanted me: astraddle behind him. It was a miracle.

"Hang on," he said needlessly. He walked the horse skillfully through the people headed for the grandstand, speaking to most of them. The old-timer with the pet fox trotted past us, heading for the dirt track behind the grandstand. He nodded, either at me or Kendall.

I nodded back. "Who's the guy with the fox?" I asked.

Kendall looked around and spotted him. "Oh," he said with a laugh. "That's old Deefy Hammersmith. Quite a character. He's been dressing up and coming to fairs and rodeos since I was a kid."

The view from my new perch was great. The small man I'd seen—if it had been Kid Corcoran—was no longer by the fence, but as we cleared the crush and headed behind the grandstand, I saw Garland and Trish Caldwell again. They were in the midst of a furious fight. He had a grip on her arm and a finger jabbing at her nose, emphasizing every word that poured from his mouth. As I watched, she pulled away, spat a few words back at him, and stalked off. Any effect she might have hoped to make was seriously spoiled by her having to stop every few feet to shake dirt from her pretty little gold sandals.

What were they fighting about? Had she finally goaded him beyond his limit of control? Unwillingly a thought flashed through my mind: the King of Swords; a man with dark hair. Garland Caldwell wore his close-to-black hair stylishly slicked back from his forehead.

The horse lurched into a faster pace, grabbing my attention. I began to bounce and slide with abandon. As we cleared the far side of the arena I saw the man in the coonskin cap standing by the fence talking to Kid Corcoran. So the Kid was here. I was glad for that.

"You okay?" Kendall hollered back at me. I nodded, which of course he couldn't see. He reached back with his free hand to steady me with a firm grip on my thigh, then picked up the pace another notch. Though faster, the ride was smoother. We took off on the racetrack, flying around the far end of the arena. I wrapped my arms around Kendall's middle and found myself thrilled with a heady mixture of exhilaration and danger—until I recognized the refrain running through my mind in time to the insistent beat of the horse's hooves against the dirt: *Death rides a pale horse. Death rides a pale horse.*

Chapter Five

Damn the Tarot reader! I thought, as we slowed to a bone-jarring trot, I will *not* let her ruin my day. Besides, she said it wasn't about Gramps, so what did I have to worry about? But hey, I hadn't said anything to the Indian woman about Gramps, had I? How had she known I was worried about him?

Kendall pulled Clover to a stop by the back of a battered pickup I remembered only too well. He threw a leg forward over the horse's head and slid to the ground, then held his arms out to me. I disembarked much less gracefully.

"All right," he said, with his usual enthusiasm. "How'd you like that?"

I laughed, only too glad to set aside my thoughts about the Tarot reader. I didn't believe in all that stuff anyway. "Actually," I said, "it was an improvement over the plane, and the truck." I even patted the horse's nose and told him he didn't look the least bit like a cow.

I looked around. On this side of the arena cars, pickups and four-wheel-drives were parked nose-in to the fence with enough room left in front for a blanket to be spread on the ground. Everyone was well settled-in with picnic lunches, enjoying the show. Farther down, the flat-bed truck had parked in a large open area, and the band was playing for a group of square dancers. Kendall threw Clover's reins loosely around the truck's bumper, got a small cooler from the cab of the truck and produced a couple of Coors. He opened one, handed it to me, and took the other for himself. Beer is not always my drink of choice, but there are times when there is nothing better. Like on a hot, hot day with the sun burning your nose, and flying dust scouring your skin, and the air filled with pungent smells of animals, hay and straw. To hell with gloom and doom, I thought, and drank deeply.

"Whooee, that tastes good!" Kendall said, echoing my sentiments. He grabbed my hand. "Come on, let's go to the chutes and I'll show you the bronc I drew to ride. I need to get a good look at the old buzzard."

We wove our way to the maze of corrals that held the animals for the upcoming events. Horses and cowboys were everywhere; Kendall knew them all.

"There's Jimmy," Kendall said. "He's my partner. We own Clover together." He pointed to a group standing by a big wooden gate. A girl wearing purple cowboy boots and short, *short* cut-off jeans clung to the gate, swinging out with it whenever it opened, and stretching up and over the top rail when it was closed to talk to a cowboy who leaned against the fence on the inside. The view she provided was greatly appreciated by the onlookers.

"My, my," Kendall said under his breath. "Look what Jimmy's found." When we got closer he called out, "Hey, Jim."

The man on the other side of the fence turned and acknowledged the greeting. His striking oriental features took me by surprise. This seemed to be my day for ethnic comeuppances. First an Indian Tarot reader, now a Chinese cowboy. Or maybe he was Japanese.

"Ken," he said, "where've you been, man? I've been lookin' for you. Hear you drew Sundog."

"Thea, this is Jimmy Chin, the best damn steer-roper in these parts." Jimmy Chin was older than Kendall, more my age. His straight black hair was cut short and close to his head and showed a few flecks of early graying. Not overly tall, he had the flexible, lean-hipped shape that give jeans a good name. Attractive. And I figured my first guess was right. Chin sounded like a Chinese surname.

"This is Thea Barlow," Kendall continued. "From Chicago, if I remember right. I flew her in from Casper this morning."

"Chicago?"

I nodded.

"You wouldn't be Max Holman's friend, would you?"

"You know Max?"

"Sure. We do some pick-up steer-roping together out at Buster Brocheck's now and then."

That name sounded familiar, but I couldn't think why. He must have sensed my question.

"Max is drilling his well on Brocheck's place. As a matter of fact, that's old man Brocheck, over there." He pointed to a rider in the arena, herding a group of calves to the other end. There was no mistaking the man or his belly. He was much more in his element here on an enormous horse than in the gimcrack-filled gift shop where I had first seen him.

"No wonder the name sounded familiar. I met him a bit ago at a store in town."

"Yeah, you don't forget someone his size easily. Old devil's still hell on a horse. He works all the rodeos around here. Contracts the calves for them." He turned his attention back to me. "Anyway, Max is drilling on Brocheck's ranch. In fact, I saw him there this morning. He's not a happy man about having to stay on the site." He laughed and added in an exaggerated drawl, "Yep, I learned some new words I ain't never heard before."

"Hey Mavis, is that you?"

I looked up at the girl still perched on the gate. She wore a too-large cowboy hat that hung over her ears, but there was no mistaking those guileless blue eyes.

"Mavis?" Kendall asked.

"Sorry about that," she said. "A little in-joke among us girls."

"We're both staying at Racy Ladies," I explained. "Our rooms are named after the Ladies of the Night who plied their trade there. My room's Mavis."

"And mine is Big Boobs Lu." She laughed as both men's eyes went directly to those accoutrements. "My real name is Phoebe Zimmerman," she said, directly to Kendall.

"Give me my hat, honey-love," Jimmy Chin said. His sardonic tone seemed to escape her. She giggled as he reached up, took the hat from her head and put it on his own.

Her brown hair was cut in one of those short-in-back, longer-in-front styles with the top layer glazed with some kind of bronzy red dye. Henna, probably. I'm sure she thought it was way, way cool.

Jimmy Chin pushed through the gate and joined us.

Phoebe rode the gate through its swing, then jumped off, flashing her exposed butt cheeks at an appreciative Kendall. Cheers and catcalls rose from the other cowboys lounging around the fence. Phoebe laughed and joined them in a good-natured exchange of insults.

Jimmy Chin shook his head and grinned at me. "Buckle bunny heaven around here."

"Buckle bunny?"

"Rodeo groupies. Looking for the guys with the biggest championship buckle. Come on," he called over his shoulder to Kendall, who'd slung his arm casually over Phoebe Zimmerman's shoulder. Her glimmering red head came up to his armpit. "Let's get a look at that horse you drew to ride."

"*Ladies and gentleman,*" the loudspeaker voice rose above its usual low drone. "*The bucking stock will be out in a few minutes, but now we've got a treat for all you out-of-towners here to help celebrate Wild West Days. A special guest. None other than Kid Corcoran.*" The name was drawn out and milked for every bit of pseudo-excitement possible. "*Last of the old-time bandits. This is a real piece of history, folks. Stand up, Kid. Let's give him a big hand.*"

At the mention of the Kid's name, Jimmy Chin stopped in his tracks. He and Kendall exchanged a long look over Phoebe's bright head. Kendall took off his hat and ran his fingers nervously through his dark curls before replacing it and tugging the brim farther down on his forehead.

"Shit," I heard one of them say in a near whisper.

It was just a brief moment, a tiny stoppage of time, then everything continued as before. I hadn't even noticed if Phoebe had reacted to mention of the Kid. She had her back turned, flirting with a cowboy coiling a rope. Still, there seemed to be some kind of a nasty undercurrent.

"Let's go," Kendall said. "Coming with us?" he asked Phoebe.

"Hey, wait a minute," I chimed in, curious. "Tell me about this Kid Corcoran. Do you know him?"

"Yeah, I'll go with you," Phoebe said, as if I and my question didn't exist. She glanced at the large-faced watch on her wrist. "But only for a minute," she said breezily, "then I'm out of here." She took both Jimmy and Kendall by the elbow and walked off.

"Tell me about Corcoran," I insisted, catching up and taking a place by Jimmy's side. "What did he do?"

He seemed reluctant to speak, but finally said, "He's just a two-bit ex-con, who made a name for himself around here a long time ago. Now they're trying to make a celebrity out of him."

Kendall added, "Pretty stupid, if you ask me."

"What did he do?" I asked again.

"Hell, I don't know. You'll have to ask some of the old-timers."

"He never should have come back here."

"It's his home, too, isn't it?" I said, feeling a twinge of sympathy for an old man nobody wanted.

Jimmy didn't answer the question. "It's one thing I hate about this town," he blurted with exasperation. "At the drop of a hat someone goes off on a wild hair about some fool thing that happened a hundred years ago and it's like the Hatfields and the McCoys again—families fightin' families; old lies and old hatreds rarin' their ugly heads."

We approached the corral and the two men broke away from Phoebe's hold, glad to change the subject and get on to more important things.

Jimmy slapped Kendall on the shoulder and said, "You are one unlucky son of a bitch to draw that sidewinder. You'll need to rake him high for the points. That might keep him from spinning."

An unusually silent Phoebe trailed reluctantly behind with me while Jim and Kendall played out their strategies.

"How's your story coming along?" I asked her casually. "Are you getting some good material?"

"Shit, I've got to kiss the old fart's ass before—" She stopped, remembering her tale about doing a rodeo story, and glared at me.

I laughed, then offered a flag of truce. "Don't worry, I knew you had to be here for Kid Corcoran. I wasn't exactly up front with you, either. I'm an editor for *Western True Adventures* magazine. I'm interviewing Kid Corcoran, too, for one of those last-of-the-living-legends kind of things. At any rate, I'm not competition," I said, trying to reassure her. "In fact, I might be a market. If you have some other kind of an angle, I could be interested in seeing your story."

Of course, there was a healthy dab of curiosity mixed in with my altruism. Was she aware of the undercurrents that surrounded the Kid? Had she talked to Hildy, the jade lady? It seemed obvious to me that even Jim and Kendall knew more than they were telling, but I was a stranger here, and small-town Wyoming tends to be very protective of its own, even unwanted ex-cons.

I was also well aware that, rightly or wrongly, writers tend to salivate in the presence of editors, and I was ready to take advantage of it. But Phoebe didn't respond as expected; she didn't jump on my offer; in fact, she ignored it.

"You were really pumping those guys," Phoebe said. "I've already done one human interest piece on Corcoran for a Riverside, California, paper," she said, totally pleased with herself. "My first by-line. The paper had me doing all their trash work, covering stupid community stuff, but I found Corcoran in an old folks' home."

I remembered the piece. "Yes, I've seen it. I have it in my file."

"A San Francisco paper picked it up and ran it, too."

Which really was a coup. "And you said your paper sent you here for a follow-up?" I couldn't help sounding incredulous.

She made an ugly little snort. "They wouldn't pay shit for anything."

"So you came on your own?"

"Yeah, why not?"

I shrugged. "Just wondered if it would be worth your while, is all." Plane tickets don't come cheap.

"The paper promised to buy the story," she said defensively. "I need more by-lines; I don't plan on being their gofer forever."

"Well, let me see the piece when you're finished. It might mean another sale for you. What's your angle going to be?"

"Oh, the usual old-geezer-goes-back-to-the-homestead kind of thing," she said, mimicking my earlier statement. She gave me another one of those wide-eyed guileless looks she did so well.

I didn't believe a word of it. Either she knew more about Kid Corcoran than I did, or she was incredibly stupid. And not for one minute did I think she was stupid.

Chapter Six

Jim and Kendall had joined a serious group of cowboys clinging to the wooden slats of a corral, weighing the various merits of the bucking stock. Phoebe and I climbed up beside them. The horses didn't look very fierce to me, but what did I know? The guys were still deeply involved in how Kendall was going to handle his ride, and speculating on which way the bronc would turn when he came out of the chute. The heat and dirt and droning loudspeaker beat down continuously, turning my brain to a numb mush.

Phoebe lost interest now that everyone's attention was on the horses rather than her. She looked at her watch pointedly and said she had to leave for an appointment. I inferred from the smug, satisfied look she threw at me that she was off to interview the Kid. Good for her.

Tiredness descended on me like a crushing weight. I felt committed to stay and see Kendall's ride, but after that it would be a nice soak in the tub for me, and bed no matter how early it was.

I must have looked pathetic. Jimmy broke away from his

discussion with Kendall and said, "Had enough? You don't have to hang around here if you don't want to."

"Oh, yes she does," Kendall broke in with a hoot. "She's my lucky charm."

His boundless good humor was endearing. "I wouldn't miss it for the world. I'm just going to look around a bit and get something cold to drink. Anybody want anything?"

They both declined, and I set off for the concession stand, thinking I might even have another barbecue sandwich if they were still serving. I opted for homemade apple pie instead, with a big glob of ice cream on top. Straddling a picnic bench, I leisurely forked the wonderful mess into my mouth and watched the action.

The loudspeaker squawked and crackled. *"Just a reminder, folks, that we're drier than sin around here, so watch your sparks and butts. While you're at it, be sure to take in the display put on by our local county fire department. All volunteers. Let's give those boys a great big hand."*

Cars and pickups still inched their way in and out of the entrance gates, mostly ignoring the ineffective hand signals from the kids directing traffic. With squealing tires, an impatient driver in an open brown Jeep swung wide around the stalled line of vehicles waiting to leave the grounds. The Jeep rocketed into a small opening at the head of the line. I recognized the driver instantly, no mistaking that strangely colored hair. Kid Corcoran sat beside her, hanging on to the seat, his plastic oxygen hose flapping in the wind as they turned out of the grounds and accelerated down the street.

Well, well, well, I thought, where were they going? Lois Lane looked pissed. Was this what she meant by having to kiss his ass? I tried to remember the conversation I'd overheard this morning between the kid and Florie. He had wanted her to take him somewhere. What had he said? "I want to see the old place"? Was that it? Had he conned Phoebe into taking him there? Could be. The thought of Phoebe having to deal with Kid Corcoran's orneriness made me smile. Ha! And she thought her paper treated her like a gofer.

I dumped my paper plate in a trash bin, and circled a stationary horse and rider blocking the way to the drink stand. Garland Caldwell stood on the other side of the animal, close to the horse, an arm on either side of the saddle, smiling up at the rider. A female, of course. Surprise, surprise. She wore a shocking pink Stetson and matching riding pants. I couldn't read what was on the sash that crossed her blouse. A rodeo queen of some kind.

Caldwell nodded at me with a conspiratorial wink. I didn't see his wife anywhere. Was there a name for male buckle bunnies? I quickly purchased a large lemonade with extra ice and headed back around the arena.

Jimmy Chin met me more than halfway. "I was looking for you," he said. "I didn't want you to leave before I had a chance to talk to you."

"Oh?"

"Yeah, Max asked me to fix you up with some kind of wheels. I should have mentioned it earlier." He had a slow smile and flashing dark eyes. Very attractive.

"Yes," I said. "Max said something about a car when I spoke to him on the phone." I wasn't about to tell this buddy of his just how uninterested in Max Holman I was at this particular moment.

"You must be dead on your feet, but would you be up for

a late dinner? I won't be finished here until around seven, but after that—say eight o'clock—I could round up those wheels for you, and we could grab a quick bite."

"That sounds great."

"Do you like Chinese? It's too late to get a reservation at Racy Ladies, but—"

"Racy Ladies?"

"It's the best place in town to eat."

"It is?" I don't know why that surprised me, but it did. I guess I was remembering Florie Dunn's rather pathetic eagerness for customers, and the general impression of nobody ever being around.

"Best food in town. Everybody hangs there, particularly on a night like this."

I suppose these *were* big doings for Rawhide.

"I adore Chinese," I said.

"I hope so."

"Food," I added quickly, with a grin that matched his. Nothing like a mild flirtation to chase the blues away. But I couldn't compete with the flash that sparkled in his dark, dark eyes.

"You know, you don't really have to stick around for Ken's ride if you don't want to. He will survive."

"Of course I'll stay. How could I pass up an opportunity to be someone's lucky charm?"

By five-thirty I'd witnessed Kendall's Ride of the Century and been duly amazed. Now Kendall was off somewhere, and Jimmy was getting ready to go help someone else prepare for a chuck wagon race. A good time to exit.

Jimmy touched his finger to my cheek. "I'll pick you up at eight at Racy Ladies. Okay?"

I nodded. Fish your heart out, Max Holman.

I welcomed the walk back to Racy Ladies; it eased some of the guilt I felt about the pie and ice cream. The approach by foot and from a different direction also gave me an interesting side view of the bed and breakfast and its small parking lot. The building was much deeper than one would have thought from the front. It looked as if several additions had been randomly tacked onto the back of the house with little attempt at harmony. Odd portions of rooms jutted out here and there from the side of the building, making it look like a three-story rabbit warren. At the rear, facing me, a flight of rickety stairs led to an open wooden porch. Another, shorter flight of stairs led from the porch to a door in a dormer. The door's window was curtained, leading me to believe it might be a separate apartment of some kind.

Web Corcoran sat on the porch watching my progress. I waved, and impulsively crossed the lot to stand at the base of the porch.

"Hi," I said, looking up at him. "Out for a smoke?"

He was silent, his gaze cold and calculating. He took a long, slow drag on his cigarette. His small frame appeared tougher, harder, more vigorous, sitting out here in the old spring-based metal chair, one foot propped on a low railing. Maybe because he didn't have his oxygen. Strange how that small length of plastic tubing could disguise, or diminish, a person's personality. I wondered how badly he needed it. I didn't see his cane, either.

"I was at the rodeo and heard you get introduced," I said. "Did you enjoy the show?"

Silence. Another long drag, but his eyes never left my face. Trying for intimidation? Or was it just his manner? Social skills are probably not something one feels obliged to hone during forty years in the pen. Or maybe he was always this way, an anti-social child, an antisocial adult. Not a bad description of most criminals, I suppose.

I remembered my conversation with Hildy in the gift store. She'd called Corcoran a murdering thief, said he'd slit his own mother's throat if he had to. It might well have been a figure of speech, but at this moment he looked capable of committing crimes much worse than those he'd been convicted of. I knew I'd fallen into the familiar trap of assuming that a quaint piece of history dredged up from crumbly old newspapers was the whole story. When dealing with the living rather than the dead it pays to remember that your little piece of history isn't history to them, it's their life.

"It was my first rodeo," I said, still trying to bring him out. "I would have asked to sit with you, but a friend took me off to inspect the bucking horses. I understand you were quite a horseman in your day."

More silence. The odds seemed good that Corcoran wasn't going to say a word to me. I pushed away from the porch, hunting for an exit line.

I said, "It's not good for you to sit out here in the heat, you know. You should be on the front porch where there's some shade." A cheap shot, referring to his poor health, but I didn't want the stubborn old coot to think he could jerk me around.

He made a little huff of disgust, flicked his cigarette onto the gravel and said, "I'm not allowed out front this time of night. Afraid I'll scare off their precious dinner customers."

Good grief. That Florie, what a bitch she was. "Oh?" Unsure of what tack to take, I chose a light one. "I thought you were a big attraction around here."

"Ain't you scared?" he asked sarcastically.

But he didn't fool me. Behind the hard eyes and bitter words I could see the lonely old man huddled in a corner.

"No," I said, eyeing him thoughtfully. "I'm not scared." Whatever he might once have been, he was now an eighty-two-year-old man in precarious health. I might not trust him, but he didn't frighten me.

"Let's meet in the morning around ten," I said, feeling much more kindly toward him. "I'm looking forward to hearing your stories. Will that be all right with you?"

He nodded, took another drag from the cigarette, then asked, "You got a car?"

"Not right now, but I will by tomorrow. Why? Do you want to go somewhere?"

"Maybe."

I wondered if he hadn't gotten along with Phoebe Zimmerman. Maybe she wasn't as tractable as he wanted. Or was he afraid he'd wear out his welcome with her?

I wasn't going to promise anything. "I'll see you tomorrow," I said noncommittally, waved, and headed off.

I could feel his eyes on my back. I turned to wave again. He stood now, one arm resting on the railing, eyeing me with such intense concentration that I quivered much as a rabbit does when an eagle wheels above. The hair on my arms prickled. Run!, instinct told me. Then he waved, a heartrending, timid little movement of his hand. Feeling ten times a fool, I managed to stroll casually around to the front of the house.

The number of cars lining the street and parking lot should have given me a clue, but I was totally unprepared for the number of people who filled the downstairs area of the bed and breakfast.

A portable bar had been set up just inside the wide doorway of the sitting room, and a man with a hawk nose and a Lyle Lovett haircut was mixing drinks with a flourish. People sat on chairs, chair arms, footstools, the stairs, the registration desk, anything remotely sitable. Some of the more agile hunkered down and leaned against odd pieces of wall, while still others stood in the more conventional cocktail party clusters. A very few sat at tables in the dining room, but that clearly was not the place of choice for the moment.

I myself stood in the hallway gaping, stunned by the noise and the transformation made on the old house by a crowd of happy people in a party mode. Florie Dunn bustled past me importantly, carrying a tray of hors d'oeuvres.

"Hi, Thea," she said, turning back. "Look, I'm really sorry that we're all filled up for dinner tonight. We like to give our guests first chance at reservations, but this morning," she made a wry grimace, "I forgot to mention it."

No wonder. She was busy terrorizing her grandfather. "That's all right," I said. "I'm going out, anyway. Don't worry about it."

"But here, help yourself to the hors d'oeuvres. They're wonderful." She stuck the tray of tiny puff pastries under my nose. "And you get a drink on the house."

"I'm a mess," I protested, holding out my grimy hands.

"Oh, nobody cares." She waved away my concerns. "You see everything here, particularly on rodeo night. Come on."

I squeezed around two men swigging Red Dog from bottles. Bits of conversation drifted by, laced with laughter. "Found a whole vein of apple green in a uranium mine out by Jeffrey City. Damned stuff was radioactive, sent a Geiger 'way to hell. Goverment tried to shut the mine down, but the guys dug it all out anyway."

A movement at the far end of the dining room caught my

eye. A shadowy figure stood in a doorway, neck craning around to peer intently at the few people sitting at the tables. My jaw dropped. It was Sheila Rides Horse, the Indian fortune-teller. She wore a white apron over blue sweat pants and a matching sweat shirt with the sleeves cut off. What was she doing here? A dishwasher, maybe? She looked up, saw me staring, and ducked back through the door.

"Thea," a voice called. "Over here." Florie Dunn stood by the little bar, beckoning me.

"This is my husband, Rocky," she said when I worked my way over to her. "Give her a drink on the house, hon. See you." And before I could ask her about the Indian woman, she hustled off, proffering her tray. In her element, I thought, watching her for a moment. More affable than I'd seen her, she seemed to enjoy making everyone feel welcome and at home. Except her own grandfather, I thought, finding it difficult to like the woman.

Tall and rangy, and as thin as Florie, Rocky Dunn exuded a kind of alert, shifty-eyed charm. The perfect host, even though his eyes were circled with smudges of tiredness, and his deep auburn hair appeared as if its wild styling owed more to fingers than to fashion.

"What'll ya have?" he asked, patiently enough for one being bombarded from all sides.

"A gin and tonic, lime. Long on tonic." I wanted to ask him about Sheila Rides Horse, but decided to wait until the noise subsided a bit and his pace slowed. "This place is a madhouse," I said, raising my voice. "How do you stand it?"

He gave me a sardonic, knowing smile. "Money in the pocket makes it music to my ears," he answered before his eyes darted across the room, acknowledging more orders from hand signals while he made my drink with one hand and something else with the other.

"How about you, Buster?" Rocky said over his shoulder as he handed me my drink. "You ready for another?"

I sidestepped a bit to see who he was talking to. Buster Brocheck sat in an overstuffed chair deep in conversation with none other than Garland Caldwell, who huddled out of sight in the corner, a captive audience.

Buster leaned over the chair arm toward Garland; his big haunches rested sideways in the seat. I caught a bit of his earnest conversation. "–over by Douglas. Found a lot of it there, nothing but frog skin, though." I grinned. First mutton fat, now frog skin. What was it with this guy? I needed to find out more. Garland's glazed-looking eyes skittered around the room, looking for rescue from any avenue, no doubt. I ducked back out of sight.

I wanted to talk to Buster Brocheck myself. Find out what made mutton fat a subject for conversation, if nothing else, but something told me he'd also be a font of information about Kid Corcoran. I just didn't want to risk being monopolized by Garland right now.

I spotted Trish Caldwell across the room deep in conversation with an elegant woman loaded down with enough silver Indian jewelry to finance a reservation casino. I found it interesting that the Caldwells were out for a bit of slumming. Evidently, Racy Ladies was beneath their touch until they discovered it was the social hot spot, then of course they had to be included. About the way I'd pegged them.

Slumming probably wasn't the right word. Trish had changed into a slim beige and white outfit that made me feel like the little match girl.

"Okay if I take this to my room?" I asked Rocky, holding

up my not-quite-finished drink. He nodded. It was time for a
serious clean-up on my part, then I'd come back down and
see if I could corner Buster, and maybe meet some of these
other people.

For the first time I wondered how Max handled this part
of his life; much of his time was spent in one small town
after another, always a stranger. Did he try to become a part
of a community, or hold himself aloof? How did he fight
the loneliness?

Starting up the stairs, I caught a glimpse of Kid Corcoran
hovering in the doorway at the end of the hall behind the
reservation desk, peering out at the crowd much like a small
boy yearning for the delights of a grown-up's party. I felt a
pang of sadness for him and stepped back to go talk to him,
but he faded from sight as quickly as he had appeared.

"Make way, everyone," a bright voice trilled from the top
of the stairs. "Here I come!"

I looked up, as did everyone else. Phoebe Zimmerman was
making an ENTRANCE.

Chapter Seven

Phoebe picked her way down the narrow staircase with cute little maneuvers around the couples sitting there or struggling to stand and get out of her way. She wore one of those long, retro rayon dresses with tiny sleeves and slinky trumpet skirt. Purple pansies sprinkled on yellow. One of those silly billfold-sized purses with a long thin strap hung from her shoulder—bright purple and hardly large enough to hold a Kleenex. A lock of hair flopped coyly over one eye.

Her face was flushed, eyes bright and flashing, wired with excitement. She laughed and executed an elaborate little jump off the bottom stair, then trailed her fingertips across the chest of a cowboy-type enraptured with her performance.

I didn't need this. I slid behind her to get to the stairs but she spun around and grabbed my arm.

"Well, *hi*, Mavis," she said with a smart-ass lilt that irritated me. "Come on, I'll buy you a drink."

"Sorry," I snapped, trying to shake off her grip. "I'm going to change."

Her fingers tightened urgently around my wrist. She smiled

brightly at everyone; all eyes were still glued on her. "Oh, come on," she said, pleading sweetly, then faked a little trip and fell into me long enough to say under her breath, "I've *got* to talk to you. It's important."

I sighed. What on earth was this all about? "All right," I said, grudgingly.

She dropped my wrist and tucked her hand through the crook of my elbow as if we were the best of friends. I could feel the energy coursing through her body; her skin nearly sparked with it. I wondered if she were on drugs, but then I remembered how my little brother used to look, standing on the sidelines, so pumped up he could hardly stand still, waiting to be sent in for his first football game. Yeah. All pumped up. That's what she was.

We went to the bar. I held my glass up to Rocky for a refill. Phoebe stepped farther into the room, instantly establishing eye contact with every man there—an amazing trick; I wish I could do it.

"And you?" Rocky asked her.

"Jack and a little spritz." Not wasting her time on the bartender, her gaze flittered back to where I knew Garland Caldwell sat, hidden in the corner. Of course. He was the best looking man in the room and, if appearances count for anything, the most prosperous. She moved artfully, putting herself in his line of vision. Our little Phoebe was a piece of work all right. Impatiently, I handed her her drink. Rocky could charge it to whomever he pleased.

"Come on," I said, ready to listen to what she had to say, but not willing to stand around watching her work a room and all the men in it. We could find a quiet place to sit in the dining room for a few minutes.

A stone skittered across the floorboards and stopped at my feet. I bent to pick it up. When I rose, Sheila Rides Horse stood close beside me, carrying a tray in one hand. Puzzled, she peered at the small rock in my palm.

"Stones," she muttered. "Everywhere I go, stones." Then her piercing glance examined my face, flashed to Phoebe's, then back to me again.

"Oh, cool," Phoebe squealed, eyeing the tray. "I'm totally famished." She took a toast point glistening with bits of asparagus and egg *en gelée*, popped in into her mouth and reached for another. Sheila offered me the tray, then Buster Brocheck spied her and jumped clumsily to his feet, an event that nearly rocked the room.

"Sheila!" he cried. "It's you. What's for dinner tonight?" At the mention of her name most of the others in the room converged on her as if she were the celebrity of the moment.

"Read the menu, Buster," Sheila said dryly, nodding at a chalkboard propped in a corner out of danger's way. I hadn't noticed it before. Handwritten in a mixture of English and French, I thought I made out a turtle soup, some kind of paté and a main dish that I swear was rabbit in some kind of guise. Good grief, I thought, and this was Wyoming, land of the chicken fried steak!

"Best cook we've ever had around these parts," I heard Buster tell Garland Caldwell, who had seized his opportunity to escape from the corner and was now trying to disappear into the crowd at the other end of the room. "Some fancy place in New York City has been trying to hire her, but she don't like cities much."

Sheila seemed oblivious to the commotion. She motioned the tray at me again and I took one of the exquisite toast points. "You're the cook ... chef?" I didn't even try to conceal my astonishment.

"Yeah," she said, with a grin that softened her face becomingly. I smiled, too, if a bit sheepishly. I knew we were both thinking about my earlier surprise at finding an Indian reading Tarot. Now this. At least she didn't know I'd assumed she was the dishwasher.

As quickly as it came, the sunshine left her face. "Are you okay?" she asked softly, a note of real concern in her voice.

"Yes, I'm fine. Why?" I looked down at my shorts, wondering for a moment if I looked that disgusting.

She shrugged. "All I can do is warn you."

"Warn me?" This again? "Of what?" I demanded.

But she moved on, wielding the edge of her tray like a shield to fend off those who invaded her space too closely. She scrutinized each face with an intensity that seemed out of place and quite strange.

An uncontrollable shiver coursed through my body.

Florie appeared with another tray. "Sheila," she said with an expression of utter astonishment, "what are you doing out here? You don't have to do this kind of work. Here let me." She took Sheila's tray in her free hand. "I'll get one of the girls to do this for you."

Sheila shrugged, looked around the room once more and headed for the kitchen. "Come see me in the morning," she said *sotto voce* as she passed by me. "I've got a room in back by the kitchen. Just be careful."

I felt like I was in a bad movie and was suddenly angry. I'd had enough of this high woo-woo stuff. And where was Phoebe and all her urgent information?

I found her cozying up to Garland Caldwell, who looked

like the Cheshire Cat anticipating a plate of cream. He also appeared a bit jumpy, peering uneasily around the crowded room. I could have told him that his wife had already seen him eyeing Phoebe. I figured there wasn't much her husband did that Trish Caldwell didn't notice. It was a wonder she hadn't killed him.

Garland handed Phoebe a drink, and hustled her off to an out-of-the-way table in the dining room.

"Phoebe," I said, stopping her. "You wanted to talk?"

"Later," she said, mouthing the word silently.

Later, my foot. Little twit. Who did she think she was? She must have sensed my anger. She broke away from Garland, waving him on to the table and actually whispering in my ear, said, "I have something to show you, you won't believe it!"

"What?" I said in my regular voice. "And when?" This was all too Valley Girl High School stuff for me.

"Shhh," she breathed, not letting her lips move. But it was the sudden cast of real fear in her eyes that surprised me, as she turned, smiled brightly at anyone interested, flittered back to where Garland waited for her. Puzzled, I drained my glass, set it none too gently on the bar, and started for the stairs, barely noticing that Kid Corcoran had abandoned his post in the hallway and was now peering through the far door of the dining room, watching Phoebe and Caldwell settle at a secluded corner table. As good as a soap opera, I thought, sick of the lot of them. I'd have to hurry now to be ready by the time Jimmy Chin got here. I dodged around the stair-sitters and ran up to my room.

I saw the Queen of Swords as soon as I opened the door.

The card, depicting a stern, determined-looking woman on a throne holding a huge saber upright, was stuck in the frame of the mirror at the upper corner. Underneath the picture were the words, Queen of Swords. I knew the card was part of the Tarot deck, but what was it doing here? Obviously, though, the work of Sheila Rides Horse. Who else? But how did she get into my room? Or was she the housemaid as well as the cook, with free access to all the rooms?

I looked around. The bed had been turned down and a pink candy rose on a long stem was placed on the pillow. A quick check through my belongings showed nothing else had been disturbed. So the maid had been here, I thought, but why would she have left a Tarot card? And if the maid *were* Sheila? Still, why the card? A reminder that I was supposed to come and spend more money with her? But I hadn't given her any money. Maybe this was just the big build-up—the warnings, the whispered, "Come see me in the morning"—then I'd be asked to cross her palm with a couple hundred to save me from some dire nemesis. Wasn't that the usual fortune-telling scam? Whatever it was, it felt like a damned cheap cat-and-mouse game and I wasn't going to take any part in it.

I took off my dirty clothes, threw them on the floor in the closet, and ran water in the tub. The card could be an advertising gimmick, I thought, still puzzling over the stupid thing. Maybe they put one in every room. "Tarot readings available, inquire at the desk." I padded into the bedroom, got the card and padded back. There was no printing on the back of the card, just a nondescript blue and white design. Whatever, I thought with disgust, and tossed it in the wastebasket.

I smoothed cleanser over my sunburned face. Later, if I thought about it, I'd look through the brochure Florie had given me with the room key. Maybe there was something in there about Tarot readings.

And, I thought, trying to bury a lingering sense of uneasiness, I'd ask Florie about security. The locks around here looked so antiquated I could probably pick them myself.

Refreshed by a bath and shampoo, I put on clean clothes and fixed my still damp hair into a fat french braid. Fairly confident I wouldn't shame myself by falling asleep over dinner, I still didn't plan on giving Jimmy Chin more than a couple hours of my time, and wished now I hadn't promised that.

I wiped the bathroom counter with a wad of tissue and dropped it in the basket. The Queen of Swords hadn't dropped to the bottom of the basket, but stuck on the plastic lining close to the rim, still brandishing her sword.

"So," I said out loud, "you don't want to be thrown out." I retrieved the card and wiped off the spatters from the soaked tissue. There was something comforting about the old girl. She sat on her throne in profile, chin up, feet planted, sword at ready. Strong, prepared. Not looking for a fight, but ready to defend herself if need be. I could use some of that, I thought.

"This is the card I worry about," Sheila's words floated in the air around me as clearly as if she were in the room. *"The King of Swords, a man with dark hair who is not what he appears to be."*

I stuck the Queen back in the mirror frame above the dresser where I found her, surprised to find my fingers trembling a bit. But what of the Queen? I wondered. Was she the King's partner in crime, or did she stand on her own?

Changing my mind, I took the card and tucked it into my purse. She didn't look like anyone's patsy. You're going with me, I thought, not entirely facetiously, I might need you. After all, no one had hair much darker than Jimmy Chin.

Chapter Eight

It was a few minutes before eight o'clock when I went back downstairs. As I expected, the cocktail hour was over and I'd missed my chance to pump Buster Brocheck for information. Rocky Dunn was alone in the sitting room, cleaning up debris. The diners sat at the tables across the hall with dimmed lighting and soft music playing in the background. Good food, or the prospect of it, tempered the conversation to a soft buzz. Snatches of mixed aromas—fresh baked bread, garlic, basil, seared meat—tickled my nostrils and brought saliva to my mouth.

Buster Brocheck dominated a large table in the center of the room. Both of the Caldwells now sat at a discreet corner table with another couple. Phoebe Zimmerman was nowhere in sight. Neither was Sheila Rides Horse or Florie. Both, I assumed, were busy in the kitchen. I sighed and picked up a couple of empty glasses and discarded cocktail napkins from the stairs.

"Hi, Rocky," I said, handing him the sticky mess.

Kendall Hauser bounced through the front door all slicked up in new jeans and a fancy shirt. He cased out the dining room, then came over to us.

"Is Phoebe around?" he asked us both.

"She was here earlier," I said, "but I don't see her now."

"She said she was going to the dance, and I just thought I'd see if she needed a ride."

"You missed the boat, Hauser, she left on her own a bit ago," Rocky said, with a leer that indicated he didn't think she'd be alone for long.

Never to be outdone, Kendall turned to me with an exaggerated Groucho Marx ogle. "How about you? You want to join me for a few fandangos out to the Legion Hall?"

I laughed. "No, you go on. Maybe you can catch her. Jimmy and I are going out for a bit of dinner."

"Whoee! Cutting the boyfriend out, is he?"

"Oh, get out of here," I said good-naturedly.

He gave me a sad-eyed, mournful look. "Dumped again," then waved and took off.

Rocky shook his head. "What a nut," he said and went back to wiping down the bar.

"I see things have quieted down a bit," I said, indicating the empty sitting room. "I hate to bother you, Rocky, but I'm a bit concerned about the lock on my door. It looks ancient. What kind of security do you have around here?"

"We've never had any complaints," he stated rather belligerently, immediately on the defensive. "The whole house gets locked up at eleven o'clock. If you're out after that just ring the bell; someone's always here to let you in." There was more than a touch of weary condescension in his voice, as if he spent the majority of his time having to deal with vaporish females. "We don't worry much about that around here."

"I wasn't so much worried about a boogieman from outside," I said dryly, "as about an invasion from within. Or can you vouch for all your customers and help?"

He grinned then, granting me a point. "The help, yeah. As for the guests, we do our best. As I said, we haven't had any problems. The guest room locks are set to be replaced next month; we're working for our Triple-A rating."

He might be confident about the help, but I wanted to know about Sheila Rides Horse. I opened my mouth to ask when the front door flew open and banged against the wall. Hildy, the pint-sized woman from the jade shop, burst in with a flurry of tiny, staccato steps, looking entirely too much like the Energizer pink bunny. She stood in the doorway to the dining room, fists on hips.

"Buster!" Her voice cut across the dining room.

Buster jumped up, jostling the table and sending his chair rocking crazily on its two back legs. He grabbed it, clattering it to a standstill, and motioned Hildy to come join the table.

She looked around disdainfully, wrinkling her nose. "I wouldn't sit down in this place if my life depended on it." She gave a hearty sniff.

As if on cue, Jimmy Chin drifted through the open door, eyed the situation and came to stand beside me.

"Hi," he said softly. We both watched Buster, red-of-face, maneuver his bulk clumsily through the tables.

"Let's go outside," Hildy said when he reached her. "How you can stand to set foot in this place is beyond me. I need some fresh air."

Buster ran his hand over his bald pate and gave Jimmy and me an unsmiling nod of recognition. He followed Hildy out the door.

The diners went back to their food.

"What's going on?" Jimmy asked, glancing at both me and Rocky.

Rocky mouthed the word, "Bitch," and went back to cleaning glasses.

"You ready to go?" Jimmy asked me, apparently ready to dismiss the little drama we'd witnessed. Not me.

"Yes," I said, already halfway out the door. I wanted to see what was happening.

Nothing very exciting, as it turned out. Buster and Hildy leaned against a parked car, deep in a one-sided conversation. Hildy was doing the talking, sending her points home with an occasional jab to Buster's chest.

"Are those two married?" I asked suspiciously, wondering if dismal couplings were going to dog my steps like an evil portent. Hildy seemed like the typical termagant, giving the old man hell for some imagined sin.

"Who, Buster? And Hildy?" he said, obviously tickled by the idea. "No, no. Buster's married to the sweetest little lady in the world. She can cook your heart out; she's been fattening me up since I was a sprig."

He guided me across the street to a Ford Bronco parked at the curb. "Well, she's wasting her efforts on Buster," I said lightly, remembering my earlier overheard conversations. "His taste in food seems to run to mutton fat and frog skin."

Jimmy had a grip on my elbow, balancing me for the big step up into the four wheel drive. At my words his fingers tightened, digging into the tender flesh.

"Ow!" I yelped and shot up into the front seat.

"Sorry." He shut the door and went around to the driver's side. He got in, started up the car, and gave me a smile. "You hungry?"

"Do you want to tell me what this is all about?"

He was silent for a moment, then said. "Do you know anything about jade?"

"Jade? No. At least I didn't until I stepped into Hildy's store this afternoon. She showed me some of the stuff she has and told me about ... I had no idea jade was found in Wyoming, but what does that have to do with ..."

"I don't know about frog skin, but mutton fat is a kind of jade, or a color of jade, a soft milky white. Prized. Hildy's father was one of the old jade men, and so was Buster's dad. Most of those old guys are dead now, and the jade's gone. But ever since the Kid came back that's all everybody talks about."

"What does the Kid have to do with it?"

"Who knows?" he answered. "I don't, but he's the villain of every story you hear. Nobody says anything for as long as I can remember, then suddenly the old guy shows up and all you hear about is how Kid Corcoran murdered Buster's father and stole tons of jade from everyone."

"Is it true? Was Buster's father murdered?"

Jimmy shrugged. "I don't know all the details; it happened before I was born. Somewhere back then, Corcoran did a stretch in the state pen at Rawlins. During the early 'forties, I think. Shortly after Corcoran was released, old Reuben Brocheck was found dead out in his winter pasture. Official word was that he fell from his horse and bashed his head on a rock. Wasn't 'til Corcoran lit out for California that everyone decided that he must've somehow killed the man."

"Why was he connected to it?"

"Kid Corcoran and Buster's dad were friends from the time they were young and later on partners in some affairs, mostly nefarious—as the old penny dreadfuls would've said. The Kid wasn't involved in anything that *wasn't* nefarious though, as far as I can tell. Anyway, during the early days of the jade frenzy they did their share of claim-jumping. Anyone in town who had anything to do with jade hunting claims to have had a find stolen from him by Kid Corcoran."

"Did they try to convict him—of the murder, I mean?"

"No, not that I know of," Jimmy said. "There wasn't any proof, no evidence. It was all just talk then; it's all just talk now."

"This is really interesting. One of the reasons I came here was to do an article on Kid Corcoran for my magazine. I've done a lot of research on him, but—"

"Your magazine?" Jimmy interrupted, surprised.

"Yeah. I'm an editor for *Western True Adventures*."

"You are? I didn't know that."

So Max hadn't told him all that much about me. I couldn't decide whether that was good, bad, or just one of those guy things.

"What do you want to write about Corcoran for?"

"Last of the old bandits thing," I said, though I was fast changing my mind. There was a lot more meat to the package than I had expected. This murder stuff must be what Phoebe was so hot to tell me about, I thought, then as quickly reconsidered. If this was the angle she was using for her story, or even new information she'd just picked up, why would she tell me? Goofily enough, she considered me the big arch rival. Or did she just feel like gloating a bit? Possible. And what had she meant about having something to show me?

But then I remembered how she'd looked, fairly dancing with electricity. I'd felt her urgency. She wasn't frightened, or worried. She was excited. She obviously wanted something from me, great little people-user that she was. And I was sure she'd get around to begging me for whatever again, if there was ever a moment when a man wasn't around to distract her. In the meantime, I'd do my own news-grubbing.

"What is it that people want from Corcoran now?"

"There's some who'd still like to see him hang."

"Surely if there wasn't enough evidence to convict him back then, no one can expect to do so now, can they?"

"No, as I said before, it's mostly just talk. I don't think anyone actually thinks he'll be brought to trial."

"Then what's all the fuss about? What are Hildy and Buster so—"

"Look, Buster's my friend. He's a good guy. He's been like a father to me in many ways. I just hate to see him go off the deep end like this. It's stupid. It's ancient history. And Hildy's the one who's lighting a fire under him."

"Why? What does she—"

Jimmy was angry. "How'd we get off on all this stuff anyway?" He pulled to a halt in front of a cluster of dingy, neon-lit storefronts. "Come on, let's get something to eat. This place may not be the fanciest in town, but it's family, and you won't get poisoned."

The Lotus Café looked anonymously like every other oriental restaurant I'd ever been in. Red tassels and plastic lantern light covers fought a losing battle with bare formica tables to provide some kind of Asian ambiance. If the place had been full earlier, it had thinned now to a few family groups still happily passing platters.

An elderly couple, so wizened and oriental in appearance that they could have been caricatures, popped out from behind the cash register to greet Jimmy with the effusive happiness of a long-lost relative. I wondered how long it had been since he'd seen them.

"Thea," Jimmy said with a twinkle in his eye, "this is my Great-Uncle Patrick O'Donnal."

I could tell by the grin on the old man's face that jokes about the family name were expected and appreciated.

But he beat me to the draw, saying with a raspy little cackle, "Funny name for a Chinaman, ain't it, but I got old sod in me, too."

"And this," Jimmy went on, "is Auntie Lee."

She bowed, stern-faced and solemn, her gray hair slicked back tightly in a knot. She had eyes only for Jimmy, and kept touching his sleeve.

"Sit, sit," she said softly, patting his arm. "I get you something special." She scurried off to the kitchen.

There was a bit of China still in her voice, more a cadence, I thought, than an accent. However, there was nothing of that in the old man; he was pure Western twang. He sat in a booth with us and immediately wanted to know everything about the rodeo, how Jimmy and Kendall had fared, who won each event, and even, it seemed, how certain horses had performed. I let them talk, content for the moment to take in the surroundings.

My eyes finally settled on a small display case I hadn't noticed before, nestled between two large fish tanks. The men were still deep in horse talk, so I sauntered over to get a better look at the two displayed pieces.

One was a bowl of deep green material carved in a lattice pattern with animal handles, ducks perhaps. Jade, I thought, pleased with my new knowledge. The second piece could be jade as well, now that I knew the stone came in many colors. But I couldn't figure out what it was. A weird shape, pale beige, almost like praying hands, but there were too many fingers. The base appeared to be entwined vines or roots, so maybe it was supposed to be a bush or plant of some kind. Eerie, almost unpleasant.

"Is that jade?" I asked Jimmy as I slid back into the booth. Both men looked at me.

"What?" Jimmy asked, as if his thoughts were still on bucking horses and steer-roping.

"In the case by the fish tanks. Is that Wyoming jade?"

The two men exchanged an uneasy gaze, then the old man said, "It is Chinese. Very old jade."

"And the one piece ..?

He seemed to know what I was curious about. "It is the bud of the lotus plant, sometimes called Buddha's Fingers."

At that moment Auntie Lee appeared with a steaming pu-pu platter. "Ha!" she said with disgust, plunking the dish on the table to emphasize her bitter words. "They are not jade," she said, "they are fakes."

Chapter Nine

Between each serving Auntie Lee went on at great length about how the family treasures had been stolen many years ago. Jade from the Imperial Palace, brought to this country by ancestors. But the gravest mistake was her husband's thinking that replacing the lost jade with similar copies would satisfy her.

"Ha!" she said more than once. "Cheap onyx fakes. Only a fool would think they were the true Stone of Heaven."

Jimmy apologized when the squabbling couple departed for the kitchen. It was obviously something he had heard many times before. I faded quickly after that, possibly overdosed on MSG. Questions about stolen jade, murder, and Tarot-reading Indians swirled together in my mind like gelatinous chop suey, but I couldn't summon the energy, or even the interest anymore to ask them.

Jimmy urged me to go to the rodeo dance with him. "It's at the American Legion Hall; a good old country dance. Your Chicago heart will love it."

I wasn't even tempted. "Thanks, but not tonight. I've had way too long a day as it is. I need to get the car Max has for me and call it a night."

As it turned out, the Bronco belonged to Max and was the vehicle he'd planned for my use. Jimmy had had the key all along and could have given it to me that afternoon at the rodeo. Choosing his moment well, Jimmy explained it all with great charm and humor. I was too wiped out to figure out if I was flattered that he'd fudged the issue for a chance to see me again, or if I was mad as hell. By the time I reached Racy Ladies annoyance had won out. All I could think about was how I could have been in bed hours ago, catching up on much needed sleep. I pulled the Bronco into the first empty spot I found.

The broad, black sky pulsed with a brilliant panoply of star patterns. Without the sun, the never-ending breeze was cool, almost chilly. I shivered, rubbing my arms, as I ran up the stairs. My hand was on the front door handle when I heard a faint sound from the far end of the porch. I swung around and caught the glimmer of bare legs stretched awkwardly on the floor. Another faint cry galvanized me and I dodged around the benches and table.

Phoebe Zimmerman lay sprawled on the floor behind the peacock chair, her head and shoulders propped awkwardly against the wall.

I dropped to my knees and grabbed her hand. "Phoebe!"

Her mouth hung open. She rolled her head feebly against the boards and opened her eyes a crack. "Thank God it's you," she mumbled. She reeked of stale alcohol. "Help me," she said muzzily. "Please help me."

"I'll go get—"

Her eyes flew open, wild with terror. "No! No one else. Help me to my room. Don't want ... don't want anyone ... see me."

"Can you stand? What happened, Phoebe?"

"Oh God, be ... careful. Shit. I'm smashed. Too much to drink," she said needlessly. "I ... help me stand."

It was a struggle, but I finally got her to her feet. She swayed a bit, clutching at the air, trying to get some balance. I just hoped she wasn't going to throw up on me. She looked like hell.

"Don't want them to see me."

"Who?"

"Anyone. Don't want anyone in there ..."

I didn't know how I could keep anyone from seeing her if they were at all interested. There was probably a back entrance, and another way upstairs, but I didn't know where it was. I figured I'd be lucky to get her in this door and up to her room, much less attempt stumbling around in the dark looking for another way in.

She clung to me and we made it to the front door. Her legs seemed to gain a bit of starch with each step. I opened the door quietly and peered into the vestibule. The dining room was dark, but light spilled into the hall from the sitting room along with soft sounds of conversation and ice swirling in glasses.

"Whoever's still here is in the sitting room," I whispered in Phoebe's ear. "I'll walk on your left and block their view. We'll go fast and head right up the stairs. Okay?"

She nodded and I felt her stiffen, trying to regain control of her body.

"Ready?" I asked. "Here we go." I took a tight grip around her waist, turning a bit toward her as if we were talking, to shield her from view as best as I could. I led her at a fast clip through the vestibule and up the stairs, not stopping until we turned out of sight on the first landing. She sagged against my arm and we paused a minute to catch our breath, then went up the last steps, and to her room.

"Where's your key?" I asked.

She looked at me blankly.

"Key to your room?" I repeated impatiently, automatically trying the knob, which of course didn't give. She twisted around looking at her hip area as if expecting a purse to appear like magic, hanging from her shoulder.

"My purse is gone," she said.

"That little purple thing? Where is it? Down on the porch?"

"I don't know. Maybe." Her voice was disintegrating into threads and her legs wobbled unsteadily.

"Come on," I said rather ungraciously, fishing out my own key. I led her to my room, propped her against the wall while I opened the door and flicked on the light. We staggered in and she collapsed on the bed with a moan of relief. For the first time I got a good look at her. Her forehead, above the right eye, looked red and swollen with scrape marks running into the hairline. There was a big tear in her skirt along the seam. Had she fallen?

"You sure you're okay?" I asked.

"Sleep. Just need ... sleep."

"Well, don't get too comfortable," I said caustically. "I'm going to look for your purse. If I can't find it I'll get another key from Florie. Then you can get in your own bed." I wasn't about to give up mine.

"Thanks," she mumbled, her voice turning mushy. When I started out she lifted her head and said with more energy, "Mavis, we need ... gotta talk ... don't listen ... The Kid ..." Then she gave it up, dropped her face and snuggled into the pillow.

How in hell do I get into these things? I ran down the stairs and out to the porch, nodding to Rocky, who was tending a handful of people, a carafe of coffee in one hand, a brandy snifter in the other.

The porch was dark, but I could see well enough by the cast of the moon and street lights. The purse wasn't on the floor where I'd found Phoebe, or anywhere else, and I wasted time pawing through all the craft items, thinking it might have been dropped among them. Nothing.

Frustrated, I went inside. Rocky hovered over an elderly couple, idly chatting with them while keeping his eye on a larger group in the corner and Buster Brocheck and Garland Caldwell, who once more occupied the two large armchairs in the corner.

I didn't want to get sucked into any conversations, so decided to look for Florie rather than try to distract Rocky. Going through the door at the far end of the dining room, I found several more small rooms stuck in odd nooks and crannies set up for eating.

A narrow hall seemed likely to lead to the back of the house. I followed it, turned a corner and saw The Kid shuffling toward me, oxygen intact, his cane thumping lightly with his steps. I would have thought it past his bedtime. Probably coming back from one last smoke. The man was going to kill himself; how ludicrous to puff away at cigarettes at every opportunity, then suck in oxygen between times.

"Hi," I said. "I'm looking for Florie. Have you seen her?"

He shrugged. "Probably in the kitchen somewhere," he said, wheezing a bit.

"And where is that?"

He wiped his forehead with a handkerchief, removed the oxygen nosepiece, blew his nose, then replaced it again. "Right down there." He jerked his thumb behind his shoulder, and moved on.

He seemed very old, moving with difficulty. I reached out

to take his arm, wanting to help him, but held back, afraid he might take it as an insult. I didn't want to damage his pride. He had little enough of that left, as it was. I watched his slow progress for a second, then went to the kitchen.

Three high school kids were cleaning up; a couple of girls were washing dishes and a boy was happily goofing off, snapping a dish towel at their bare legs.

"Hi," I said. "Is Florie around?"

"I dunno," one of the girls answered with a giggle. "She was here awhile ago. Try the pantry."

I looked in that room, and several others, but she wasn't there. I was getting no place fast. "Thanks," I said distractedly. As I crossed the hall again, I noticed that the Kid had made it to his room. I hurried back the way I came.

I'd just have to get a key from Rocky. I'd already been gone too long; Phoebe was probably dead asleep, or passed out by now and I was going to have a hell of a time moving her.

When I reached the vestibule, I said, "Rocky, I need to speak to you." At the sight of me, Buster rose and stepped forward. I turned my back on him, grabbed Rocky's arm and drew him towards the registration table.

"I need a key to Phoebe Zimmerman's room. We came in together, but it seems she's lost her purse. She's in my room. I offered to get a key for her."

"We're not supposed to—"

"She's had a bit too much to drink," I said with one of those grimaces you hope speaks a thousand words.

"Oh, well ..." He went behind the registration desk to the antique key cupboard that hung on the stairwell wall. "She's in Hard-Nosed Lu, isn't she?" He opened the cupboard's door and ran his finger over the keys hanging there. "The other key isn't here. She must have both of them." He scratched his head. "Oh, wait a minute." He fumbled around in a drawer under the rack, peering at tags. "Here's one." He handed it to me. "Just have her check in with Florie tomorrow and tell her she has extra keys, okay?"

"Sure." I turned for the stairs, but Buster Brocheck stood in my way, a big grin on his face.

"Hey, there," he said. "I understand you're Max Holman's girl. I just wanted to say howdy. That Max is a right nice young man."

I smiled weakly, so tired and frustrated I wanted to scream "Out of my way, you blithering fool!" But of course I didn't. It wasn't his fault that I found myself serving as an extremely reluctant Good Samaritan to a drunken woman I didn't like very much. Besides, I didn't want to alienate him, though I couldn't remember exactly what it was I wanted to talk to him about. Unfortunately, drink seemed to make him effusive.

"Max spends a fair bit of time out to our place," he said, "and I want to tell you you're welcome, too. The little woman would love to see you." He chuckled, and poked me playfully in the ribs. "But you're gonna have to watch out for her. She's got a soft spot herself for Holman."

"I'd be glad to meet her," I said, inching up the first stair, "but right now—"

"Come on now, young lady, it's too early to be going to bed. Join us for a drink. I want you to meet my friend." He laid his big ham hand on my elbow. I hung onto the stair rail.

Rescue came from a unexpected quarter. "Last drink, Buster," Garland Caldwell called, holding his glass in the air. He cast me a sympathetic look. "Rocky's getting ready to close up. I'm going to finish this and be on my way."

Buster loosened his grip on my elbow. "Go ahead," I said, easing away from him. "Join your friend. We'll have a chance to talk later." I dashed up the stairs, not at all happy that I now owed one to Garland Caldwell.

Going directly to Phoebe's room, I unlocked the door and turned on the light. The room was similar to mine, simply furnished, but without a bathroom. The bed covers were turned back as mine had been and a candy rose placed on the pillow. I grabbed the rose and jerked back the covers, so I could just dump Phoebe on the bed.

Tossing the candy on the dresser, I noticed a Tarot card stuck in the mirror. The Knight of Wands; a young man in full armor riding a prancing steed, and holding a rather ridiculous-looking wooden club with sprouts growing out of it. It meant nothing to me, but at least answered one question: the cards must be in every room. I didn't give it another thought.

Leaving the light on and the door open, I crossed to my room, which I hadn't bothered to lock. The door opened to darkness and the stale reek of unpleasant odors. Phoebe must have roused enough to turn the light off. I flicked on the switch.

Phoebe lay on the bed as I'd left her, her impossibly bright hair a splash of color on the pillow. A knife—a large kitchen knife—protruded from her back.

Chapter Ten

"Phoebe," I cried, dropping to my knees beside the bed. My hand instinctively grabbed the knife, wanting to pull the ghastly thing out, but the instant my fingers touched it, I knew I shouldn't. My hand recoiled off the handle and dropped to her neck, searching futilely for a pulse. Nothing.

Be calm, be calm, I told myself, but all I could do was stare at the one open eye I could see, and the faint stain of pink-tinged drool that crawled across the pillow.

I stumbled to my feet, retching, trying to release the scream that seemed stuck in my throat. I ran out of the room and careened down the stairs.

"Rocky!" I croaked, still unable to produce a proper sound. "Call the police. Phoebe ... Phoebe's dead!"

"Wha—?" Rocky gasped, stopped in the process of urging the last customers toward the door. Everyone gaped at me, unsure of what was happening.

"What did she say?" someone asked.

"Who?" from another.

My legs collapsed and I sat down hard on one of the steps.

With a look of incredulity, Rocky pushed past me and ran up the steep flight. Some of the others who stood closest to him would have followed, but my presence on the stairs stopped them.

I sat in a state of shock, unable to move, or speak. I watched, heard the confusion, but couldn't take it in. All I could think about was the feel of the knife when my fingers wrapped around the handle, the awful sensation of outraged flesh clutching fast to the blade. My stomach churned.

Buster Brocheck and Garland Caldwell stood close to the front door, too far away to have heard my feeble croak.

"What's going on?" Buster asked, his great head swinging from side to side like a confused bull. "What's happened?"

Garland shrugged, one hand on the doorknob, his alert, inquisitive eyes skittering around like a buck deer trying to decide whether to run or not.

"Someone's dead."

Rocky clattered down the stairs behind me, muttering, "Shit, shit, shit."

He seemed surprised to see people still hanging around downstairs, waiting for answers. "Come on, guys," he said. Garland had already disappeared out the door, but Buster stood there, blocking the way.

"Get a move on. We're closed," Rocky said. With impatient shooing motions, he herded everyone out the door like a bunch of chickens, then headed for the phone.

Florie came in from the dining area, took one look at me and asked, "What happened?"

"Phoebe," I mumbled, rather incoherently. "Phoebe Zimmerman. She's dead." At least my voice had come back.

Florie's hand flew to her mouth and she went to Rocky, who was still talking into the phone. She listened a minute, then she too dashed upstairs, pushing past me much as Rocky had. She returned almost immediately, her face contorted and her fair skin tinged a faint green.

Rocky covered the phone's receiver with his hand, mouthed something at her, jerking his head toward the back of the house. She stared at him blankly for a moment then, with a strange look of panic, pushed behind the registration desk, knocking it askew, and rushed through the door at the end of the hall.

She had gained some measure of composure when she came back to stand beside Rocky again.

"They'll be right here," he told her, hanging up the phone.

She nodded. "He's asleep." They spoke in low voices which nevertheless carried plainly to my ears.

"I'll wait upstairs," Rocky said. "You watch her. Don't let her get away." They turned in unison to stare at me hard-eyed and fearfully, as if I were some kind of alien lowlife.

That shocked me out of my stupor. I jumped up. "Wait a minute, for God's sake. You can't think I killed her."

Rocky eyed me skeptically, holding up his hands in a pacifying manner. "Just sit down. The police will be here in a minute," he said, then took a wide berth around me and went back up the stairs.

Now that I was on my feet, it didn't seem possible to sit again; the shock was gone. From the look on Florie's face I knew it would be impossible to try to talk to her. So we just stood and looked helplessly at each other until the sound of a car screeching to a halt outside and feet pounding up the front stairs propelled me to the door.

"Come in," I said to the uniformed man, for all the world like a society matron greeting her guests.

There were two of them. A beefy, unsmiling man seemed

to be in charge. The other, younger man carried a duffel bag and kept a few steps behind his boss with the uncertainty of a new puppy. Rocky appeared at the top of the stairs.

"Hi, Dwayne," he said. "Where's the sheriff?"

"Out of town," the officer named Dwayne answered shortly, as if his competence had been questioned.

Rocky shrugged. "Up here."

The two men trooped up the stairs. Not knowing what else to do, I followed, as did Florie.

The three of them went in my room and eyed the body. Florie and I hovered awkwardly in the doorway.

"Who is it?" Dwayne asked.

Rocky said, "Her name's Phoebe Zimmerman. She rented a room this morning." Rocky jerked his head my way. "She found the body."

Dwayne glanced at me briefly, then looked around the room. "Anybody else been in here?"

Rocky shook his head. "No. I came up after she told me about it, then called you right away."

I looked at Florie, expecting her to say she had gone upstairs, too. But she remained silent, her eyes on Phoebe. My mouth dried and I averted my eyes. Florie said nothing.

Both of the officers had taken out notebooks and were jotting things down, then the younger one unzipped the duffel bag and took out a camera.

"Get some ID first, Buck," Dwayne told him, pointing to my purse on the dresser.

"That's my purse," I said, going to the dresser. Buck stopped me when I reached for it.

"*Your* purse?" the officer named Dwayne asked, turning his full attention to me.

"Yes," I said. "This is my room."

"*Your* room?" Hard-faced, he eyed me with a raised eyebrow.

I nodded miserably, suddenly realizing how tangled I was in this, and how strange my explanations were going to sound.

"Phoebe's room is across the hall," I offered. The officers shouldered past me. Following close on their heels, I stopped abruptly at the sight of the darkened room.

"Wait a minute," I said. "I left the light on in her room and the door wide open." The door was open now, but only ajar. "Did you turn the light off when you came up?" I asked Rocky.

"No. I didn't even go in there."

"Was the light on?" Dwayne asked him, carefully flipping on the switch with the end of his pen.

"I don't know." He shrugged. "I don't think I noticed one way or the other."

"You came up here," I said pointedly to Florie. "Was the light on then?"

"Of course it wasn't, or I would have noticed," she said angrily, as if she thought I was lying. Why would I lie about such a stupid thing as that?

"Then is there another way up here?" I insisted. "Someone had to turn the light off."

Neither Rocky nor Florie answered, as if my questions didn't matter. We stood in Phoebe's room, peering around as if something was going to jump out of thin air to explain everything away.

Dwayne opened the closet door. "Well, is there?" he asked, poking Phoebe's luggage with his foot. When no one answered, he turned and glared at Rocky.

"What?" Rocky asked nervously.

"Is there another way up here? Any backstairs?"

"Well, yes," he said uncertainly, gesturing in the direction of the hallway.

I looked over my shoulder, then went to the archway I'd noticed earlier. Four steps up led to a short hallway and a door named Madame Juju. Two other doors were unnamed, closets or storerooms, maybe. At the end of the corridor, a narrow flight of stairs descended to the lower floors. I turned back to see the others crowded behind me.

"Madame Juju?" Dwayne asked.

"Honeymoon suite," Rocky said, leading the way back down the four little stairs.

We formed an uneasy cluster in the hall, both officers writing in their notebooks.

"Anyone in these other rooms?" Dwayne asked.

"No," Florie said. "Jenny Frisco's rented, but they're on an overnight pack trip in Wind River. They'll be back tomorrow, or the next day."

Buck strung some yellow tape across the open door to Phoebe's room, then took the camera back into my room and began to take pictures.

Reality struck like a cudgel. Not only was Phoebe dead, she had been murdered. Someone had intentionally taken her life, plunged a knife deep into her back while she lay helpless, sleeping—in my room. My stomach churned with horror and a sudden shot of fright. Who? Why? Had someone meant to kill me, but got Phoebe by mistake? No, that couldn't be. Nobody could have mistaken that red hair for mine, unless, I thought uneasily, Phoebe had roused from her drunken stupor, turned the light off, and the killer had struck in the dark.

I played with the idea. I'd left the light on in my room when I went to hunt for her key, because I didn't want her thinking she was tucked in for the night. When I returned the light was off, but Phoebe lay on the bed in the same position as when I'd left her. She hadn't moved. Whoever had done this must have stabbed her, switched off the light, and left the room. It made sense. No matter what way I looked at it, the choices were chilling: the killer either knew who his victim was, or it was a random act of murder.

Or robbery, maybe? I remembered the woman downstairs wearing a fortune in silver jewelry. Could someone have been skulking around up here, waiting for an opportunity? My brain bounced crazily from thought to thought.

Then a picture entered my mind. The Kid, hovering in doorways, watching. Oh, God, I thought. Kid Corcoran, a resident criminal. Could he ...

I covered my face with my hands, trying to still the wild mix of images that came to mind. *Stop*, I told myself, breathing deeply. *Think*. I leaned against the wall, willing calmness to take over. Could the Kid have done this?

I had seen him downstairs. I remembered watching his slow progress down the hall toward his room, then, after looking for Florie in the kitchen area and heading back to find Rocky, I'd again seen the Kid at his doorway. It had taken him that long to go a fairly short distance. At that point, would he have been able to scurry back through the hallways, up the backstairs, stab Phoebe and hide himself in the upper hallway before I ran up and discovered her body? I'd been delayed only a few minutes more. At the rate he was moving, the Kid wouldn't have even gotten up the stairs in that length of time.

And what about the light in Phoebe's room? If neither Florie nor Rocky had turned it off, then ...

"Whoever killed Phoebe had to be hiding up here when I found her," I said aloud.

Rocky and Florie had huddled close together, watching the officers in my room.

Florie jerked around. "Why would anyone be up here?" She spat the words at me as if I'd accused her of dirty house-keeping, then began to cry. Rocky put his arm around her shoulders and pulled her close, but she'd found a convenient vent for her anger.

"This is your fault," she accused me between sobs. "None of this would have happened if you hadn't come here." She covered her face. "This will ruin us," she said. "We've worked so hard, now ... nothing."

Crap. "I simply meant that if neither one of you turned the light off in Phoebe's room, someone else must have."

"Don't try to blame any of us," she yelled. "You did this."

"Me?" I said, equally outraged.

"All right, you two," Dwayne stepped into the hall. In his hand he held the book I'd bought at Hildy's store, *The Story of Jade*. "This yours?" he asked me, riffling through the pages. "You some kind of jade expert?"

"I don't know much about it at all," I said, suddenly aware that maybe the purchase of the little volume had landed me in the midst of a local battlefield. "I just bought it today at the gift shop across the street."

He snapped the book shut and switched his penetrating gaze from me to Florie. "Where's the Kid?"

"Asleep," she said. "In his room downstairs."

"You sure?"

She nodded.

"Buck," he called. "Call the damn coroner, see what's keeping him, and get us some help here. We gotta secure these rooms."

"Want me to call the Sheriff's—"

"Nah, we don't need anybody from the damn Sheriff's Department. We can handle this. Call McConahy. He'll come in. And Roscoe. While you're down there check on the Kid. Go with him," he gestured to Florie.

"You want me to wake him up?" Florie asked.

"Not yet, just make sure he's there. Don't worry, I'll get around to him later," he said with enough sarcasm to indicate no one had to point out a prime suspect to him.

Florie caught the implication as well, and it was like seeing one of those cartoon light bulbs turn on above her head. Her mouth dropped open and her eyes flickered from one of us to another. *Aha,* I could see her thinking, *this is a way to get the old man out of my hair–send him back to prison.*

"He was with her," she said, licking her lips nervously, "that Zimmerman girl. She gave him a ride to the rodeo."

"Yeah?" Dwayne looked interested. "Is that right?"

Florie nodded. "I don't know where all she might have taken him."

Whoever said blood is thicker than water didn't know this woman. I didn't mind being eclipsed as chief suspect by any means, but I knew the old man couldn't have done this particular deed.

"I don't know what he and Phoebe might have been doing, but I saw your grandfather downstairs at about the time this must have been happening."

"We'll talk about it later," Dwayne said. He gave us both a cold, fish-eyed stare, and slapped the jade book in his palm over and over again until I thought I'd scream.

"Go on down, Buck," he said, finally, and motioned Florie to follow him. "Send the guys up when they get here. Check around downstairs and keep an eye on the Kid's room. You."

He pointed to me. "Stay here where I can see you." To Rocky he said, "You can do what you gotta do, just don't go anywhere. When we get some more help here I'm gonna want to talk to all of you."

"What about my things?" I asked, wondering for the first time where I was going to sleep.

"You can have them when we're through in there," he said, then added, "Anything, that is, that isn't needed for evidence."

Chapter Eleven

I sat on the floor of the upstairs hallway, leaned against the wall and tried to get comfortable. Feeling like a misplaced person with all my belongings impounded, I dully watched the flare of the flashbulb playing around the interior of my room—and tried not to imagine what the camera focused on.

Exhaustion had set in, my eyes were dry and gritty, the lids at half-mast. Somehow it seemed important that I try to figure out this light thing, since nobody else was interested. Who had turned it off, when and why, and did it mean anything? But it was difficult keeping my mind off Phoebe, lying there on my bed. Impossible to believe that such an outrageous, in-your-face, look-at-me personality could be so abruptly silenced.

I couldn't bear the stillness of her death, that she hadn't moved, that she lay on the bed exactly as I'd left her. She'd had no knowledge, no chance to struggle, to fight for her life, just that sneaky, insidious snuffing between one breath and another. Outrageously unfair.

My throat tightened, and I wiped a hand roughly across my eyes. No, I thought, gulping a bit, I didn't want to think about

Phoebe. Think about the damned light. Someone—come on, face it, the killer, murderer—had been lurking around up here, watching me while I prepared Phoebe's room and then discovered her body. And why, the minute I'd run downstairs, turn the light off in Phoebe's room? Trying to draw attention away from the room? But why? Why did the killer stay up here just to turn out the light in Phoebe's room? It didn't make sense.

Buck came back upstairs, followed by a disheveled older man who looked like he'd just stumbled from bed. They joined Dwayne in my room.

Dwayne had told Buck to keep an eye on the Kid's room. Who was watching it now? Maybe some more of their help had arrived.

I struggled to my feet; my legs were cramped and my butt sore. I had to move around and I wanted to tell Dwayne how I'd reached my conclusion that the Kid couldn't have killed Phoebe.

Dwayne stood in the door of my room giving orders to those inside. I went over to him and said, "I just want to explain to you why I think Kid Corcoran couldn't have done this: when I was downstairs, trying to find a key to Phoebe's room, I met him in the hallway; there's no way he could have gotten back up here in time."

Dwayne stared at me gravely, and I realized that he didn't know anything about me running around looking for Phoebe's key. He hadn't even begun to find out what had actually happened. I made one of those helpless gestures, and mumbled, "I'm sorry. I'm really tired."

He took my elbow. "Let's go downstairs. I'm ready to take your statement."

I was only too glad to get away from that room. I led the way down the stairs, and made a beeline for the sofa in the sitting room, sinking into it with a tremendous sigh of relief.

"Sit there," Dwayne said unnecessarily, "I'll go round up the Dunns."

I closed my eyes and nodded to him. Nothing had felt so comfortable to me in my life as this couch, at that moment. I leaned my head back and tucked my legs up on the cushions. As I began drifting off, I remembered reading somewhere that as far as the police were concerned, nothing signaled guilt as much as a suspect who falls asleep as soon as he's brought in. Something about the release of nervous tension ... or something ...

The next thing I knew Dwayne was shaking my shoulder. "Wake up, there. Wake up." My head rolled on the armrest with the motion.

"Wha ..?" I pried my eyes open. Dwayne stood over me, Rocky and Florie to the side, all staring at me. I struggled to sit up, and rubbed my eyes. My mouth was dry and I could feel dried saliva crusting the corner.

"I need to get a statement from you," Dwayne said. "You two can wait in there," he told Florie and Rocky, pointing to a table in the dining room. "But get Miss Barlow here some coffee, if you've got some."

The coffee helped, but not much. My head felt as if it were stuffed with old dust rags, but I did my best to tell my story clearly and in great detail. I started with my first meeting with Phoebe here at Racy Ladies, and then at the rodeo.

"She told me she worked for a small paper in California. Riverside, I think. She did local community news stories. She discovered Web Corcoran in a nursing home there, and wrote a piece about his early career as Kid Corcoran, when he was being mythologized as the last of the old-time bandits. It was a good story and was picked up by one of the larger papers around San Francisco. I have a copy of it in my briefcase, if you're interested."

"And she came here to talk to the old fart again?" he asked with some disbelief.

I shrugged. "I wondered about it myself, but I guess she thought a follow-up about how he felt going back to his childhood home would be worthwhile." As it turned out she'd stumbled onto a better story than she could have expected, but I didn't go into that.

I gave him Jimmy Chin and Kendall Hauser's names as others who had spoken with her at the rodeo.

But we spent most of the time on the sequence of my finding Phoebe drunk on the front porch, through to her death in my room. We went through it three or four times, interrupted by frequent arrivals of yet one more person come to help, who had to get instructions from Dwayne as to where to go and what to do.

And then a young guy in white pants and shirt arrived, carrying a folded stretcher in one hand. He snapped his fingers, bopping around to whatever he heard over his headphones and took the stairs two at a time. Soon he and the coroner came back down with Buck on one side balancing the stretcher and its blanket-shrouded burden. Dwayne got up and helped them out the front door.

I felt cold and drained and found it hard to concentrate when Dwayne plopped back down in his chair. "Now, where were we?" he asked, thumbing through his notebook.

So we went over it again. I worried about the quality of his note-taking, and wished I could peer over his shoulder and edit as he went. Again I made a special point of telling him I'd touched the knife handle, so he wouldn't be surprised if my prints showed up on it, and spelled out the few deductions I'd reached on my own about the light in Phoebe's bedroom. I even told him about Phoebe's grabbing me earlier in the evening, insisting she had something of great importance to tell me.

"And it was ..?

"She never got around to telling me."

"So you have no idea what was on her mind?"

"No, she ..." I hesitated, unsure if I should mention the gossip-based conclusion I'd reached on my own. Still it seemed in my best interest to leave nothing out.

I tried to choose my words carefully, not wanting to incriminate anyone else, particularly the Kid. Florie would handle that well enough on her own. And it was just gossip, after all.

"I heard," I said, "that there was a lot of talk around town about the death of Buster Brocheck's father, and that Kid Corcoran might have been involved in it."

Dwayne snorted with more emotion than I'd seen from him all night. "That's putting it lightly."

"Well," I said, "I just figured that if I'd heard the ... the rumor, Phoebe might well have also and, uh ... wanted to gloat about it or something."

"You two were rivals?"

"No. I didn't even know her. I mean, not before this morning."

"But you were both here to get stories about Kid Corcoran?"

"Well, yes, but there wasn't any rivalry. I didn't care what she wrote about. I'm just interested in the old stories about the Kid, his early career."

"Yeah?" He made no attempt to hide his skepticism. "And you don't know nothing about any jade, I suppose."

"No, or ... what exactly do you mean?"

"Most everyone around Rawhide thinks the only reason Kid Corcoran would dare come back to town is because he's got some kind of stash hidden somewhere. It seems he never could hang onto money, but he sure had some affinity for rocks. You know anything about that?"

"No, I don't. I wasn't even aware there was such a thing as Wyoming jade before this morning."

"But you know it's jade we're talking about when the Kid's name comes up?"

"Well, yes. I told you I'd heard gossip about the Kid."

"And when you talked, or, uh ... interviewed," he gave a nasty twist to the word, "the Kid, did he give you any special information that led you to believe he was in town for a specific purpose?"

"I've only spoken to him briefly. I haven't interviewed him as yet."

"Don't suppose you and that Phoebe woman were planning on doing a bit of jade hunting yourself, were you?"

"No, of course not. I came to Rawhide to spend some time with a friend and to interview Web Corcoran for my magazine at the same time."

"And who is this friend?"

"Max Holman. He's drilling a well on Buster Brocheck's ranch."

"He that geologist I hear's running around out there?"

Good grief. I didn't want Max to get pulled into all this jade business, too. "He's an oilman."

There was a dangerous undercurrent here that seemed to be coiling around me like a beast from the deep. If only I weren't so tired. And there was something in good old Dwayne's voice, or attitude, that had raised my antennae, made me wonder if maybe *his* daddy had been a jade man, too. What kind of an axe did he have to grind? I didn't even want to contemplate the thought. At least not now. The frequent stops to catch up on the note-taking were getting harder for me to handle. I should have loaned him my tape recorder. I leaned my head back on the sofa again and fought to keep my eyes open.

The doorbell's ring startled us all. Florie shot from her chair, but the door burst open before she reached it. Max Holman strode in the room, loaded for bear.

Chapter Twelve

"For God's sake, Thea," Max said, "what's going on?" Before I could even register his presence, he'd pulled me to my feet and wrapped his big arms around me. "Are you okay?"

I nodded, still semi-stupefied by surprise at his sudden appearance. His rough chin scratched blissfully across my cheek.

He pulled away, looked into my eyes for a moment, then gave me one of those quick head-to-toe surveys. "My God," he said, "you look awful."

"Thanks a lot." I found myself grinning like an idiot, delighted to hear this typical Maxian greeting. How could I have imagined for one minute that I didn't remember what he looked like? The eight months since we'd seen each other disappeared in a flash. "You look pretty awful yourself."

His dark-brown hair was tangled and a hard hat had left a matted flat crease that circled his head. A streak of grease ran through one of his Tom Selleck eyebrows, and the ever-present dark beard-shadow had turned into visible stubble. Still, his very presence seemed to dominate the room.

He looked down at himself with guilty surprise. "Guess I

should have changed," he muttered, glancing behind to see if his boots had tracked up the floor. "Buster came straight to the rig from town, said something had happened here and you might need help."

"It's been a nightmare, Max. Phoebe—Phoebe Zimmerman—a girl I met, is dead," I said, hopelessly unable to condense everything he needed to know into a few sentences.

"Murdered," Dwayne said, ready to take control again. "In this one's room," he jerked his head at me.

Max eyed him coldly. "And you are ..?"

"Officer Dwayne Muldrew, police."

"Where's the Sheriff?"

"Out of town," Dwayne bit the words off.

"Can't this wait?" Max demanded. "It's the middle of the night. She's in no shape to talk now. She needs to get some sleep."

"And who are you?"

"Max Holman."

"Ah, the geologist." Dwayne touched the tip of his pencil to his tongue and made a notation. "Know everything there is about rocks, huh?"

Max gave him a puzzled look. "I'm not a rock man; I'm a petroleum geologist. What does that have to do with this?" Then to me, "Did you call a lawyer?"

"She don't need a lawyer," Dwayne said. "Yet. Now sit." He pointed Max to a table in the dining area. "Or I'm going to take her down to the station."

"It's okay, Max," I said wearily. "I'm just telling him what happened. I'll be with you in a minute."

His heavy-lidded eyes looked tired and the creases that fanned their corners seemed cut a little deeper in his tanned face than I remembered; but he looked wonderful to me.

"Please, Max," I said, urging him towards the other room. "We're almost finished."

Reluctantly, Max joined Rocky and Florie, who stood a few feet away taking it all in. Florie sat back down at one of the tables and Rocky and Max leaned against the sideboard. Dwayne settled himself in his chair and began to review the notes he'd taken. Sinking onto the sofa, I contented myself with watching Max across the room. Rocky had poured coffee for both of them and Max seemed to be plying him with questions. Good, I thought. No way could I manage another string of explanations.

As it turned out Dwayne had pretty much finished with the questions, and I couldn't think of anything pertinent to add.

"Well, that about does it for now, Miss Barlow. Except for this." He leafed through his notebook and plucked a card from between the pages. "What's this?" He handed it to me.

I turned it over in my hand, but I knew what it was. The Queen of Swords.

"It was in your purse."

"Yes, I know," I said. "It's a Tarot card. I found it in my room, stuck in the mirror frame. I guess they put them in all the rooms; I saw one in Phoebe's room, too. For some reason I just threw this in my purse."

Dwayne stared at me, as if waiting for me to say more. I wrapped my fingers around the card, remembering why I'd taken it with me. Protection. Had the indomitable Queen saved me from the dark man, The King of Swords? Under other circumstances might I have been in Phoebe's place? Or was the queen playing another game? Like "Throw the little fool into a pool of dark-haired men and see what kind of stuff she's made of"?

Across the room Rocky and Max were still talking, their dark heads close together. Then there was Jimmy Chin, and Kendall Hauser. Even Dwayne had black hair liberally shot with gray. If I went by hair color the Kid was the only safe person around. I rubbed my eyes. I was too damned tired to think about this crazy stuff now.

"What's it for?" Dwayne asked, plucking the card from my hand.

I stifled a huge yawn. "Fortune-telling. Sheila Rides Horse, the cook here, reads Tarot for people. I thought maybe this was how she advertised. You know, putting cards in the guest rooms. Do you know her?"

"Yeah, I know who she is. Hangs out at the Center Bar a lot. You say there's one of these in Zimmerman's room?"

I nodded.

He stood and hitched up his pants. "The guys should be about finished. You can have your purse and suitcase back if they're through with them."

We went upstairs. Max and Rocky followed and stood to one side. Dwayne went first to Phoebe's room and ducked under the yellow tape. I didn't have to cross the barrier to see that the Tarot card was no longer where I'd seen it.

Dwayne ducked back under and went over to my room, waving the card in front of him. "Any of you guys see a card like this in the other room?"

The two men working in the room came to the doorway. "Nah," said one. The other shook his head.

"It was stuck in the mirror," I offered.

They stared at me a moment then repeated, "Nope," to Dwayne.

"When did you see it in her room?" he asked me.

"The only time I was in there: when I got the key from Rocky and was getting ready to get Phoebe to her room. I don't remember noticing the card one way or the other when the Dunns and I were in the room with you earlier. Did any of your men take pictures in there? If so, they might help pinpoint when the card disappeared."

He contemplated the card some more, then seemed to dismiss it. I don't think he appreciated my suggestions.

"Did anyone tape off the back stairwell?" he asked his men.

"I didn't. Buck was doing the taping."

Dwayne disappeared into the small upper hallway and returned almost immediately, shaking his head. "Tell Buck I don't want nobody using those back stairs 'til we're done with them," he roared at the men. "Get 'em taped top and bottom." But we all knew it was too late. Anyone and his dog could have been up and down the stairs freely the last two hours and no one would have been the wiser.

"You finished with Barlow's purse and suitcase?"

One of the men handed Dwayne a plastic garbage bag, which he passed on to me. My emptied crochet sling bag and all its contents were in the bottom, along with some fine powder I assumed was from the fingerprinting process. The man returned with my suitcase held upright in his arms. It was unzipped, everything in it jumbled and hanging over the sides. He set it on the floor at my feet.

I stared at it numbly. "What about the things I put in drawers," I asked, "and the bathroom? And my briefcase?"

"Later," Dwayne said. "You can't sleep in there, either."

"As if she'd want to," Max said, coming to stand beside me. "Rocky's given you another room, free of charge."

"Here?"

"Half the town's hanging around outside trying to find out what's going on. You don't want to run that gauntlet. Besides, it's three o'clock in the morning, not the best time to hunt for another room. All my stuff's out at the rig. I'll move you out there tomorrow, or we'll make other arrangements, but for tonight—right now—we're taking this room." He pointed at the archway to Madam Juju. "I'm staying with you," he stated firmly. "You're not spending the night alone."

I was in no condition to argue with anyone, even if I wanted to. I heard Max tell Dwayne that I was through for the night and if he needed to talk to me tomorrow I'd be available. He picked up my suitcase without zipping it and tucked it under his arm. "Come on." He took my arm. "Let's go."

He led me up the short flight of stairs and into Madam Juju. As soon as the door closed behind us Max wrapped me again in his big arms. I was inert, but appreciative.

He drew back to look at my face. "Hi," he said, and flashed the glorious smile that had always made my stomach lurch a bit. Smoothing my straggling hair away from my forehead—God only knew what I looked like—he proceeded to kiss me long, tenderly.

"Are you okay?" he asked seriously when we finally came up for air. "Finding her ... was it too horrible?"

I nodded, burying my nose in his shoulder, but words wouldn't come. I was all talked out. Thank God I didn't need them with Max.

"Look," he said. "I have to get back to the rig first thing in the morning; you can come with me if you like. I'm going to get someone to take over for me out there. I thought we'd be at completion by the time you got here, but we ran into a bunch of hard—Hell," he said, stopping for another kiss. "We'll talk about that later."

Finally, he murmured into my ear, "I've got to shower. I'm going to go find Rocky and round up a toothbrush and paste and whatever else he can come up with. I'll be right back."

He was about to the door when I remembered there was one thing I needed to know. "Max," my voice sounded like a creaky hinge. "You went fishing?"

"What?"

"You went fishing."

"When? What are you talking about?"

"I called you back at the rig, a little while after we first talked this afternoon. The man said you went fishing."

"Fish— Oh." He grinned. "We had a broken drill stem. I was helping the guys fish it out of the hole."

"Oh," I said, and grinned as well. "Good." I stretched out on the bed to wait for his return.

I vaguely remembered hearing the shower run, and Max crawling into bed beside me. When his arms wrapped around me, I discovered I wasn't nearly as sleepy as I had thought I was.

A sharp clicking noise woke me later and I lay there only partially awake, listening, wondering what the sound was. Then it stopped and sleep rolled over me again.

Another noise pulled me partially alert again. A soft scuffling, in the bathroom ... or the hallway ... A thunk. Close. I shot up, heart pounding, clutching the sheet in my lap. The door had closed. Hadn't it? My eyes searched the room. Nothing unusual, the bathroom door was still partially open, as we'd left it. I rested a trembling hand on Max's shoulder. He turned, mumbled a sleepy, "Hmm?" and pulled me down and close, snuggling into my back. Another noise, definitely in the hallway. Jumpy, I thought, I'm just jumpy. After all, it is a hotel. I relaxed into Max and dissolved again into deep sleep.

In the morning I woke slowly, still clinging to vivid dream images. Gramps was there. We were going fishing, and I was holding onto his arm. *Now stay with me*, I kept telling him. *Don't go away.* I was anxious, because I knew I had to protect him from something, but I didn't know what. It didn't seem to matter that sometimes he looked like Gramps and sometimes he looked like Web Corcoran. I knew it was Gramps, and I felt warm and happy just being with him again. Snuggling into the soft bed, not ready to open my eyes yet, I let the dream images drift slowly away.

Mind pictures of last night's events replaced them, snippets that seemed astonishingly real in that wonderful alpha state of clarity that exists on first waking.

The scene on the porch replayed behind my eyes: Phoebe stretched out on the wooden floorboards, me kneeling beside her. Fear filled her eyes and befuddled voice. Fear. "Don't let them see me" she'd said. I'd taken it for pride at the time, now it seemed more sinister. And hadn't she said "Be careful," more than once? Again, I'd put a totally different spin on it, thought she was worried about the way I was pulling her to her feet.

I was wide awake now, afraid to open my eyes or move, for fear I'd lose these elusive memories. It seemed so clear to me now: she'd been trying to warn me about something, but who had she been afraid of?

What else had she said? Upstairs ... She'd collapsed on my bed, I was about to leave and she'd risen up—why hadn't I noticed the urgency of it?—and said something like "We've gotta talk," and she mentioned the Kid. Said "Don't listen ..." Had she meant don't listen to the Kid, or was she trying to tell me something else about him? Her speech had been so boozy and disconnected that I hadn't even tried to understand.

I repeated her words over and over in my head, so I wouldn't forget them, then jumped out of bed, scrabbled for paper and pen, and wrote everything down. That done, I sat back on the bed and looked around. It took a moment to remember that this was a different room; I wasn't in Mavis any more. I got up to look at the picture on the wall. *Madame Juju*, the placard underneath the photograph read, *real name, Catherine Nederland.* The sepia-tinted picture showed a plump, wrapper-clad young woman with frowsy short hair posed seductively on a chaise. Probably hot stuff for its day.

My watch showed a few minutes after nine. I must have slept the sleep of exhaustion, both physical and mental. Not surprisingly, Max had already left. I smiled and stretched, luxuriating in the memories of being with him again. I could see a note propped against the fringed lamp on the dresser. *Couldn't bear to wake you* it read. *Rest well, this is the last chance you get, we have things to do! Be in by three to get you. Love, Max.*

My suitcase was on the floor and the plastic bag filled with my purse and its contents was on the dresser. I took a quick shower and pulled on some jeans and a light shirt, investigating the room as I did so. More spacious than Mavis, nicer furnishings, great brass bed, and a larger bathroom, with, thank God, a shower.

I stood in front of the mirror brushing my hair and letting my mind wander when it suddenly occurred to me that there wasn't a Tarot card tucked in this mirror's frame, which, of course, reminded me of Sheila Rides Horse.

Where had she been during all of last night's commotion? Did she have anything to do with the missing Tarot card from Phoebe's room? She had a room somewhere in the back of the house, she'd said. Had the police talked to her?

I quickly pulled my hair back, wrapping it carelessly with a scrunchie. Sheila had said to look her up this morning and I was damned well going to. I hurried out.

On impulse, I took the back staircase. The yellow tape had been removed, and I was curious about where it led. The stairs were steep, narrow and wooden. Anyone using them would have to take extreme care not to be heard. Two short landings changed the direction of the flight before it ended on the main floor in another hallway. One could truly get lost in this maze. To the left of the staircase was a windowed door to the outside, and to the right the hall dead-ended with a sharp turn into another passage.

As if by magic, Florie appeared there and looked at me with some surprise, as if she were expecting someone else. She seemed flustered and harried. As if already the day wasn't going well for her.

"Oh, it's you," she said. "Our guests usually use the other staircase." Her tone was more matter-of-fact than unfriendly. "There's coffee, juice and rolls on the sideboard in the dining room."

"Thanks," I said.

She eyed me curiously, hesitating a moment as if there were something she wanted to say, but then she turned and disappeared as quickly as she had appeared.

I looked out the grimy window, trying to orient myself, and tried the door handle. Locked. I didn't recognize anything outside, but figured this must be the back of the house—an easy, private way upstairs for anyone who had a key.

I followed the turn into the hall that Florie had taken. It brought me to the wider passage that I remembered from last night. The kitchen was to my right, and the curtained outside door that led to the side porch where the Kid went to smoke was at the far end. On the opposite wall was a door with an ornate brass knocker; on a hunch, I used it.

Sheila Rides Horse opened it. "I've been waiting for you," she said, and pulled me in.

Chapter Thirteen

Filled with a brisk urgency, the woman motioned me to a small table and two chairs. She wore a loose cotton dress and her feet were bare. Impatiently, she tucked her dark shoulder-length hair behind her ears.

The small room had all the trappings of a low-rent studio apartment. Some cupboards and a two-burner range in a corner, next to a sink with a red-checked curtain around its base. A metal bed covered with a bright, star-patterned quilt took up another corner. A partition marked off the third corner into what was most likely a bathroom.

A comfortable recliner sat in front of overflowing book-shelves of the plank-and-cinder-block variety which lined every inch of available wall space.

Sheila followed my glance as if seeing her surroundings with new eyes. She shrugged and grinned. "It's free."

Without asking she poured two cups of coffee from a dented metal percolator, and urged me again to one of the chairs at the table. She sat opposite and pulled a packet wrapped in a dark blue velvet cloth from the pocket of her dress.

I tried a few sips of the bitter, boiled coffee, but couldn't hack it. Sheila drank deeply of hers.

"Do you have the Queen of Swords?" she asked without preamble.

"You mean the card you stuck in my mirror?"

She grinned. "Yeah."

"How did you get into my room?"

She shrugged. "We need the card."

"Well, I'm afraid the police have it."

"The police?"

"Yes."

"Where was the Sheriff?"

"Out of town," I answered automatically, feeling a bit more sympathetic towards Dwayne. "What's this bit with the sheriff?"

"He's a good man. Knows what he's doing. Don't tell me you got Dwayne Muldrew out here investigating?"

"That's who we had. He hasn't talked to you yet?"

"Not yet."

"Where were you last night?"

"Out." She took the cloth from the packet of Tarot cards and began to shuffle them. "We can work without the queen."

"You mean with an incomplete deck?"

"Oh. No, that card wasn't from this deck. I have lots of decks. If I want to project cards out into the world I use those. This deck always remains complete."

So many questions were roiling around in my head I didn't know where to begin. "But why did you put a card in my room?"

"I wanted a significator."

"A what?"

"A card that represents you. It can be used as the base of a reading."

"But why? Look, I haven't a clue about any of this. You're going to have to tell me a lot more."

"The cards have been warning me about something for a long time now. I'm just not sure what it's all about."

"Why not? I thought that's what you did?"

As she talked, she dealt the cards into five piles as if for a hand of cards. "Tarot doesn't stand up and shout at you. It speaks in symbols. The meaning isn't always clear, or can be read in different ways."

"What are you doing?" I asked, watching her slap the last few cards into their respective piles.

"Cleansing the deck." She gathered the whole mess up again and shuffled. "Getting rid of past influences, or if you prefer," she said with a sly little smile, "just another way to shuffle."

I loved watching her hands on the cards. It was as if each finger vied with the others to caress the cards in their own individual manner. Between shuffles, she held the pack enclosed in both hands like one would a baby bird.

"When the readings speak with urgency," she said, "repeatedly showing the same cards over and over again, you better take notice. 'Pay attention!', they're saying. *Do* something." She shrugged. "But it doesn't always make it any easier to know what's going on."

"Yesterday," she continued in her rather monotonous voice, "at the fairgrounds, the same cards showed up in your reading that I've been seeing over and over again in mine. It spooked me. I didn't know if I was influencing the cards, or if you're mixed up in whatever's brewing around here. I still don't know. That's why I want to do another spread for you. Maybe we can figure it out."

"And the Queen of Swords in my room?"

"I picked her to represent you. I wanted the card to absorb your surroundings, catch your vibes. Did you handle the card?"

I nodded.

She shrugged, one of her favorite expressions. "Well, it doesn't matter now. Good old Dwayne's put his spin on it; won't do me any good."

"It would have made a difference?"

"Yeah, I think so. Could have given the reading a better focus."

"But what about Phoebe? I saw a card in her room, too. Did you put it there?"

"Yeah. I didn't have any contact with her, but seeing as how she came to Racy Ladies same day as you, I thought I'd cover all bases. The Knight of Wands."

"Why that card?"

"It suited her. Youth, energy, ambition. Impetuous, devious."

"Did you take her card? It's not in her room anymore."

"It's not?"

"No," I said, not at all impressed with her show of innocence; she was not good at dissembling. "No, it's gone. It disappeared sometime after I found Phoebe's body." There could have been more windows of opportunity, but the most likely time for the card's disappearance was in the few—very few—minutes between my finding the body and Rocky running back upstairs to check on my story.

Had the same person who turned out the light in Phoebe's room also taken the Tarot card? Had the killer done both of those things? I licked my lips nervously.

Sheila gazed at me quizzically and cocked her head. "I didn't kill Phoebe Zimmerman," she said, as if she'd been reading my mind. "I couldn't help her, either. And I can't be responsible for you. All I can do is read the cards." She gave a little snort. "Sometimes I don't do that so hot. If the cards indicate you're part of the forces swirling around me, then at least you'll be warned. All I can do is read the cards. You gotta depend on your own insight." She snapped through a final shuffle, and placed the deck in front of her. "And my knowledge." She turned the top card over.

Even I recognized the King of Swords. She ran her fingers over the face of the card, shaking her head in wonderment. "He's appeared in every spread I've done for myself in the last three months. And in your reading yesterday. Sometimes upright, sometimes, like now, upside down. He's a dark man, both hair and soul." Her voice became soft and thready. "Strong, ambitious, and powerful. Ruthless. He's jerking me around, forcing my fate. I don't like it."

"You're sure of all that?" I asked dubiously; it sounded like a bunch of rubbish to me.

"Yes, I'm sure," she said with a sense of finality. "The King of Swords isn't always a bad guy, but this time he is."

"How do you know?" I asked, still awash with skepticism.

"By the company he keeps." She flipped over the next two cards. "Death and Sorrow"—she indicated that I should turn over the next. I did—"and Turmoil," she intoned, tracing the pattern of the lightning bolt, the couple flailing through the air.

She could have stacked the deck, I thought, staring at the cards in amazement. I didn't want to believe, because these were the cards I'd seen before: the grinning skeleton of Death and the sundered Tower. The third card, in the middle position, I didn't know, but it depicted a fallen body pierced by numerous swords.

I thought of Phoebe and how I'd actually touched the knife that took her life. A gush of sorrow welled up from some hidden part of me I'd not been aware of before, engulfing me in a dark cloud of misery. My vision blurred. I couldn't think. I couldn't speak. Tears that should have been shed last night poured down my cheeks. My breath caught in sobs.

Slowly, the flood began to recede. Sheila watched without expression. "That's the card speaking to you," she said.

I wiped my eyes with the back of my hand, wildly embarrassed by the unexpected outburst of emotion. "She was so young," I said, offering the only excuse I could think of, "so full of life."

"I couldn't help her," Sheila said, reaching behind her to hand me a box of tissue. I blew my nose and got up to throw the tissue in the wastebasket. My toe kicked something that went rattling across the floor.

Sheila half-rose from her chair. "What is it?"

"A pebble," I said, picking up a small piece of gravel. "It must have been stuck in my shoe." I started to throw it away with the tissue, but she said she wanted to see it. I handed it to her.

She turned it over in her palm. "Rocks and stones. Everywhere I go, inside or out, I'm kicking up rocks and stones. I've never done that before. And now you're doing it." She shook her head and put the pebble at the end of a row of stones that lined the windowsill. She motioned me back into the chair. "I want you to handle the cards now. Cleanse the deck first."

I followed her directions, then gathered the cards, shuffled, and cut the deck in three stacks. Sheila picked them up.

"You are a strong woman," she said, as she began to lay out the spread, "but you rule from compassion. That's why I chose the Queen of Swords for you. Your heart is as big as your sword."

"I don't have a sword," I said, attempting a bit of levity.

"Then get one. You will need a sword."

Chapter Fourteen

Sheila Rides Horse studied the spread of cards silently, elbows on the table, head propped in her hands. I'd witnessed the constant cleansing of the deck, the repeated shuffling by both Sheila and myself, yet in a layout of fourteen cards from a pack of seventy-eight, there they all were again. A preponderance of the suit of swords: struggle and animosity. Swords everywhere, in fact. And, of course, the King. This time the Queen of Swords was next to him.

"See," Sheila said, shaking her finger. "He means you harm, but you are strong. Just be careful."

Yeah, and get a sword, I thought.

The others were there as well, the Tower, the Hanged Man, and the awful sword-pierced body of the Ten of Swords. And no matter how she tried to soften the Death card by calling it transition, I saw it for what it was, and it chilled me.

"Did you see Phoebe's death in the cards?"

"I saw someone's death. I thought it would be mine," she said, much more calmly than I could have managed. "I can't burden you with this," she said, dismissing the layout. "It's too dark, and just a warning, anyway. I can read for myself, but I don't want to put things in your head that might not happen. You're never bound by the cards, you know, there is always free will."

"But—"

"There are other things here that I will tell you." She brushed her fingers across a few of the more innocuous cards. "You have a lot of unresolved issues in your life involving relationships and you're fighting the solutions." She spoke quickly and lightly. "The answers are there. Why are you afraid of them? And again I see a new career, or at least a new venture, involving people and houses. Service of some kind, I think. Maybe you like to cook, too?"

"I like to eat," I said, with a little laugh, much relieved by this lighter mood. "Where did *you* learn to cook?"

"The orphanage. Sister Fortunata."

"Here in Rawhide?"

"No, South Dakota. Got dumped there as a newborn. Sister Fortunata took me under her wing. She was a bit of a rebel herself." Sheila stretched and rested against the back of her chair. She too seemed relieved by the respite, a brief escape from the doom-saying cards. "She taught me Tarot, and how to escape into books. I found an old Escoffier Cookbook when I was around twelve. She let me experiment in the kitchen. Always encouraged me. Been cooking ever since." She gazed out the window a moment, lost in her reverie. "She was like a mother to me. A best friend. She died two years ago. A part of me went with her." It was the longest speech I'd heard from her. "Tell me about your grandfather," she said, with an expression on her face that made me think she really wanted to hear what I had to say.

"How do you know about my grandfather?" I said, startled. "You mentioned him yesterday, too."

She gave another of those expressive shrugs. "The Tarot opens all kinds of windows. I see lots of things. I don't always know where they come from."

Now it was my turn to gaze out the window, thinking about Gramps. "I can't let him go," I said, finally. "He was my beacon. He brought adventure to my life. The world and everything in it held glorious promise whenever he was around. He gave me years of advice, wise counsel, unquestioning love. My parents were hard-working, busy people. He was the core of our family, kept us all vital and strong. I can't bear to see him dwindling away."

"And now he is—"

"The cranky old shell of the man he used to be. Feeble and bedridden by choice, resigned, waiting to die. I want to shake him, I want him to rise up and fight, to regain the brilliance he shed so generously on us. I want him to cherish every minute that's left to him." I paused a moment, trying to sort out my feelings. "Most of all, I'm afraid my light will diminish and die when he's gone."

For some reason, we both looked back down at the spread of cards. Perhaps we'd had enough of self-revelation.

"You have the answers," she said. "Remember the Hanged Man, strangled by life patterns he won't give up. Tear them away. Run toward the new and what is waiting for you. And as for this," she said, indicating the cards. "We are in it together. I am here, and here." She pointed to two different cards. The tenor of her voice dropped and became nearly toneless. Her eyes focused on something I couldn't see. "We must be fearless, but careful."

With a shudder of her heavy shoulders she rose to her feet. She was nowhere near them, but the collection of stones on the windowsill clattered to the floor, bouncing and rolling around our feet. I jumped out of my chair, knocking it over. The hair on the back of my neck bristled with alarm.

"Help me find the dark-haired man," Sheila said, stretching a hand out to me. "Fly with me." Her voice dropped to a whisper. "Fly ... We'll find the King ..."

She dropped back into the chair, her glazed eyes fluttering shut.

I was out of the room like a shot, skin crawling, breath coming in frightened little gusts. I hurried through the maze of hallways toward the front of the house. Way too weird for me. I desperately needed some good strong caffeine.

I found coffee, juice and breakfast rolls on the sideboard in the dining room. Rocky stood behind the registration desk, sorting out keys.

"Hi," he said, as I shakily poured myself a cup of coffee. "Did you sleep all right?"

"Yeah, like the dead." I grimaced at my word, took my coffee and stood by the desk watching him, sorely needing company.

"How about you?" I asked. "I bet you had a long night of it."

"You're not kidding, I ..." He looked at me sharply. "Are you sure you're okay? You look like you've seen a ghost."

"No, I'm fine. I just needed some coffee," I said with a pathetic little laugh. "I've been talking to Sheila Rides Horse."

"Oh, yeah? She's quite a character." He pawed through the pile of keys, reading tags, looking for matches. "But let me tell you, if she was as psychic as she thinks she is, she could have saved us a bunch of trouble last night."

"Psychic?"

"Yeah. Reads fortunes, too. Florie says she has visions. She's a strange one all right. I don't believe in any of that crap, myself."

I couldn't argue with his opinion of Sheila. Still, there was something about her. Stolid and rather lumpish, yet intelligence fairly leapt from her eyes, and her fey sense of humor continually took me by surprise. I found myself liking her—at least now that I wasn't in the same room with her—regardless of my suspicions, which never quite disappeared.

"She's the best damn cook I've ever known. She's put us on the map, let me tell ya." He snagged another key, put it with two others and hung them on a hook.

I asked, "Have the police found anything out yet about Phoebe?"

"You mean who killed her?"

I nodded.

"No. At least not that they've told me. The cops didn't leave 'til early this morning, but I guess they'll be in and out all day."

"What do you think, Rocky? Do you have any ideas?"

"About what?" he asked nervously.

"About Phoebe, who could have killed her." I couldn't believe he hadn't done some speculating. "I mean, what was going on down here at the time? Did you notice anything unusual? Did you hear anything upstairs at all?"

"No. Not a damn thing."

"I know Garland Caldwell and Buster Brocheck were having after-dinner drinks. Had they been here all evening?"

"Oh, you know, they kind of come and go. Buster left after dinner for a while and then came back. Caldwell and his wife left; he must have taken her back to the motel because he came by here later, alone, and he and Buster sat over drinks. They were having brandies. Caldwell's a good spender. There were four or five other people here, too. I gave all their names to the police."

"And none of them were moving around the house, going to the restroom?"

"I don't remember anything like that."

And what about Rocky? Had he been tending bar all that time? I sighed and sipped my coffee. "It just seems so unbelievable that people could be sitting and talking so normally downstairs when something so horrible is happening upstairs."

"Yeah, it gives you the creeps." He had the door of the small hanging key closet open, putting matched sets of keys on hooks as he found them. "I just wish the Sheriff was in town. He knows what he's doing."

"Is, uh, Dwayne all that bad?" Only in Wyoming would I be calling a police officer—who was diligently trying to pin a murder on me—by his first name.

Rocky shrugged. "He's all right, I guess. We went through school together. Never seemed like he had a brain in his head, is all."

But I needed to know something else.

"Last night, Rocky, while we were waiting for the police, you went upstairs to stay with the ... the body. Did you wait in Phoebe's room or in the hall?"

"In the hall. Why? What do you want to know for?" He frowned, instantly prickly.

"I'm just wondering who took the Tarot card out of Phoebe's room, and when they could have done it." Actually, I was quite positive *who* had taken the card—Sheila Rides Horse— but *when* was the crucial question.

"Oh, that," Rocky said, losing interest and going back to his keys. "I wasn't about to wait in there where she was so I stayed in the hall."

It wasn't conclusive, I thought. I supposed it was possible that Sheila could have slipped upstairs while the police were working in my room and whisked the card away then, and not in those few moments that were only available to the killer. Why was I finding it so hard to believe that she might have wielded the weapon? The knife had probably come from her Racy Ladies kitchen. Maybe she *was* a crazed killer; she was certainly spooky enough. Still, I couldn't convince myself. It didn't track for some reason.

"Do you have your key to Mavis?" Rocky asked, hanging two others on a hook labeled with that name.

"Yes, it should be in my room upstairs. I'll bring it down. I don't plan on ever going in there again." I looked the keys over with some interest. "I guess I should get a key to Madame Juju. How many keys to each room?" I asked.

"Should be three for each guest room. We keep two on the hook and a spare in the drawer. One of the Hard-Nosed Lu keys is missing," Rocky added casually. "Don't know what happened to it."

"You have two?"

"Yeah."

"Then the other one is in Phoebe's purse. It's her purse that's lost." I made a mental note to remind Dwayne about that. "The two keys hanging on Lu's hook are the spare that you gave me last night—I'm assuming the police found it in her room where I left it and gave it back to you?"

He nodded.

"Then the other key hanging there must be the one that was missing last night. Whoever took it must have returned it."

"Are you saying that someone stole the key and used it to get into Phoebe's room?"

"All I'm saying is it wasn't there last night when you were looking for it. Now it's here."

"I don't like your—"

"Oh, come off it, Rocky. That's a great-looking key cupboard, but face it, anyone could take anything out of it any time they wanted, and return it, as well. You don't even keep the silly thing locked."

He gave a weary sigh and ran his hands over his hair and then his face. The dark smudges under his eyes were more pronounced than ever.

"You're right, I know it. That's why I'm trying to sort this mess out," he said, dejected. Then with a burst of anger, "We've never had to worry about this stuff before." He slammed the door of the little cabinet. It whapped in place, then slowly bounced back open. "Now I've got to come up with some other system." He began picking through the keys again, matching and hanging.

I got a refill of coffee and brought him back a cup, too.

"Thanks," he said, with an apologetic smile. "I'm pretty frustrated at this point. And look, Thea, I'm sorry that Florie sounded off at you last night. She was really upset."

Weren't we all, I thought dryly.

"We never did think you had anything to do with Phoebe's death."

I wondered if it was a real apology, or if he'd just changed camps, ready with Florie to shift all blame on the Kid.

"All of us were upset, Rocky."

"Florie's right, though. This could really ruin us, particularly with people like Hildy Gilstrom bad-mouthing us to all the tourists. She'll love this turn of events," he said bitterly.

"What's her problem?"

"She's got a bug up her butt about most everything. Her father used to be a big man in this town. Used to own this building. Not in the glory days when it was the fanciest whorehouse north of Denver—that's what we're trying to restore it to look like. Hildy's father owned it much later. Not that there weren't prostitutes here then, too, but it was a sleazier business then, undercover. Anyway, Hildy's father came on hard times and sold the place, which was fine for Hildy then. She didn't want that kind of thing, a whorehouse, in the family. But now that Florie and I bought the place—hell, they were going to tear it down and build a gas station here five years ago—and began making a success of it, you'd think we'd stolen her birthright."

"Does she still have an interest in it? Did you buy it from her?"

"Hell, no. It's been through a dozen owners since her daddy sold it."

"Doesn't seem very reasonable."

"Reason doesn't have any meaning to Hildy Gilstrom. I'd like to wring her neck."

I let that one alone.

"And now she's all hot under the collar because Florie's grandfather's here. Says it's our fault for bringing a criminal element into town. As if we had any choice in the matter."

"You didn't?"

"Hell, no. He just showed up one day about two weeks ago. Sicker than hell, too. Had to get a doctor and everything. Bronchitis. He's not an easy patient. He had some wild idea about going out to the ranch to live. We couldn't let him do that. Nobody's lived out there for a couple of years, not since

Florie's mom died. The old house has gone to ruin. No water, no electricity, no nothing. Florie's mom had a nice trailer out there for years, but we hauled that to town and sold it after she died. There's nothing out there for him."

"Was Florie's mother Corcoran's daughter?" I asked.

"Yeah. She wanted us to take over the ranch. We tried it a while, but neither Florie or I liked it much. Damn hard work. Florie's mom helped us buy this place. We would've sold the ranch when she died, if we could've. Man, we could use the money; this place sucks up dough like a vacuum cleaner. But the Kid wouldn't hear of it, ornery old coot."

"Does he own the ranch?"

"It belongs half to Florie and half to the Kid. Neither one can sell without the other's permission." He threw some scraps of paper in the wastebasket. "Here," he said, handing me a key. "To Madame Juju. Again, I can't tell you how sorry I am for all that's happened. You know, we'd really appreciate it if you'd stick around here. I mean, keep your room at Racy Ladies for as long as you're in town. It would sure help us out. Kind of show people that the place is still okay regardless of ..."

"I'm not sure what my plans are going to be."

"We'd let you have Juju for no cost to make up for bad experiences." Nothing like a free room for an enticement.

"Well, for right now that's fine with me. What do the police say? Are they going to release those two rooms to you? And I wonder when I'm going to get the rest of my things back."

"Yeah, Dwayne said we could have Hard-Nosed Lu back tomorrow. I'm not even thinking about renting Mavis again for a long time. Don't think it would set well with folks. We'll just close it up for now."

"Sounds like a good idea. On second thought, Rocky, why

don't you let me have all the keys to Madam Juju? I think I'd feel a lot better."

He handed over another key.

"And the third?"

"I gave that to Max last night."

"Oh, of course," I said, feeling stupid for not thinking of it. I bet he'd even left it in the room and I hadn't noticed. I hadn't bothered with a key this morning, forgetting again that the door didn't lock automatically behind me. Well, I'd get it in a minute. First I'd have another cup of coffee and one of those rolls.

I picked a particularly luscious-looking roll dotted with pieces of apricot and took it and another cup of steaming coffee to a table and sat down. I've always found that the third cup of coffee is the best. The first two are necessities, but the third is to be savored and enjoyed. If the situation had been different I would have leaned back, smacked my lips and uttered a contented "Ah."

I happened to glance up and saw Kid Corcoran standing in the doorway.

"You got a car?" he asked without preamble.

Chapter Fifteen

The lightness took over. Sheila Rides Horse rose from the chair with the gauzy airiness of a dragonfly and darted from her room. Delighted, she soared, caught by the wind until the earth snatched her feet, pulling her to the ground. Walk, she was told. She must walk. Plodding steadily across the light sandy soil, she lengthened her stride, aware that she was not alone. Two figures walked ahead of her, one on the right, the other on the left. She knew they would not turn around, that she would not see their faces.

For now she kept her eyes forward, taking her time, not wanting to get lost in this other world. She observed the landscape, mentally record-ing the occasional cactus, the scattered boulders jutting up from the stark terrain, and the pointed mountains in the distance. Confident that a part of her inner mind remained alert and aware, she let her eyes drift to the figures accompanying her. Sheila knew who walked on her left. She recognized the nun's habit of Sister Fortunata even though she wore a hood rather than a cowl. A dove fluttered, hovered and sometimes rode on the nun's shoulder. A bobcat paced protectively beside her. Sheila felt warm and comforted, honored by her presence.

An old man walked abreast of the nun on Sheila's right, dressed in a loin cloth and leggings. Dark, weathered skin clung loosely to the lean bones of his back. He limped arthritically on bowed legs. An Indian shaman of some kind, Sheila thought, or maybe a chief. She shrugged. What did she know of Indians? Not much.

An eagle wheeled over the old man's head and behind him a silver and green snake slithered majestically, carrying its head unnaturally high like a sentinel. Scenery began to pass by as if she were on a train. Great stone cathedrals, crumbling grave yards, monuments topped with angels sped by on one side, burial platforms, tepees, hogans and medicine wheels on the other.

The shaman spoke. "You belong to us, daughter. You are welcome."

"You didn't want me," Sheila answered angrily. "You threw me away."

"Don't deny us. We will give you strength."

"I don't know who I am."

The eagle swooped low, his feathers changing into iridescent darkness as he landed on her shoulder.

"You are Crow," the shaman said.

Sister's familiar voice floated on the air. "Your soul is divided. Accept them, Sheila, or you will lose a part of yourself. Look to the distance." She pointed ahead where the passing panoramas met in the distance and became one. "You will need us both if—"

A thunderous cry rang out, hammering her eardrums. Sheila dropped to her knees in agony, covering her ears. The nun and shaman disappeared, replaced by a gigantic man running toward her, brandishing a broad sword. Bellowing with rage, he whipped the weapon in wide arcs of destruction. Sheila struggled to her feet; terror clutched her belly. She tried to run. The sword whistled past her ear.

"No," she screamed, "not here!" Stumbling back, she bumped into her chair and sat with enough force to knock it over backward, tumbling her across the floor of her room. She lay there, breathing hard, letting the adrenaline drain away.

She crawled to the bed, her hair and face dripping with sweat. Her body shook with the unnatural chill of fear. She pulled the star quilt up to her chin. Her cards were still on the table, but she didn't need them to tell her what the vision meant.

Sister Fortunata had always urged Sheila to make peace with her background, but Sheila wasn't interested in the past or a mother who had dumped her as a naked newborn with nothing other than a name and no clues as to where she had come from. The orphanage, the sisters, were good enough for her. She had been nurtured and loved.

Out of love, Sheila had made a few attempts to appease Sister. Making her Indian dress had been one of those attempts. But as she got older, she found she didn't need Indianness to survive or even to succeed. She scorned the culture freaks who insisted her only worth was in being as Indian as possible. She remembered someone once asking her what tribe she belonged to, and she had answered "South Dakota Catholic."

But Sheila knew that none of this was the true meaning of the vision, either.

The message was of an imminent crossing-over. Sister Fortunata, and the shaman, wanted to ease her coming passage over to the other side.

Chapter Sixteen

The Kid wore the same khaki pants, or another pair just like them, and a white T-shirt, no oxygen. Probably been out smoking.

"Care to join me for a cup of coffee?" I asked, temporarily ignoring his question.

He hesitated a moment, then, doing a fair job of masking his impatience, went to the sideboard, poured himself a cup of coffee, and joined me at the table. Good thing. I wasn't about to commit myself to any chauffeuring until we'd had some conversation.

I wondered how much he knew about last night's events, and figured there was only one way to find out: I said, "You look like you got a good night's sleep." And he did. He looked refreshed and much more vigorous than he had last night. "Did you manage to sleep through all the ruckus?"

"Most of it. Too bad about the girl."

He eyed me with an unblinking stare that seemed like a challenge of some kind.

"Yes," I said. "It was pretty horrible. I can't imagine who, or why anyone would want to kill her."

He shrugged. "Probably in the wrong place at the wrong time." He took a couple slurps of coffee, then said, bleakly, "They're gonna pin it on me. You can bet on it."

"Have the police talked to you?"

"Yeah, they been here, bright and early."

"What did they say? What makes you think they're going to pin it on you?"

"An ex-con is easy game. They'll be back, you'll see."

"It won't be that bad. I told them you couldn't have done it because I saw you downstairs at a crucial time. And they checked your room. They know you were asleep."

"That won't matter to them." He shook his head at my naivety. "You got a car?" he asked again.

"Yes. Why?"

"I want to go out to the old place before they come and get me. Out in the country; it was my folks' homestead. I was born and raised there."

"Where is it? How far out?"

"'Bout thirty miles out Donkey Creek Road."

Which, of course, told me nothing. "How long does it take?"

"Twenty, thirty minutes is all." He had the dignity not to beg. But I could tell how badly he wanted me to say yes. His hands worked nervously, one gripping the other with enough tension to whiten the knuckles and pop the tendons on the age-spotted backs.

He caught me looking at them and reached for his coffee mug, cradling it in both hands. A pretty cool customer, I thought. "I saw you leave the fairgrounds with Phoebe yesterday. I thought she might have taken you to the country."

"She gave me a ride to the rodeo and back is all. And a run by the store for smokes. I asked her to take me to the country, but she wouldn't do it," he said querulously.

"What was she like? I really didn't know her very well."

"Oh, I dunno," he said, staring down at his coffee. I suspected he didn't spend much time thinking about other people's personalities. "Young, pushy."

"You'd met her before, though, hadn't you? When she interviewed you in California."

"Yeah, asking all the same questions again. Gets kind of tiresome."

I'd assumed the important info Phoebe wanted to tell me was something she'd gleaned from the Kid, but maybe not. I didn't want to blatantly pump him, mainly because I didn't think he'd fall for it.

"I guess I can check with Florie, and see if it's okay to go out there."

"I ain't no ten-year-old kid needs to get permission."

Whoops. "I'm not worried about permission as much as by your health. You sure you're up to it?"

"Wouldn't ask if I wasn't," he said with some belligerence.

"Well then, why not? We can talk on the way and I'll get my interview at the same time. But I can't be gone for very long. Okay?"

He nodded.

I drained my coffee cup and said, "I'll go get my things and meet you out front." I needed to change my shoes, having learned the hard way from my first trip that the Wyoming countryside was no place for sandals. I'd also need to get something to write on. My notebook and tape recorder were in my briefcase and still in the hands of the police. But my camera should be in the suitcase.

I grabbed another sweet roll and went upstairs. The doors to Mavis and Hard-Nosed Lu were shut, and presumably locked, with a couple of strips of yellow police tape strung across them. I felt an odd sense of removal, finding it hard to recall the horrors of last night with any sense of reality, more like a hazily remembered nightmare. I halfway hoped Florie might be cleaning rooms upstairs. If so, I would have told her I was taking the Kid out. As it was, I didn't feel like running back downstairs to hunt her up; besides, I was willing to take the Kid's word for it that he could stand the trip.

My only real concern was the chance of missing Max. So I left him a note telling him where I'd gone and propped it on the dresser. I looked briefly for the room key, but it wasn't on the dresser or nightstand and I couldn't imagine where else Max would have left it. He must have taken it with him. It didn't matter, I had two more.

I put on some Keds and grabbed my string bag from the plastic sack and a few other things I might need. I didn't want to bother reorganizing the whole mess right now. I got the camera and fresh film from my suitcase, the notepad from the nightstand and threw them in the purse, too.

In the process I saw the notes I'd made that morning, recalling Phoebe's last words to me, and stopped to re-read them. They didn't seem nearly so profound as they had earlier, nor could I imagine they'd convince Dwayne that she was trying to warn me about something. Oh well, I thought grimly, you had to have been there.

It would be nice if people who were going to run around warning you of things could be a bit more concrete. Something a little better than "Be careful," or "He's a man with dark hair." Phoebe had mentioned the Kid's name, which might be damning in Dwayne's eye, but I still felt I should tell the police about it. They could do what they wanted with the info. I was sure Florie would find much more damaging things to throw against the old man.

No matter what else the Kid might be mixed up in, at least I felt comfortable in my own mind that he couldn't have killed Phoebe. That's all I cared about now.

The Kid was waiting in the vestibule, and I was relieved to see that he had his oxygen carrier with him and a light jacket over his arm. I resisted taking his arm to help him down the steps and he managed very well on his own, though he did stop for a brief coughing spell at the curb and spat into the gutter.

"Which way do we go?" I asked, pulling away from the curb.

"S'pose we could swing by the nursing home for a minute first?"

Here we go, I thought. First change of plans. I should have expected it. But the nursing home, of all places? Why did he want to go there? Oh, well. "I don't know why not. Which way?"

"To the left."

He directed me to a low, sprawling brick building. One end was a clinic and small hospital, and the other, with nicely kept grounds and rows of wind-weary geraniums, was a nursing home. Not beautiful by any means, but then nothing could really make amends for the unfortunate name scrawled over the arched entrance gate: Evening Repose. That would take the heart out of the most chipper.

Riddled with curiosity, I bided my time, knowing full well that sooner or later I'd lose my couth and be as nosy as the next guy.

We stepped into a broad foyer decorated with furniture, which looked like it was never sat upon, pictures on the wall, and lots of potted plants, but the brave attempt at homeyness wouldn't have a fooled a six-year-old that this was a place for anything other than the sick and dying.

The Kid paused, sniffing the air like a wary wolf. His lip curled with distaste as he glanced nervously around before going any farther.

"Put this back in the car, would you?" he said, handing me his oxygen carrier and hose, as if fearing he might be caught and caged if he looked too much like "one of them."

He stood, clutching his wadded-up jacket as I left. He nodded curtly to a dark-haired lady at a desk and headed down a corridor. When I returned he was nowhere to be seen. Not surprising, of course, but I was bursting with curiosity as to what he was doing, or who he might be visiting.

I lurked in the foyer. Straight ahead was a dining facility flanked by two wide corridors, and to my right a common area with a large TV. Two elderly men, who appeared to be comatose, sat slumped in chairs in front of the screen. I wondered how long they had been there, if anyone ever came to check on them. A livelier group, two in wheelchairs, clustered around a table in the corner, playing cards. A small woman moving turtle-paced towards them with the help of a walker cast me a shy smile of welcome that tugged at my heart.

The dark-haired lady dressed in a trim summer suit paused by a door marked Office, smiled and asked if she could help me find somebody.

"I'm here with Web Corcoran."

"Oh, he's probably visiting with old Kate. I'll show you the way." She led me down the corridor to an end room, chattering all the way. "We're so glad that Kate finally has someone to come see her. It's helped her ever so much, though

at her age," she made a little moue of sympathy, "you know ..."
She shook her head, then perked right up. "Still, she's much
more alert than she's been for months."

She motioned to the propped-open door of the end room,
then bustled back towards her office. The name tag by the
door said "Kate Webster." I peeked in.

A heavy-set woman sat in an armchair by the window
with a crocheted robe over her lap. Her sparse white hair stood
in feathery clumps all over her head. I didn't see the Kid.

"Okay if I come in?" I asked from the doorway.

The woman turned alertly at my voice. "Come ahead,"
she said, shielding her eyes with both hands in an effort to
see me better.

I stepped over the threshold and saw the Kid on his knees
in front of a dresser, struggling to close the bottom drawer. He
turned and looked at me. I couldn't tell if he thought my
presence an intrusion or not. Pulling something from the
drawer, he impatiently rocked it shut and got to his feet.

"This is Kate Webster, an old friend of mine," he said,
and tossed a sweater on her lap.

"Do I know you?" Kate asked me in a quavering voice.
"Did you bring me my lunch?"

"No," the Kid said, "she's just visiting, Kate."

I moved closer so she could see me better. And she tried,
poor dear, squinting through thick glasses, but I suspected
her eyesight was next to nil. She appeared to be very old. Her
soft doughy skin hung in puddles under her chin, swaying
softly with every movement of her head. She wore a flowered
cotton dress or duster with a front zipper and a thin blue
sweater over her shoulders.

"Come closer, dear," she said, and stretched her hand out
to me.

I took it and held the gnarled bony fingers in both of mine. "Have you come to take me home? You know they don't feed me very well in here."

I looked to the Kid to help me out.

"Not yet, Kate," he said, bending close to her. "Soon. I'll take you home soon."

She looked up at him and a gleam of lucidity lit her eyes. She pulled her hand from mine and shook a finger at him gleefully. "Ha!" she said with a delighted cackle. "I know you! Remember those meals we used to have out to Forty Miles? You rascal, you!"

"Sure do, Kate," the Kid said with the first real smile I'd seen from him. "We gotta go now, but I'll be back. Behave yourself, you hear?"

"You better come back and see me, Fancy Pants." She cackled again.

Fancy Pants! The Kid looked chagrined. I struggled not to laugh. We left Kate happily talking to herself.

Once outside, the Kid stopped and rested a moment. He coughed and spat into the gravel drive. "Nobody should have to live in a place like that. Worse than a goddamned prison."

I stood by, ready if he needed help getting into the Bronco, but he managed on his own.

"Are you really going to get her out?" I asked as we drove away.

"No way I can do that," he said with a little huff of disgust. "Wish I could. She don't remember half of what anybody says, but I figure it makes her feel good to talk about it." He shrugged.

"How old is she?"

"I don't know. Older than me, I guess. Must be eighty-five

or more. She's about the only person left around here that I know."

"It's nice of you to go see her."

He snorted again. "She don't remember nothing longer than fifteen minutes."

"Still, she enjoys it while you're there," I insisted. "Where to now?" I asked, glad to change the subject.

He pointed and we drove through town, out past the fairgrounds, and headed for the country. I noticed without commenting that this was the direction he was going when I saw him with Phoebe in the Jeep.

It was a beautiful day. Hot, but with a stiff breeze easing the main burn. Traffic thinned quickly to just an occasional vehicle. I whizzed by a flat-bed truck; I wanted to see that long stretch of empty road in front of me.

I'd forgotten how dry Wyoming could be in July. Even the sagebrush looked crisp and dusty. But I hadn't forgotten the vast stretches of emptiness broken only by bare rocky hills and hogbacks. Now I felt like I was in Wyoming. This was what I'd wanted to see again. Bare skies clear to the horizon.

"Do you mind if I roll down the windows?" I asked, turning off the air conditioning. "It's beautiful! I want to smell the air and feel the heat."

"Okay by me," he said, but his look said he thought I was crazy. He himself couldn't take his eyes off the Bronco. Like a kid, he opened and closed the glove compartment several times, moved his seat back, forward, up and down. Fiddled with all the gadgets he could find and watched enviously how I handled the controls and foot pedals.

I laughed. "Roll the window down, Mr. Corcoran." He grinned and did so. I sucked in a deep breath of hot dry air, and drove with my arm resting on the windowsill. I felt wonderful.

I'm sorry, Phoebe, truly sorry, I thought, but after last night we really need a beautiful day. Unfair as it was, I wanted to forget all of last night and get on with my life. I would get a quick interview with the Kid, give him an hour out at his ranch, and be done with it. Max and I could get on with our agenda and forget the rest of this stuff. If I could whistle, I would have.

I should have known better than to call down the gods in that particular manner.

Chapter Seventeen

We turned off onto a graveled road. "This place where we're going," I asked, "were you born and raised there?"

"Yeah. My folks homesteaded the place. Then my brothers and me had it."

"Brothers?"

"Two of them. Youngest died. Diphtheria. My brother Boyd, he stayed on the ranch. Me, I had an itchy foot. Times were tough and I couldn't sit still. Boyd was a good man. I let him alone and he run the place anyway he liked. Always had a room for me if I needed one. He and his wife raised my oldest girl, Arvilla."

"You were married?" I'd assumed he was, but you never know, even in those days.

"Yeah. She took off with some sailor boy when I was in Rawlins."

It took me a minute to realize that he meant the state pen at Rawlins, Wyoming.

"Took the two youngest kids with her. Never saw 'em again. Left the oldest, Arvilla, with Boyd. They raised her like she was their own and left her their share of the place when they died. Didn't have kids of their own. Arvilla was a good girl. She wrote me pretty steady, kept me up on what was happening around here. Sent a newspaper now and then. Didn't cut me out of her life like that daughter of hers, Florie."

Strangely enough, I found myself mentally defending Florie. After all, she hadn't even been born when the Kid began his last prison stay forty years ago.

"All that Florie wants to do now is sell the old place. Her mama wouldn't't've done that; Arvilla ran the place herself 'til she died last year. Cancer."

His one link with the outside world. I voiced my sympathy. "That must have been hard for you."

"Yeah," he said after a lengthy pause. "I would have liked to see her again."

On the other hand, it couldn't have been easy to be the daughter of a man who spent his life in and out of prison, nor one who had been basically dumped by both parents. I'd be willing to bet that both Arvilla and Florie had paid dearly for the relationship, particularly in a small community like Rawhide. A rather tawdry, depressing story. Not what I wanted for the magazine. Nor me either, for that matter. Not today. This was a day for escapism.

"That was all later in your life, wasn't it? Tell me about the early days when the papers called you the Nickel Kid. Did that nickname come before or after Kid Corcoran?"

"I was always called Kid even as a young squirt. That Corcoran kid. But the papers started calling me the Nickel Kid back in the late twenties. I stuck up this bank in the little town of Bliss, Utah. Dropped a bag of nickels some young kids glommed onto. Told everybody I gave it to 'em, I suppose, thinking that way they wouldn't have to give the money back. So the paper called me the Nickel Kid. After that I kinda made a point of throwing some loose change around."

Building his image, I thought wryly.

"'Course, nobody knew who I really was then, it was just The Nickel Kid Strikes Again, sometimes right across the top of the paper."

His moments of fame. Well, I guess that must have been heady stuff for a poor, young kid. And this was exactly the kind of material I wanted.

"Donkey Creek Road is up here a ways," he said. "You'll want to turn right at the next turnoff." He went back to admiring the Bronco, running his hand over the dashboard, checking out the gauges. I wondered how long it had been since he'd driven a car. We turned onto the graveled road.

He shook his head in wonder. "Things sure have changed. Used to be nothin' but dirt tracks up here."

I hated to say the obvious, that after forty years one would expect changes.

He snorted cynically. "Someone out here must be a County Commissioner. That's the only way you could get any road work done; bet that hasn't changed. Probably that Brocheck boy."

"Brocheck? What Brocheck boy?"

"Always called Buster, far as I know."

Good grief. I guess the mountainous Buster had been a boy, or at least a young man when the Kid left Rawhide. "Does he live out here?"

"Yeah, 'bout four miles beyond our place, as the crow flies. Longer by road."

I started to tell him about Max drilling a well on Brocheck's land, but decided not to. I wanted to keep Max to myself at this point. And get on with the interview.

"Tell me some more of your stories. I gathered that part of the pleasure the press took in the Nickel Kid's exploits was your, uh, ineptness, and the fact that you were never very successful, if you don't mind my saying so." My understanding was that the sobriquet came not from largesse with odd change, but because he never got away with much more than a nickel.

He didn't take offense, just chuckled a bit. "I was a kid. Didn't do much planning, just grabbed an opportunity if I saw one. Fell off my horse once, right in a bunch of cactus. He was a right ornery critter, that horse. Some local fool posse was chasing me, so I had to ride the saddle with my backside loaded with stickers. Hurt like hell. But they didn't catch me. Should have. Small town law wasn't much in those days, which is why I stuck to small towns."

Things haven't changed much, I thought, thinking of Dwayne. And I wished he hadn't impounded my tape recorder. I didn't want to lose any of the details of Corcoran's stories.

"Look," I said. "Would you like to drive?" The road was decent here, and there certainly wasn't any traffic to worry about. "Then I can take notes while you talk." His look of amazement delighted me.

"You bet," he said eagerly.

I remembered how painful it had been for Gramps when he had to quit driving. He saw it as a humiliating defeat, and it marked the beginning of his downhill slide.

The kid and I exchanged places and after a few brief instructions we started off. After a hesitant, jerky start, he drove easily, his face glowing with pleasure.

The joy of driving made the old man garrulous. I scribbled

furiously, taking down the comparative merits between a horse and an old jalopy for use as get-away vehicles.

"The train jobs were the worst. I never liked them. You never knew who might come out behind ya. I never set out to hurt nobody, and I was always afraid something awful might happen on one of them trains. There was this guy Lovett once, who tried to do a train. Damn thing was loaded with Marines on their way to California. They were hot on his tail in a minute. I had enough trouble without running into a mess like that."

His stories were wild and funny and most likely apocryphal, but I knew what my readers liked. The Western myth. The cavalier gentleman robber. I'd throw in a few caveats at the end of the article, and a brief overview of the Kid's life from the 'forties on.

I closed my notebook and asked, "And when did they find out who the Nickel Kid really was?"

"Got caught in 'forty-two. Found out I was that Corcoran kid from Rawhide, so's I got the moniker Kid Corcoran. Didn't matter to me, I was always called Kid. Did fifteen years in the state pen. Moved to California after that."

By my calculations that meant he'd had not much more than ten years of freedom during the late 'fifties and 'sixties before his final stretch of forty years. All that time in prison, and now an old man. And if his granddaughter had anything to do with it, he'd be back in the pen to end his days.

"This is it," he said, turning onto a dirt road. Ahead I could see a large barn rimmed with rusting machinery nearly hidden by tall weeds and nodding sunflowers. Scattered outbuildings littered the grounds, all showing various stages of neglect; some, abject dilapidation.

Off to the side, and set back a ways, stood an abandoned two-story house shaded by a couple of ancient gnarled cottonwoods. Peeling green paint worn to the boards in places gave the building the mottled look of moldy cheese. Most of the windows were boarded; those that weren't, were broken. Depressing. I glanced at the Kid, but it didn't seem to bother him. He brought the Bronco to a whiplash stop and opened his door. He exited the high step nimbly enough and reached in back for the oxygen carrier. I climbed out, too.

Hooking up the oxygen briefly, he held the nosepiece to his nostrils for a minute, but then left it by the car. So he could have a cigarette.

"That's the house my brother built," he said. "I helped him a time or two myself. Hasn't been lived in now for a long time. Arvilla had herself a trailer house over there." He pointed to a large concrete slab with a tall light and electrical pole at one end. "Looks like, anyway," he added. A sagging four-strand clothesline still stood behind the slab.

"This wasn't the house you were raised in then?" I asked, still staring at the decrepit ruin.

"No. We had a house on the actual homestead site when I was a kid. It's gone now. Site's up the road a bit," he said, pointing to a rutted trail that wound around behind the barn. "That's where I really want to go." But he wandered off towards the barn and its cache of old machinery.

"Mind if I look in the house?" I asked.

"Go ahead."

I guess I'd expected some kind of emotion from him, some show of nostalgia at finally seeing his old home, but maybe he'd spent too many years hiding his feelings. Well, he could look at old machinery if he liked, I thought. I walked toward the old house, which held more interest for me than rust.

Piles of tumbleweeds lined the scattered remnants of fence that marked off the yard area. The grass was long gone, taken over by hardier weeds and ground cover. Vandals, active even here, had sprayed patterns and unreadable slogans on all the reachable areas. Hunks of bare wood hung off the front door where someone had jimmied the lock.

I pushed the badly warped door open with some difficulty and stepped inside. The uneven floorboards creaked and groaned with my steps, as if pained by the intrusion. Man and animal footprints scuffled the dirt and blown-in debris on the floor.

Generally speaking, I like old houses and seldom pass a chance to explore one, but this place had a nasty feel to it, that awful sense of eyes watching. What a cliché, I thought, trying to laugh at myself. I must have seen too many bad movies. Forcing myself farther in, I peered into the dimly lit kitchen area, but didn't enter. Cupboard doors hung open or were torn off and thrown on the floor, even the sink had been pried out. A sound behind me made me whirl, heart thumping. Nothing. A breeze gusting through broken panes sent dry leaves dancing, or was it scurrying feet? Rats. I shuddered. Above my head a fine mist of dirt drifted down from the ceiling, as if someone waiting quietly above had shifted weight. It was all I needed. I turned and fled.

The Kid stood by the car, smoking.

"Why don't they tear that place down?" I asked, hoping my nonchalance covered the true fear I'd felt. "It's creepy."

He grinned. "That's a good house." It was probably as close to making a joke as he ever got. "I made Arvilla promise never to get rid of it as long as I lived."

"Why on earth not?"

He shrugged and ground his cigarette into the gravel.

I sighed. After all, what right did I have to judge other people's sentimentality? Personally, though, I thought the place should be relieved of its misery. Shoot the blasted thing as you would a horse with a broken leg.

"Let's go to the homestead," the Kid said.

"Walking distance?"

"Used to be," he said, dryly. "Don't know about now."

"We'll drive." I headed for the Bronco. He looked longingly at the driver's seat, but I wasn't about to turn complete control over to him. I handed him the oxygen carrier and said, "Here, you better hook this back up."

He took it, but set it on the floor of the front seat and climbed in. Nothing was easy with him, everything a struggle of wills.

He was right, the distance would have been an easy walk, a half to three quarters of a mile, maybe. But not for him. I was glad for the heavy vehicle. The road was no more than a dimly marked trail.

There wasn't much to see, just a large clearing with the big rounded hump of an ancient dugout to one side and a pile of boards and rubble beyond. A small barn with a rock base—actually nothing more than a shed—stood at the other edge of the clearing. The boards were weathered to a soft gray, and the door hung loosely off its hinges. Only the rock foundation, its stones fit together with care, stood square and strong. The rest of the structure tilted wildly off center, looking as if the next strong wind would finish the job. Though that was obviously not the case, since it hadn't toppled yet, and strong winds were a given around here.

"Is that as old as it looks?" I asked the Kid.

"My daddy built it with his own hands. First building on the homestead, put it up before the house."

The Kid walked slowly around the pathetic little structure, shaking his head. "I didn't know if it'd still be standing." He stood staring at it a moment, then turned away. "Ever see a dugout before?" He pulled at the still-intact door, but it didn't budge.

"As a matter of fact, I have," I said, remembering some unpleasant experiences from my first visit to Wyoming. A dear friend of mine had nearly died in a dugout, because I had been too frightened of the lizard-filled place to go in and look for her. I didn't like dugouts much.

"How about a soddy? You ever seen a sod house?"

"No, I haven't," I said, with some interest. "Is there one around here?"

"Used to be one not far from here. There's a road goes up there, through the north pasture. I could show you."

"Not today, but I might take you up on it another time." Maybe, I thought, but probably not. "Where was the house?" I asked.

"Over there, by those trees." He pointed to some shrubby cottonwoods and willows that marked a meandering creek bed.

"I'm going to walk over there," I said. "Will you be all right?"

He nodded. "Nothing there to see."

I didn't care, I wanted to get away from all this man-made garbage. The junkyard mentality drove me crazy. Never tear anything down, never haul anything away. Everything left to collapse into ugly piles of rot and rust. A desecration of the land, as far as I was concerned. I picked my way through cactus and fallen strands of barbed wire still attached to broken-off posts, all lying on the ground ready to snare the unsuspecting.

Stripping some leaves from a sage brush, I crushed them in my fingers and held them under my nose, breathing deeply of the pungent, dusky smell. Soft, rolling countryside stretched in front of me, broken only by an occasional ridge.

As if to make the picture perfect, a horse and rider appeared, shimmering in the heat from behind trees farther up the creek bed and in a slow, graceful canter, came toward me. I climbed a small, rocky hillock to watch as he crossed the dry creek bed below me, standing in the stirrups, his flanks strong and lean. John Wayne couldn't have done it better. I recognized the horse, Clover, before the rider. Then he swept off his hat. Jimmy Chin.

Chapter Eighteen

His blue-black hair glistened in the sunlight. "Well, hi," he said, as surprised to recognize me as I him. "What are you doing out here?"

I gestured behind me. "I brought Web Corcoran out to see his old home place. No one else would give him a ride."

"I was on my way to Brocheck's for some roping practice when I saw the dust trail from your car. Thought I'd see what was going on. I kind of keep an eye on the place for Florie."

"Do you live out here, too?"

"No, not really. I live in town. It's my uncle's place."

"Your Uncle Patrick O'Donnal that I met?" The Chinese Irishman.

"That's the one." We exchanged smiles and he dismounted his horse. "Our land abuts this place a mile or so to the west. Been in the family for years. I keep my horses there. Pat and Lee's kids run the place."

"How interesting. I ..."

"It's one of the very few old ranch properties owned by a Chinese family," he said, guessing my thoughts and my hesitation in voicing them. "My great-grandfather, Ah Chin, came here as a Chinese laborer in the late eighteen hundreds. Worked for the railroad, then in the coal mines in Rock Springs. He was one of the few survivors of the Chinese massacre there."

"Oh no," I said. "I've read about that; one of the ugliest cultural disasters in western history." Hundreds (well, the actual number was still in dispute) of Chinese miners were killed by their white fellow workers who saw them as threats to their jobs. Shades of today.

"Yeah, he was part of the despised 'yellow horde.' He hid out in the hills for months, then came this way and got a job cooking at the ranch. Ended up buying the place. It's still called the Ah Chin place in these parts, though no one by that name has lived there in ages."

I saw Jimmy staring over my shoulder, and turned around. The Kid stood a few yards away, watching us.

"Do you know Jimmy Chin?" I asked.

The Kid shook his head. I made the introductions. They exchanged nods and a few words, and I noticed that neither one of them made an effort to shake hands. A tad frosty.

The Kid lit another cigarette. "You live on the Ahchin place?" He pronounced it as if it were one word.

Jimmy nodded.

"That old soddy still there? I was telling her about it."

"Yeah, I think so, what's left of it. Mostly caved in, now."

Jimmy addressed his comments to me. The Kid turned and walked away. Well, I wasn't going to attempt smoothing any waters, but it did please me that the Kid had made an attempt at civility.

"I better be on my way," Jimmy said. "I was sorry to hear about the trouble at Racy Ladies last night. Is it true that you found the body?"

"Yes." I suppose there wasn't anyone within a hundred miles of Rawhide who hadn't heard by now.

"Do they know who did it?"

"Not that I'm aware of."

"Is Max here with you?"

"No, I'm meeting him in town later."

Jimmy eyed me with some concern, hesitated, then said, "Do you think it's a good idea to be out here alone with ..."

"The Kid? I'm sure it's all right. Don't worry. Besides, we're about ready to go back to town now."

"What's he doing, anyway?"

"Looking around, kicking tires. He's afraid the police are going to pin the murder on him and send him back to prison."

He didn't say so, but I could tell Jimmy didn't think it was a bad idea, either. "Well, keep your eyes open," he said. "There hasn't been a killing in Rawhide for as long as I can remember. Now, after this guy shows up, look what happens. Seems strange to me." He mounted his horse. "Tell him to watch those cigarettes, too, would you? We've already got one brush fire going out past Brocheck's."

"Is it close to Max's well?"

"No. And they've got it under control anyway."

I assured him we'd be very careful. We said goodbye again, and for a few minutes I watched as the horse ate up the distance and the two became smaller and smaller.

I went to find the kid, impatient now to get back to town. I wanted time to check in with the police before Max got to town. I'd give Dwayne the notes I'd taken about Phoebe's last words to me. I was less certain about mentioning anything about Sheila Rides Horse. I thought I wouldn't. Dwayne would question her himself; let him reach his own conclusions.

The Kid was inspecting the barn's rock foundation. "Let me get a picture of you, and one by the dugout, too," I said. At least they'd be picturesque. "Then we've got to head back. It's getting late." I got my camera from the car and began to snap pictures. "You said the sod house wasn't far from here. Your folks must have been close neighbors with Jimmy's relatives then."

The Kid gave an expressive snort. "Damn land grabbers, them chinks. They would have taken this place, too, but my folks beat 'em out of it," he said with satisfaction. "Let's go back to my brother's house. I want to poke around there a bit before we go. Maybe you can help me with a few things."

"What do you need help with?" I asked as we drove the short distance back to the abandoned house.

"Want to see if there's anything left that I remember."

"All right, but don't spend too much time, okay?"

He said nothing, and I hoped there wouldn't be a test of wills getting him away from here. I pulled the Bronco up in front of the deserted house and stopped. If he wanted to go in the old relic he could, but I wasn't stepping foot in that moldering pile again.

"Pull around to the side," he said. "Back in, there by the porch."

I did as he asked. He wouldn't have to walk so far; he was bound to be tired by now. I took the oxygen unit out and handed it to him. "Here," I insisted. "Use it."

"I ain't going to carry that thing around," he said.

"Then take a few whiffs before you do anything else. I don't want you keeling over on me."

He did so grudgingly, sucking in five or six deep breaths to satisfy me. Then he took the tubing from his nose, dropped it on top of the carrier and walked around behind the house.

I followed and watched, puzzled, as he lifted a board away from the base of the house and pulled out an ancient garden spade. The shovel's blade was completely covered with rust and had a clump of dirt clinging to its edge. The dirt looked newer than the shovel.

"What are you doing?" I asked, as he dragged the spade to a corner of the yard and began pulling away clumps of tumbleweed with his hand.

"I hid some of my things out here a long time ago. Wondered if they were still here." He began to dig. The dirt seemed friable enough, probably a much-used garden area. After a few minutes, the shovel rang against something hard. Sweat sprang out on the Kid's forehead and his breath came in short gusts.

"Here," I said, "let me help." I took the shovel from his hands, working it against the buried object to loosen it, then scrabbled for it with my hands. I pulled out a sharp-edged, roughly triangular rock the length of my forearm and about eight inches thick.

A reddish rind and patches of glossy black showed through the dirt; I brushed it off. It looked just like the pieces I'd seen at the store. Jade. Black jade.

Surprised, I looked up at the Kid. "This is jade, isn't it?"

He nodded. "It's mine, don't worry about that. No matter what anybody says." He picked up the spade and began to dig again in another spot.

"You shouldn't be doing that," I said.

"This is my nest egg. Only money I got. I ain't going to no nursing home, or no prison, neither," he added, stomping the shovel deep in the earth.

I ran to the Bronco and got the oxygen. I didn't want him passing out on me, or dying, for God's sake.

"Here," I said, handing it to him. "Hook yourself up." I took the spade from him again.

"Just hit another," he said, working the plastic nose piece into place.

I fished out a smaller, roundish lump, so anonymous-looking I never would have been able to identify it as anything other than rock. He took it from me, hefting it admiringly. "Will you help me then?" he asked.

"I don't know," I said, feeling angry and used. All I could think of were the stories of stolen jade. I didn't want any part of that.

"This ain't stolen," he said, as if reading my mind. "I found this just like everyone else did. Fair and square."

"Then why did you bury it?"

"Hell, everybody hid their jade 'til they got it sold. Some Chinaman used to come to town every few months on a buying trip. I just never had a chance to get back here and get mine. I done nothin' but think about it all these years." He gave me a sliding, sidelong glance. "I'm going to get me a trailer house and move out here. Bring old Kate, too."

"I thought you said you couldn't do it."

"If I can swing this," he indicated the jade, "I might be able to. Without money I can't do nothin'."

I knew he was manipulating me, but this was his land, and I had no way of knowing that the jade wasn't rightfully his. And who could blame him for wanting a place of his own, a way to avoid that fate worse than death, the nursing home.

The thought of the Kid and Kate trying to make it out here on their own boggled the mind, but so what? There were bound to be organizations that provided help in such cases. More power to them, I thought, better to go out fighting than dwindling into some awful twilight zone. Gramps should have been so lucky.

"I'll give you thirty minutes of my time," I said, "then we're leaving."

Piece by piece, as I dug them out, the Kid loaded the rough jade into the back of the Bronco. I dug up six more sizable pieces and a cluster of fist-sized and smaller pieces that were a breathtaking emerald green.

"What's frog skin?" I asked at one point, leaning on the spade to rest a minute.

He didn't hesitate. "Trash jade. Got a rough, bumpy rind like a toad and it's a dull, ugly green. Not worth nothing. What do you know about frog skin?"

"I heard a man talking about it. That and mutton fat."

"What man?"

"Buster Brocheck," I said, digging again. The thirty minutes were up; this would be the last piece.

The Kid came back from the Bronco cradling a large, heavy, light-colored piece cradled in his arms. He grinned at me. "This here's mutton fat," he said. "Worth good money. The Chinee will pay maybe eight hundred bucks, maybe more now. They make carvings out of pieces this size. Sell 'em for big money."

I was pooped and had lost a good deal of interest in jade. The ground in this particular spot was packed harder than the rest, or maybe my muscles were just registering a complaint. I was about to give up when the shovel rang out again. I chopped at the dirt on top, threw a few shovelfuls to one side, then got on my hands and knees and lifted out a medium-sized lump of dirt.

Brushing the dirt off, I uncovered a pale claw-like hand. I dropped the disgusting thing with a cry of alarm, then looked closer. The Kid reached down to pick it up, but I pushed his hand away and brushed more dirt from the repulsive thing. I'd seen something like this before. A cluster of bony, arthritic-appearing fingers with curved-in tips rising from a base of finely carved leaves and tangled roots that formed a stand. A lotus bud. Buddha's Fingers.

I rose to my feet holding the strange but exquisite carving. "You stole this, didn't you?" I said to the Kid. "From Auntie Lee."

"I don't know any Auntie Lee," he said. He wouldn't look at me.

"Jimmy Chin's Auntie Lee, or from her family. You stole it a long time ago and it's been hidden here all these years. I saw a replica of it in their restaurant."

From where I was standing now, I could see another spot of freshly dug earth close to the corner of the house. "Someone's been digging over there, too." The Kid followed my glance, but remained silent.

A lot of things began to fall in place. The broken lock on the front door; the Kid's lack of feeling at seeing his home again; the spade found so easily in its hiding place with its clump of fresh dirt.

I was furious. "You were out here yesterday, weren't you?" I threw the jade back down in the dirt. "With Phoebe. Why didn't you tell me? Why did you lie about it?"

The Kid said nothing, he just picked up the carving.

"Come on," I said wearily, heading for the Bronco. "Let's go. I've had enough of this. Come on," I repeated, opening the car door. A reflection in the glass gave me warning of the rusty spade swinging in a big arc toward my head.

I ducked, but not quickly enough.

Chapter Nineteen

I groaned and tried to roll over on my side. Spears of pain shot through my shoulder and neck, and every movement brought torturous pricks and stabs. Pinned to the ground. An image played in the darkness behind my eyes: a shrouded, prone figure pierced with swords. Lots of swords. More than five. I tried to count them ... more than eight. Ten. The Ten of Swords. Sorrow. I fought to open my eyes, wanting the picture to go away. I moved again and what felt like a ragged saw blade tore through my arm—I cried out in agony, clearing some of the fuzz from my head. This wasn't sorrow, I thought. This was *pain*.

My eyes squinted open, blinded at first by the light. I was lying face down in a thicket of dead bushes, cactus and weeds. Broken branches and sticks and pine needles pricked and poked me everywhere. There was even a twig up my nose. I pulled it out gingerly and tried to sit up. Unbearable pain coursed through my shoulder, neck and head. I stopped, panting. But now that I knew my bed was just stickers and needles, and not the dreaded Tarot swords, I managed to move through the pain and get to my knees.

I was in the bottom of a gully, or a dry creek bed, wedged in between a small pine tree and a broken-off tree stump. I'd landed on a spiky pile of sagebrush, tumbleweeds, yucca and other brush.

Still dazed, I looked up at the lip of the gully about ten feet above. I must have fallen. Memory edged with panic began to return. The Kid! Where was he? What had happened to me? I remembered digging up a pair of hands. My head whirled. Oh, God, could that be right?

I staggered to my feet. Raging pain in my right shoulder turned my arm into a useless hanging thing. To my horror, I saw that a long cactus spine had completely pierced my numb hand. I tried to pull it out, but couldn't. My head reeled with every movement and something was terribly wrong with my eyes. I blinked, trying to clear the haze away.

I had to get out of here. I ran the fingers of my good hand over a huge goose egg on the side of my head. What kind of blow—the shovel! I remembered the instant's glimpse of the blade swinging toward me.

Oh, God, I thought, my head clearing a bit more. The Kid had hit me. What a fool I'd been to trust him. Had he tried to kill me? Why? Because I knew he had the jade? And suddenly I remembered it all. The jade he'd buried in the yard and me, helping him dig it up. Stolen jade. And he'd lied to me about Phoebe. She had brought him out here yesterday. Did that mean he'd killed Phoebe, too? Most importantly, where was he now? He might be eighty-two years old, but hardly harmless.

I stood still and listened, but heard only the clatter and whir of insects and the soft song of a meadowlark. I was in the deepest part of the gully. I hadn't fallen, so the Kid must have thrown me into the gully.

I pressed my useless arm close to my body, trying to still the motion that brought agony. I inched my way to the shallow end of the ditch where I could easily climb out, stumbling over weeds and brush. Every time I caught myself with my good left hand I collected more stickers and burrs in the palm. I pulled them out with my teeth, and spat them on the ground.

Crouching at the end of the gully, I stopped to listen again, but heard nothing. Taking a deep breath, I stood slowly until I could see over the edge.

I was north of the old house; I could clearly see its side and the yard where we'd been digging. The Bronco had been moved from where I'd parked it, into the large open space between the house and the cement pad where the trailer once stood. The driver's-side door and the tailgate were open, but no one was around. The area seemed deserted. Where was the Kid? What was he doing?

Silence hung heavily in the air. I crept up and out slowly, following the lip of the gully back the way I'd come, heading for the protection of a small grove of cottonwoods. Reaching a tree, I collapsed against the rough bark, huffing for breath. From here I could see the point where I'd been dumped in the gully—it was about twenty yards from the house. How had the Kid gotten me here? He didn't have the strength to drag me that far, and the weed- and scrub-covered ground didn't show any signs of tire tracks.

My eyes hurt and the blurred vision made me dizzy and nauseous. All of the pain had coalesced into a giant body-wide agony. I had to get out of here and get to a phone. The Bronco was my only chance. I peered out from behind my hiding place: still no sign of life. I wanted to make a run for the Bronco, but didn't think I could make it.

The Kid had to be in the house, or in one of the outbuildings, but you'd think he'd make noise of some kind. The silence was palpable.

So I just did it. Stumbling and weaving, but moving as quickly as I could, I headed for the next point of protection, the house. Sticking close to the wall, I moved to the front, where I could see the Bronco. Again, I'd raised no alarms. Nobody yelled, nobody popped out from behind anything. So what the hell. I wrapped my good arm around my injured one, ran for the car and threw myself onto the front seat.

I nearly screamed with the pain of landing on my injured arm, but struggled to get upright. Slamming the door shut I reached awkwardly with my left hand for the keys. They weren't there.

I scrabbled around frantically, tears of frustration running down my face. My purse was on the seat; I dumped it out—no keys. I searched the glove compartment, the dash, the floor. Nothing. Cautiously, I re-opened the door, craning around to see if the Kid had appeared. Nothing. None of the racket I'd made had roused anyone. If the Kid was around, he wasn't nearby.

Less frightened of being caught, I searched the ground under, around and back of the Bronco. The jade was gone, too. Damn the Kid! I thought, he'd taken the keys with him. But where had he gone? And how? I couldn't think, couldn't sort anything out right now.

But I needed to get to a phone. The police. Buster Brocheck's ranch was around here somewhere; Max would be there. For the first time I thought to check my watch. Between the badly scratched crystal face and my uncertain eyes, I could barely make out the time. I thought it said something past four o'clock. If that were true, Max would be in town looking for me, or maybe even on his way out here. I would walk to meet him. Yes, I thought, struck by the perfect logic of it all, that's what I would do. I might even be able to hitch a ride. I refilled my purse, grabbed it out of the car and slung it over my good shoulder.

I looked back at the old house. The empty, staring windows reminded me of the awful feeling I'd had inside. The feeling of being watched, not alone. What if someone had been in the house? What if someone had been there all along watching the Kid and me? What if it wasn't the Kid who'd hit me with the shovel? Maybe the Kid had been attacked, too, and was lying in a ditch somewhere. Fear wound around my belly. Maybe I should go look for him.

I hesitated for a moment, uncertain, but only for a moment. Nothing could make me stick around this horrid place. I needed to get help. Propelled by apprehension and the dizzy certainty that this was my best chance, I stumbled off, headed for the county road. At least there I had the chance of meeting a car.

Once there, I quickly realized that I was in much worse shape than I'd been aware of. I felt sick, disoriented and frightened. Walking in the thick gravel became a problem of enormous proportions, and every stagger sent my head reeling with dizziness. I could no longer distinguish the pain from my injuries from the raging headache that beat my brain to mush. I didn't even hear the approach of a pickup behind me until the short blast of the horn shocked me into a whirling lurch that sent me to my knees.

The vehicle pulled to a stop beside me; it was a wonder I didn't get run over, flopping around in the middle of the road. Shakily I got to my feet while the driver burst out of the car and ran to me.

"Hello there!" she said. "Are you all right?"

It was ... what's her name. The jade lady. If I closed one eye and squinted through the other, I could see her fairly well.

"What are you doing out here?" she asked, peering at the side of my face. She took my arm, opened the door, took a few things off the seat, threw them underneath, and helped me in the truck, clucking like a mother hen.

"Can you take me to town?" I asked, as we drove off. "I think I need to see a doctor."

"You need a hospital, young lady."

"Just hurry. I don't feel so good."

"We'll get there in a flash. Don't worry." She gripped the steering wheel intently, sitting on the edge of the seat so her short legs could reach the pedals. "What were you doing out here in the middle of the road?"

I tried to talk, afraid of dimming out. "Brought the Kid— Kid Corcoran—to see his old home." And I'd seen the King of Swords, I thought woozily, riding a pale horse.

"He did this to you?" she asked, wide-eyed with interest.

"The King ..?"

"What? The Kid. Did he do this to you?"

"I don't know, maybe." I tried to keep my eyes open, closing them sent me off on a wild, spinning carnival ride. Nausea clutched my belly and rose threateningly up and down my throat like an out-of-control elevator. I held myself tight, fighting the pain from the jostling, bumpy ride.

"I told you he was dangerous," she said. "He killed that girl last night. Why in the world did you take off with him?"

"Don't know where he is. He's gone. Lost."

"What were you doing out there?"

"Looking around," I said. I heard my words slurring together. Mushy, to match my brain. I squinted at her. Hildy, I thought, snatching her name from the ooze. The jade lady—but I shouldn't talk about the jade, not until I could think better.

"You found that girl last night, didn't you?" she asked. "I told everybody something like this would happen if they let that man stay in town."

"He didn't kill ..."

"What do you mean?"

"He couldn't have killed her... I saw him ..."

"Saw him where?"

But I couldn't remember. Couldn't remember why I'd been so sure the Kid hadn't killed Phoebe.

"What did he talk to you about? Did he say anything about jade? Everyone knows he has jade hidden around here someplace." She chattered on and on, throwing questions at me. "Were you trying to find out where the jade is? What did he tell you?"

I couldn't think. She frightened me. Where was Max? Why hadn't he come looking for me?

My mind spun out. *Hands*, I thought with a rush of panic. *I dug up hands, clammy dead hands tied together at the wrist with ... something ...* I jerked alert. A hurricane cloud billowed towards us. No, a pickup.

"Stop!" I said, grabbing on to the dashboard. "Max. He's ... he's looking for me." But we barreled on. "Slow down!" I screamed, totally losing it. She gave me a furious look, and stomped on the brake.

The two vehicles came to careening halts in the loose gravel. The pickup backed with a roar to parallel the car.

Max! Thank God.

He ran to me and opened the door. "My God," he said after one look. He raised a questioning glance at Hildy. "She's got to get to a doctor. I've been trying to keep her talking, poor dear," Hildy said. "Follow me." Max kissed my cheek. "I don't want to move you. We're almost there, just hang on." Slamming the door, he ran back to his truck—with a spray of gravel he turned and followed us into town.

I concentrated on not passing out, not throwing up. Through the haze that covered my eyes, I could see Hildy hunched over the wheel, grimly silent, intent on driving.

Oh God, I thought, *could the King of Swords be a woman?*

Chapter Twenty

Max carried me into the hospital, which I thought a bit much, but kind of nice anyway. They put me in a large open examining area that could be divided into cubicles by curtains. The place was empty, so they didn't bother with any curtains, just laid me out on an examining table.

The nurse was a large woman with a broad smile and a straight no-nonsense haircut. She held out a clipboard, glancing from Hildy to Garland. "Who wants to fill this out?" Max took it. "Whooee," she said, turning her attention to the goose egg on the side of my head. "What happened to you?" She probed the wound gently. "What's your name, honey?"

"Thea," I said, wincing as she began cleaning the area. "Thea Barlow."

"No kidding?" She stopped to give me a look of delighted curiosity. "You're the one who found the dead girl, aren't you? And now somebody's rung your bell, huh? What's going on around this town?" She worked quickly and precisely, talking all the time.

"I found her staggering around in the middle of the road,"

Hildy said, bustling from one side of the table to the other in an exaggerated mixture of excitement and concern. "I don't know the answers to half of these questions," Max said, tossing the clipboard on the chair in disgust. "And she doesn't need to be bothered with them now. There's enough information on there to get her admitted. We'll fill out the rest later."

"You have a headache, honey?" the nurse asked me.

I nodded, then wished I hadn't.

"Don't surprise me none. What did you get hit with?" The nurse held two fingers up in front of my face. "How many do you see?"

"Two, fuzzy."

"Sounds like a concussion to me. And you're in luck. The doctor's here delivering a baby. We've had a rash of them recently. Generally he's only here two, three days a week. I'll go get him so's we can get you started on some painkillers. Be right back."

"That outlaw Kid Corcoran did this," Hildy announced to no one in particular. "Didn't I say this kind of thing would start happening when he came to town? First that girl last night, and now this. They ought to run him out of town."

Max stepped close, jostling Hildy away from the bed. "Max," I said, clutching his hand, trying to gather my wits. "Call the police. The Kid is missing. I don't know where he is ... I thought he hit me, but maybe someone else was there. He might be lying in a ditch somewhere. And your car, Max, it's at Corcoran's place, but I lost the keys ... I think I left the door open too, and I need to tell the police—"

"Hey, slow down. The police can wait. We're going to get you taken care of first."

The nurse came back with a glass of water and some pills. She was followed by a nurse's aide and two other women who looked like office help. They stood around the perimeters and stared at me. I heard one of the office types ask Hildy, "Is she really the one who found the body?" That was all she needed. Hildy had found her audience.

"You're a celebrity," Max said dryly, squeezing my hand.

"Here we go, honey." The nurse handed me a tiny paper cup of pills. "We'll start cracking that headache. I bet it's a doozy."

She and Max helped me to sit up. I swallowed the pills obediently.

"Let's take a look at that shoulder, now. Okay, people, time to get out of here." She jerked the curtains closed.

The doctor came and went, I was poked and probed and cleaned and daubed and finally put to bed in a dimly lit hospital room, which was fine by me. I passed in and out of sleep, barely aware of what was happening. Others came and went, but all that mattered was that Max was usually by my side.

Four or so hours later, the nurse woke me to take vital signs and give me another dose of painkillers. I stretched cautiously. The headache still pounded, but feeling had returned to my arm and hand, and, thank God, my eyes had cleared. I was hungry as hell.

As if on cue, Max came through the door with a bundle of clothes in one arm and insulated food carriers in the other. A rose stuck out of his shirt pocket.

"Hi," he said. "Clean clothes for you." He dumped them in the closet. "And," he cracked open one of the carriers, wafting it under my nose, "Sheila Rides Horse sends her best wishes."

I sucked in the heavenly aroma with the eagerness of a puppy at his food dish. "Umm. Wonderful."

"You're looking much better," Max said, more seriously. "How's the headache?"

"Still there, but much better."

He checked out my head wound and the colorful assortment of Band-aids, cuts and bruises on my arms. He kissed me lightly, then took my hands in his. "Before we get to the food," he said, "I need to know if you're up to seeing some visitors."

"Who?" I asked, surprised.

"Phoebe Zimmerman's parents. They'd like to see you, if possible. They're in the lobby talking with the doctor. He helped with the autopsy."

I must have looked stricken.

Max said, "You don't have to. The doctor said it's entirely your decision."

"Oh, Max, of course I'll see them."

"Good girl." He patted my hand. "I think they need to talk to you. They seem like nice people."

He rolled up my bed, then left, and returned shortly with the couple in tow.

I saw immediately why he'd championed them. They were older, an average-looking couple, neat, trim and prosperous. Bereft was the only word to describe the lost expressions on their faces. I ached for them.

"I hope we're not bothering you," Mrs. Zimmerman said.

"Of course not," I held out my hand. "Please come in." Max offered them the two chairs in the room, but they waved them away.

"No, we won't be staying but a minute," Mr. Zimmerman said.

What does one say? "I'm so terribly sorry," I began. "Phoebe was a beautiful girl, so full of life and laughter, it must be a terrible loss for you."

"Yes," Phoebe's mother reached for her husband's hand and clung to it. "She was our only child. It's ... been such a shock."

And I could tell it was; there was a bewildered look to them, as if they couldn't quite accept reality.

"We were told you were the last person to talk to her, so we wanted to meet you. I suppose it's silly."

"Of course it's not silly." I could understand their hunger for connections of any kind.

"And we understand you helped her in some way that night," her husband carried on his wife's train of thought as if it were second nature for them. "We wanted to thank you for that."

"I didn't do much. I didn't know Phoebe well, I'd just met her. She'd ... she'd hurt herself some way and I helped her, well, to my room, is all. I just wish I'd done more."

"She'd had way too much to drink," Mrs. Zimmerman said with an understanding look. "They told us that."

"She was a headstrong girl," her husband chimed in. "A handful sometimes, but she was a hard worker and full of ambition. I admired her for that." He paused, his eyes filling with tears.

His wife stroked his arm. "She was so excited about this new story she was after."

"Oh?" I said, interested. "Did she talk about it? What did she say?"

"Nothing much, actually, just that it was going to be another one about the Nickel Kid. I guess he's called Kid Corcoran around here."

"But there was more to it than that, dear. She claimed she was going to get another by-line, bigger than the first. She got phone calls from somebody, making inquiries; made her perk up her ears; said she was sharpening her newshound nose."

So, I thought, she *had* had some kind of lead before she came here; she was onto something more than just the jade stuff and gossip she'd come across here. What? I wondered. And how much a part did that knowledge play in her death?

"When was this?" I asked.

"Just two, three weeks ago. Shortly after the first piece was rerun in the San Francisco paper." His voice rang with pride for his daughter. "Teased me to death, said she was on to something big, if I'd just help her get out to Wyoming. So, of course I paid for her ticket." His shoulders slumped and his voice dropped to a whisper. "Wish I hadn't now."

"It's not your fault, dear," his wife consoled him, probably not for the first time. Then gently to us, "She could always wheedle her daddy out of anything."

There was one of those self-conscious moments when nobody knew what to say, until Phoebe's father filled the void.

"Well, thank you for letting us intrude on you."

We exchanged some more words of sympathy and they left.

"Oh, Max," I said. "How heartbreaking for them."

"Yes. I noticed they didn't say anything about murder."

"I think they're still trying to accept the fact that she's gone. The horror of the rest will come later."

I wanted to get up and sit in the chair, in fact I was ready to put on my clothes and get out of there, but Max insisted I stay in bed.

"Give yourself a chance. The doc says you're doing great and he'll release you in the morning, but they like to keep concussions overnight." He rolled the bed back down, and sat on the edge.

"What's happened, Max? Have they found the Kid? Did you see Florie? What did she say?"

"They haven't found the Kid. I did talk to Florie, and I'm going to stay in Madam Juju until you get out of here. Remind me to get a key from you before I leave."

"They should be in my purse, wherever that might be. Did you eat at Racy Ladies tonight?"

"Yes. In fact, I joined Garland Caldwell and his wife for dinner. News gets around fast; he was quite concerned about you."

"He's quite concerned about anything in skirts."

Max grinned. "Anyway, they send their best to you. He seems like a decent guy." I rolled my eyes. "Well, a little gung-ho, maybe." Max laughed. "He thinks he's getting an inside look at the real wild west, and by now is expecting a shoot-out at every corner. And, of course, Buster doesn't help, filling him full of crazy jade-hunting stories."

"He was there, too?"

"Yes, but we can talk about all that later." He got off the bed and reached for the food carriers. "This is from Sheila."

He swung the tray across my lap, whipped out napkins and silverware from the top container and arranged them on the tray. He took out the first dish and uncovered a thick, creamy slice of paté studded with capers and pine nuts, and ringed by an assortment of crackers. "This is for both of us. Sheila said you have to share."

From his pocket, he pulled the rose, which was drooping a bit by now, and propped it in my water glass. "This," he said, placing it on the tray, "is from me." He leaned over and kissed me tenderly and smoothed my hair away from my face.

"We will talk about the serious things; I want to know exactly what happened to you," he said softly, "but let's make time for this, too. Okay? I about went crazy when I couldn't find you in town this afternoon."

He sat back on the bed and, with elaborate flourishes, thickly spread a cracker and offered it to me.

Heavenly. We dug in.

We talked about the little things. His job, my job, how my parents were, our plans for the next few days, all the things we would have said to each other if there hadn't been a Phoebe, or a murder or Kid Corcoran. A small bowl of richly flavored consommé followed the paté, accompanied by thin triangles of pumpernickel.

"Help," I said, happily. "I have to rest, or I'll never be able to eat again. I hope Sheila remembered that I'm an invalid."

"Yes, that's why the consommé. I had the most incredible chowder over there tonight that I've ever eaten in my life."

"Thank you for this, Max. I didn't realize how badly I needed some quiet time."

"Okay, we can talk now, then we'll have the next course." He moved the tray out of the way so he could sit closer to me. "I called the police, as you wanted me to, and Dwayne came out. The doc didn't think you should be bothered tonight, so Dwayne will be back to see you in the morning. But he talked to Hildy and me. Or rather," he said wryly, "Hildy talked to him. We told him what little we knew, that you'd gone to the country with the Kid, that either he, or some mysterious other person, bashed you on the head, and that now the Kid was missing."

"Did they go look for him?"

"Well, that is the sheriff's jurisdiction out there, so Dwayne called them. They were going to send a man out, but because the sheriff's out of town and it's a holiday weekend they're understaffed. I don't know how they settled it, but someone went out there to look for the Kid. They didn't find any sign of him."

"But how hard did they look, Max?" All I could think of was all that land, all those weeds, all those buildings, all that junk. An elephant could have been hidden out there and not be found for a week.

"I don't know, Thea. We have to assume they know their job."

"But—"

"I called again, before I came here. I know someone's been to Corcoran's ranch. I gave them a second set of keys to the Bronco. It's still there, they locked it and I'll get it back when they're finished with it. The Kid hasn't turned up. They claimed they did a thorough search, but I also got the distinct impression that they think he's skipped out."

"What did Florie say?"

"Not much," he said. "I couldn't figure her out. I told her everything I knew. Part of the time she seemed genuinely worried about the Kid, and at other times I got this kind of hidden elation about something. We didn't connect."

"She's not happy being burdened with her grandfather. I guess he just showed up one day, and here she is with an ex-con on her hands and the town in an uproar. I think she hopes he'll be convicted of Phoebe's murder and sent back to the pen. In fact, I think she's pushing for it."

"Incredible. I'd never met the woman before. I've eaten there a couple of times, but mostly I stay in the country at the rig. I've met Rocky a time or two. Buster raves about the place; he likes his food. In fact, he's the one who took me to dinner there the first time. He's a great salt-of-the-earth kind of guy. I like him a lot. Do you know Buster?"

I told him about the few times I'd met him. The frog skin and mutton fat. And how I first met Hildy the jade lady. "Did you know the buzz has it that the Kid killed Buster's father?"

"No kidding? When was this?"

"A long time ago, I guess. 'Forties, I think."

"Where did you hear that?"

"From Hildy Gilstrom. Her daddy was one of the old jade men. Or, wait, maybe it was Jimmy Chin who actually told me about the murder and stolen jade."

"Jimmy Chin? What does he have to do with this?"

"That's what I'd like to know." I was rather enjoying Max's astonishment. There's nothing like being the purveyor of choice bits of gossip, rumor and innuendo. "Jimmy claims to be disinterested, but there's no love lost between him and the Kid."

"Hold on," Max said, standing up and pacing. "I knew Buster's dad was into jade, he still has some impressive pieces in his home, but he never said anything about murder, or stolen jade. He's the one who told me about the Kid in the first place, didn't say anything against him." He stood, hands on hips, eyeing me with a mix of bewilderment and exasperation. "How in hell did you get messed up in all of this? Lord, woman, you haven't been here two days yet."

So I told him everything. Well, everything except the Tarot stuff. Somehow I didn't think he was ready for that.

"I was so sure the Kid couldn't have killed Phoebe that I had no qualms about taking him to the country. But the rumors proved right, the Kid had a stash of stolen jade buried in the old flower borders of his brother's house. And I helped him dig it up."

"I can't believe it, Thea. Why did you do it?"

"I don't know. It seemed so logical at the time. He told me the jade was his nest egg. He has a friend living in the nursing home here, named Kate. He doesn't want to end up there as well, and I don't blame him. He had plans for the two of them to move out to the old home place. Talk about the halt leading the blind. Still, it just tore my heart out." I made one of those helpless gestures. I couldn't believe myself, how easily I'd been taken in. "And I believed him when he said the jade was rightfully his."

Max sat back on the bed. "What made you change your mind?"

"I recognized the last piece I dug up, a carving of a lotus bud. It's called the Fingers of Buddha. Very strange looking piece." I grimaced, remembering how I'd mistaken it for real bones. "There's a replica of it in the Lotus Café, and I heard at great length from Jimmy Chin's Auntie Lee how the real thing, and some other family heirlooms, had been stolen from them many years ago."

"You're sure it was the same thing?"

"Yes. I mean, how many jade masterpieces of Buddha's Fingers would you expect to find in Rawhide, Wyoming?"

He grinned. "So what did you do then?"

"I accused him flat-out of lying to me."

"And he said?"

"Nothing. I must admit I didn't give him much opportunity. I was really steamed. I stomped off to the car, and next thing I knew I woke up in the ravine."

Again, he popped up and began pacing like a restless animal. "Did you see what hit you?"

"I saw something reflected in the car's window, enough to make me duck. I *thought* it was the shovel, but whether I actually saw it or not, I'm not certain. When I came to and started remembering things, I know I believed that the Kid had whomped me with the shovel."

"Logical conclusion. He was the only one there."

"But now I'm not so sure, Max, and it really bothers me."

I told him about my unsettling exploration of the old house, or non-exploration. "I had a distinct feeling that I was not alone in that house, but it was more than that. How could the Kid have rolled, or even pushed, me into the gully? It's not that close to the house. He doesn't have the strength to drag me that far. I mean, I saw how just a few digs with the shovel nearly did him in."

"Could he have put you in the Bronco?"

"He might have been able to hoist me onto the tailgate, drive to the edge and dump me over, but there weren't any tire tracks. I was right there afterwards. I know I was pretty loony-tunes at the time, but even then things didn't seem right. I looked; there weren't any tire tracks anywhere around the edge of the gully."

We sat silent for a moment, contemplating possibilities.

"The Bronco was moved from where I'd parked it." I said, thinking out loud. "The jade we dug up was gone. If he wanted me out of the way so he could take off with the jade, why not just steal the car? I can't help wondering if a vagrant wasn't in the house watching us all the time. Maybe that person attacked me and the Kid, too, and took the jade."

"Vagrant, Thea? Come on, this isn't Chicago. You don't get casual vagrants thirty miles out in the country where there isn't any food. But he could have had an accomplice, and they both took off with the loot."

"Yes, but then why bring me in on it? Why risk letting me

in on his secret cache of jade, unless I was his only chance for retrieving it? He knew I was sympathetic."

"A patsy for any hard-luck story," he said. I knew this wouldn't be the last I'd hear of it. "You could have been killed."

"Well, maybe," I said, sheepishly. "But—"

"It's not up to you, Thea, to figure any of this out." He took my hands in his, massaging them lightly, running his fingers over the various cuts and scrapes. "That's what the police are for—actually the sheriff's department, now."

"Is the Sheriff back in town?"

"No, not 'til next week, but his deputies are on it."

"It's just that I feel so responsible, Max. I have this awful feeling that the Kid might be lying in a ditch somewhere, injured like I was, but without a chance of saving himself."

"My sympathy's at a low ebb. He may be an old man, but he's no saint. He put you in an unfair position, and if he's the one who whopped you, left you for dead, then I'll gladly wring his neck all by myself. He's probably high-tailed it out of here with his precious jade. Leave it to the authorities, Thea. They'll find him."

I sighed. I knew he was right. I smiled at him and asked, "So what's the next course? I'm ready to eat again."

We finished the food, light, airy bluegill fillets that melted in the mouth, and berries with clots of fresh cream for dessert. My eyes were drooping.

Max kissed me goodnight and brought me my purse from the closet. I found the two keys to Madam Juju in my billfold where I'd put them. I gave one to Max.

"What did you do with the other key?" I asked sleepily. "The one Rocky gave you last night."

"I left it on the dresser for you. Didn't you find it?"

"No. I might have overlooked it, but I didn't see it anywhere. Another missing key, Max." But I was too sleepy to worry about it now.

***

I awoke in the middle of the night feeling quite refreshed and perhaps a little too full of Sheila Rides Horse's wonderful food. All my body parts seemed to be working surprisingly well, I thought, flexing my arms and legs. The shoulder was sore to the touch, but the arm felt quite alive and useful. Only the headache remained, but reduced to a much gentler throb. Of course, I looked like hell, with livid cuts, scratches and a crazy variety of Band-aids, half of which were the kiddie kind, scattered all over my arms and legs. Small price, I guess.

I went to the bathroom, drank some water, paced around a bit and decided I was too restless to go back to bed yet. Slipping on the hospital-issue robe and scuffs, I wandered out into the hall.

"Hi there," said the night nurse as I walked past her desk. "You're looking pretty good. How do you feel?"

"Surprisingly well."

"Good. Let me know if I can get you anything."

Hers was a new face. She seemed pleasant and ready to talk. But I knew what the subject would be and I just couldn't face going through all the details of Phoebe's death again. I smiled my thanks and moved on. It felt good to move around and get some of the kinks worked out.

I walked the corridors, what there were of them; it was a very small hospital. Each time I passed, I stopped at the nursery. Three little cribs were positioned close to the window. Two boys and a girl. The baby girl looked brand new. I rested my forehead against the cool glass, and lost myself in admiration. Yes, I thought, I would like this.

I'd been moved by the love I'd seen in Phoebe's parents

for their daughter and for each other, and how they were using that love to find ways to fight their grief. And I thought about the rest of us who had once been this new. Phoebe, who hadn't had her fair chance, me, Max. Gramps, who had given up, and the Kid, wherever he was, who wouldn't go easily, and even old Kate down the hall. What a strange passage it was.

I stretched, flexed my legs some more and opened the swinging doors at the end of the corridor enough to see what was on the other side. It was the connecting corridor to the nursing home wing with a nice long hallway. I pushed through the door, thinking I'd walk the long hall and maybe peek in on Kate. Few people were stirring at this time of night. I waggled my fingers at the two aides doing paperwork at a desk by the entry and went on my way.

Kate's door was open. She sat in her rolled-up bed watching a small television pulled up close to her eyes on a hospital-style lap tray. I couldn't tell if she was awake or asleep.

"Are you awake, Kate?" I said in not much more than a whisper.

Her head bobbed up. "Who is it?" Nothing wrong with her hearing.

"It's Thea Barlow. I was here this morning [was it really just this morning?] with uh ..." I wasn't sure what to call him, then decided she probably knew him the same way as everyone else. "I was here with the Kid."

"Of course you were. I remember," she said, defensively. "Did you bring me my lunch?"

"No, it's not quite time yet." I vowed that the next time I visited I'd bring some snacks.

"Come sit down, dear. Where's the Kid? Didn't he come with you?" She sounded very lucid.

"No, not this time." What could I say? I hated to promise he'd be here tomorrow or any other time, when I was dreadfully afraid that none of us might ever see him again.

She caught whatever hesitation lurked in my voice. "Did something happen to him?" She clutched at my hand apprehensively.

" No ... I ... I just haven't seen him recently, is all."

"Oh, dear." She became increasingly agitated, twisting her fingers, worrying the enlarged knuckles. "They're after him, you know." Her voiced quavered, and her dim eyes flittered helplessly around the room. "Someone's trying to kill him."

Chapter Twenty-One

"Now, now," I said, murmuring soothing sounds. Holding her hands gently in mine, I tried to quiet her fears while still discovering what she meant. "Tell me more about it, Kate. Who's after him?" Did she really know something, or was this just another quirk of her mind?

"I don't know," she said. "Some men, hoodlums, I imagine. They're hunting him down. Gonna steal him blind." Then she dropped her fear to register what sounded like a major annoyance. "He tells me these things, but he thinks I don't remember," she said indignantly. "I'm not as dumb as he thinks. He's got lots of valuables and we got to keep them safe, so's we can go home."

"Home? Where's home, Kate?"

"Why, out to the country," she said, as if surprised that everyone didn't know this. "He's got a grand, big old house out to the country. Are we going home tonight? Are you going to help me get my things ready?"

"Not tonight, Kate." Had the Kid really promised her they'd live in that awful house? Whatever, she wasn't going to forget the Kid's grandiose plans as quickly as he thought. I massaged her knobby fingers.

She chuckled, her mind quickly switching to another channel. "We was wild ones, I tell ya. Ol' Fancy Pants, he'd come down to Plumber Street, sneak in an' wait for me. Then we'd run off and go honky-tonking all night. Out to the old Forty Mile house. Do you remember that place? They had some fine bootleg. Oh, we had good times, all right."

"I'm sure you did," I said, wondering how I could get her back on the subject of who was after the Kid without alarming her too badly. "Why do you call him Fancy Pants, Kate?"

She puzzled that over a bit. "Can't rightly remember. He had a likin' for fine clothes, he did. Used to love them gambler's-striped trousers, maybe that was it." She chuckled again, replaying the good times. "Yep, he was Fancy Pants and I was Madame Juju."

"Madame Juju!"

"Yes." She sounded offended by my surprise. "Those railroad turks liked Frenchy stuff, so I gave it to them. Made me some good money, too. They was always asking special for me."

"You mean you were ... uh ... in Racy Ladies?"

"Racy ladies! Ha ha," she chortled, as if I'd made the joke of the century. "That's a good one. You bet we were, honey."

I laughed, too. "No, I didn't mean that. I meant the house where you lived, uh, worked."

"The house on Plumber Street."

Now that I thought about it, Racy Ladies didn't sound like a legit name for a whorehouse; it was more like a catchy name for a tourist attraction. Which it was.

But I wanted to be sure. "Was it here in Rawhide?"

"Well, of course." She shaded her eyes and squinted at me.

"Who are you, anyway?" She pushed the tray and TV aside and squirmed restlessly in the bed.

"I'm a friend of the Kid, Kate," I said, readjusting the pillow behind her head and smoothing the covers. "I just wanted to know what the Plumber Street house looked like, is all."

"Why didn't you say so?" She huffed querulously, motioning me to the dresser. "There's pictures over there. In the top drawer."

I got them, eagerly thumbing through to see if any showed buildings. "I think I'm staying in the Plumber Street house, Kate. It's been turned into a bed and breakfast—a kind of hotel. I might even be in the room you used."

"Is that right?" she asked, but I wasn't certain she understood.

"Here, is this it?" I took a small, severely cracked photograph to her and adjusted the light over her shoulder. The picture showed three women standing in front of a house that looked very much like The Racy Ladies Bed and Breakfast.

She held the picture up close to her thick glasses. "That's it. And this here is me"—she put her finger on one of the women—"and that one on the end is Clarise Bagwell; she run the house. The Kid couldn't stand her. He used to sneak in the house all the time. We'd feed him dinner, take care of him. He never paid for anything. Hid out there a time or two when the law was after him. He knew every hidey-hole in that place. Used to hide his stuff all over that house."

Something, the secretive connotations of "hidey-hole" maybe, sparked an instant memory, something I'd completely forgotten: being wakened in the middle of the night by strange noises.

"What did he hide?" I asked. "What do you mean?"

"Oh, clothes and things," she said cagily. "His belongings."

Loot was probably more like it. I remembered the fright

I'd felt, thinking someone had been in my room—Madam Juju. If the Kid had been accustomed to hiding things there in the past, could he have done so now? Would he have had the guts to enter the room even with Max there? If so, I thought, he must have been desperate. Why? What did he have that he needed to hide?

"He hides stuff in here, too," Kate said.

"What?" I'd been lost in my own thoughts.

"He hides things in here. Doesn't think I know what he's doing, but he can't fool me. My eyes may be bad, but there's nothing wrong with my ears."

"Here? He's hiding things here in your room?" More jade?

She threw back the covers on the bed, and moved her legs slowly over the side of the bed.

"Wait," I said. "What are you doing?"

"I'm getting out of this bed. People die in bed. I'm gonna sit in my chair."

"I don't think you ..." But there was no stopping her. I rushed to help, afraid she might fall. Taking her arm as she slipped out of bed, I got her settled in the recliner with an afghan over her shoulders and lap.

"Look in that bottom drawer over there," she said, with the eagerness of a child. "He put something in there; let's see what it is. I want to know what he's up to."

So did I. I was certainly as curious as she. The dresser was cheap and the drawer hard to open; they needed some WD-40 around here. I remembered the Kid struggling to get the thing closed, and how slickly he'd covered his actions by pulling out a sweater for Kate when I appeared. I hadn't suspected a thing. If he'd brought something in with him, it must have been under his jacket.

"This is a sorry place to hide anything," Kate complained. "I shoulda told him that. People're always snooping around. Steal ya blind is what they do. I heard tell from a lady down the hall that ..."

She chattered on and I got the drawer halfway open, crooked, but open far enough to run my hand under the piles of soft clothing. Nothing. Impatiently, I jerked harder and the blasted drawer came all the way out onto the floor. I swore under my breath, and picked the thing up to put it back on the glides. If I hadn't been on my knees with my nose practically to the floor trying to see how to fit the drawer in, I wouldn't have found the newspaper-wrapped package in the empty space under the drawer. I grabbed it, and uncovered a long, flattish green vase beneath two layers of newspaper wrapping.

Its elegance took my breath away, even with dirt still clinging to the cuts and hollows of the carved dragon handles. I remembered something Hildy had said about the "feel" of jade, and for a moment sensed what she meant. The cool stone caressed my fingers and became one with its beauty. I wanted to hold it forever, contemplate the artistry and the play of light on the subtle colors.

"What are you doing down there?" Kate's words pulled me from my trance. Quickly, I wrapped the treasure up in the dirt-sprinkled paper. My covetousness shocked me. I'd never wanted to own anything as much as I wanted that vase. Reluctantly, I put it back where I'd found it. It seemed well enough hidden from casual nursing home thievery.

I'd have to tell the authorities about it, but was afraid Dwayne would see Kate as an accomplice, particularly with her background. She'd be better off not knowing the piece was here. I rocked the drawer back in place and shut it.

"What are you doing?" she asked again.

"Just closing the dresser drawer." I hoped she'd forgotten what she'd ask me to do. Could I be so lucky? I rose and went back to her chair. "Don't you think you ought to get back in bed? It's really late."

"No, they're going to bring me my lunch on a tray. Then nobody can steal my food."

Good, I thought, she's off on another track. But then the old threads began connecting and she said, "When's the Kid coming back? Where is he?"

I sighed. "I don't know." It was time to get out of here. "Look, I have to leave now."

"What did you find? What was in the drawer?"

"Nothing; you were wrong; the kid didn't hide anything there." The less she knew the better.

"Did you take it?" Her voice was ripe with suspicion. "Are you stealing from me, too?"

"No, but I'm worried about the Kid, Kate. Can you tell me anything more about who's after him? Is it just one person, or a bunch of people? What did the Kid tell you? I need to know who's after him."

She began to fret again, picking at the stitches in the afghan folded over her lap. "I don't remember," she said, fear beginning to build in her voice and on her face. "I don't know who you are. You're hiding things from me, aren't you?"

I touched her soft cheek, and ran my hand over her tufty hair. "It's okay, Kate. Please don't worry. Everything will be all right." May God not strike me dead, I thought. "I'm going to get your lunch now."

I stopped by the dimly-lit desk where the two aides were drinking coffee and chatting.

"I've been visiting with Kate," I told them. "She insisted on getting out of bed and into her chair; I don't know if you want to put her back in bed or not."

"I'll go check on her," the older woman said. "It's not unusual. She doesn't sleep much at night."

"Could you take her some kind of a light meal now?"

The two looked dubiously at each other. "Well," one said listlessly, "I guess we could get her some cereal. She likes Cheerios."

"And how about some toast and jelly?" I suggested impatiently. "Anything to make her feel like she's getting a treat."

"There might be some of that cake left, too," the blond said, warming to the thought of a late-night snack.

"Thanks. I think she'd really enjoy that, and if there's any problem about the cost, I'll be glad to pay." I gave them my name on a piece of paper.

I suppose I was taking a chance that Kate might blow the whistle on me, alarm the aides about me stealing things from her, but I couldn't worry about that now. I had to talk to Max.

The jade vase had obviously been buried in dirt, but it wasn't anything I'd seen before. Had the Kid recovered this piece when Phoebe took him to the country?

What had Phoebe meant when she said she had something to show me? If it had been that vase I could understand her excitement, but I couldn't imagine the Kid turning it over to her. Maybe she'd spirited away a different piece when the Kid wasn't looking? I just didn't know. Again, it seemed more and more apparent that another person was involved. Sheila's dark-haired man? Phoebe could have been working for him—and perhaps murdered by him. If that unknown person had been lying in wait for the Kid at his ranch to find out where his jade was hidden, then the chances were great that the Kid was either dead, or lying in a ditch somewhere, alive, but unable to help himself. How long could he last out there on his own? I had to get Max.

I scurried back to the hospital wing.

"Still up and around?" the night nurse asked as I passed her desk. "You probably ought to get some rest now."

"Yes," I said. "The exercise did me good. I think I'll really be able to sleep."

"How's the head?"

"Not bad. Pounds a bit if I move too suddenly, or bend over."

"Well, we have some Tylenol if you think you need it."

"Yes, please." I might as well get what help I could, because I had no intention of staying in bed the rest of the night. I took the medication when the nurse brought it and let her tuck me in. When she left, confident I was settled for the night, I bounced back up and quietly changed into the clean jeans and T-shirt Max had brought for me. I slipped down the hall and out the front door, with no problem. If they wanted to sue me they could.

The brisk wind whipped my hair and brought gooseflesh to my arms. Now and then a strong gust tweaked my nose with the faint scent of wood smoke. I wished I had a sweatshirt. If it weren't for the wind I would have enjoyed the odd sensation of walking through quiet residential streets in the middle of the night without fear.

There were no cars on the street, though I could hear traffic closer to the center of town. An occasional house showed the glow of a television between a crack in the curtains, or even a front door left open to catch the cool night air.

I hurried as I got closer to Racy Ladies, pushing against the wind, worrying about how I'd get into the place. I had a key to Madam Juju in my pocket, but the house itself would be locked at this time of night. I could always ring the bell and have Rocky or Florie let me in, but I thought they might feel obliged to report the whereabouts of a wayward patient to dear old Dwayne. I wouldn't risk it unless I had no other choice. I didn't want to get caught up in endless stupid arguments about why I needed to spend the night in a hospital bed.

If only there'd been phones in the rooms, I could have called Max to open the door for me. On second thought, I was sure he wouldn't be at all pleased with what I had in mind. Best to take him by surprise, too.

As far as I could tell, Racy Ladies was dark, except for a lone light in the vestibule; this was not surprising for past midnight. I decided to check all the doors first to see if one could have possibly been left open. Rocky claimed to lock everything at eleven o'clock, but ...

He didn't lie. All the doors were tightly secured. I stood on the side porch off the parking lot feeling frustrated, when it dawned on me that the window to one side of the porch railing was to Sheila's room. The curtain was drawn, but I could see the row of stones lining the sill. Weird as she was, I couldn't imagine that Sheila would give a damn one way or another if I'd skipped out on the hospital.

I got a handful of gravel from the parking lot and leaned over the railing, tossing pieces at her window. Nothing stirred. Impatiently, I threw what remained in my hand with enough force to wake a deaf person. Again no response. She must be out. Now what?

I straddled the railing and leaned over to get a closer look at the window. It was the old-fashioned type with a thumb lock that holds the top and bottom sashes together in the middle of the window. The sashes weren't evenly lined up, so I figured the window couldn't be locked. Wrapping and weaving my legs and feet between the porch rails for support, I reached farther over and pushed up on the sash. Much to my surprise the window opened easily. I hesitated a moment, but quickly convinced myself this couldn't be considered breaking and entering as long as I officially had a room in the place. More like being locked out, I'd say. And no one could accuse me of sneaking, which implied a certain amount of stealth and quiet. It's a wonder I didn't wake the whole neighborhood.

The rock collection on the windowsill clattered to the floor when I slid across the sill on my stomach and when I turned my legs loose of the porch railing they banged against the side of the house with the resonance of a kettle drum. The few minutes hanging upside down, to say nothing of the fall to the floor, set my head to pounding again, and my injuries set up a howling of their own. Thank God for that last shot of Tylenol.

Dragging myself to my feet, I shut the window, replaced as many of the stones as I could find, and limped painfully toward the door. Just as I grabbed the knob, the door jerked open from the other side, pulling me face to face with a towering Indian wreathed in curls of smoke that snaked across the dark cavernous face and high up into the air.

Chapter Twenty-Two

I think I screamed. I know I wanted to, but all I could hear was my pounding heart. The curls of smoke drifted away and I recognized Sheila Rides Horse blocking the door like a monolith. She put her hand on my chest and pushed me back into her room.

"What are you doing here?" Her voice rumbled.

I stumbled back, eyes wide. "What are *you* doing?" I gasped. She wore her beautiful doeskin dress with a simple headband across her forehead. In one hand she carried a smoking herb bundle and in the other a wand of eagle feathers with strands of bundle-tipped rawhide dangling from the bottom.

"Purifying," she said, wafting the herb bundle much as a priest would wave a censer. Then she sighed and flipped on the light switch. The apparition disappeared into stolid Sheila. She looked dreadfully tired. She wiped her eyes with the back of the hand holding the feathers. "I'm making peace with my background; maybe that will help. I purified the house." She held the bundle high, wafting curls of smoke to the four corners of the room. "And what are you doing in my room?"

I lifted my face, inhaling the essence of sage, basil and other herbs I couldn't identify. Regaining some courage, I spoke quickly.

"I'm sorry, Sheila." Nervously, I gave her the aw-shucks-we're-such-great-buddies smile. "All the doors were locked and I needed to get in to see Max. Your window was open"—just a tiny stretch of truth—"so I came in that way. I didn't bother anything, really."

She didn't seem terribly interested. She looked me over carefully. "You got hurt; you could have been killed. I told you to be careful."

I am being careful, I thought, sidling toward the open door.

"Did you see the dark-haired man?"

"I've seen nothing but dark-haired men," I said caustically.

"Have you found the King of Swords?" she demanded impatiently. This was nothing but serious business as far as she was concerned.

"No," I said, equally serious. "I did not see the person who bashed me in the head. I'm worried about Kid Corcoran, Sheila. Do you know where he is?"

She went to the window, opened the curtains and stared silently into the night. "He's under the stars," she said tonelessly. "Lying on the ground. There's a dome nearby, and buildings collapsing." Her voice rose with anxiety. "The Tower! The old man is there."

"Is he dead?"

Another lengthy pause. "I don't know." She turned away from the window and rubbed her eyes. Her voice returned to normal. "His power is gone, but that doesn't mean he's passed on."

"I need to look for him."

"You need to stay away. You need to hide. Be careful."

I'd heard this before. I started out the door and stumbled on a stone that darted off my shoe. Sheila snatched it up.

"It's not a new one, Sheila. I knocked your collection off the window sill when I came through. I picked most of them up."

"Why stones? It's like they're falling out of the sky, trying to tell me something. Why am I being sent stones?"

She wasn't really asking me, but it seemed obvious and I didn't need cards to tell me so. "Jade," I said. "Jade is a stone, a rock."

"But it was a bush I saw," she said, still perplexed. "I had a vision, a warning vision. A strange, flesh-colored plant, whose branches were hard as stone, but they grew, wound around me, tried to take my life."

I edged toward the door, afraid she was wigging out again, then it dawned on me what she was talking about.

"Oh, my God, the lotus bud! I've seen it. It's not a plant, Sheila, it's a jade carving of a lotus bud." I held my cupped hands upright in imitation, fingers spread and curling. "Buddha's Fingers."

"Yes, that's it," she said with wonderment. "Jade. I'll be damned. So it's about money after all." She grinned, but it wasn't a pleasant sight. "I been looking in all the wrong places. Now I can find the bastard." She pushed me out the door unceremoniously. "I need to go."

"But the Kid—" The door shut in my face.

I couldn't get rid of the picture of the Kid, lying injured, or worse, on the ground. A dome, buildings falling down. I supposed it could mean a city, or town. But I'd last seen him in the country and the small weathered barn was as close to collapsing as any building I knew about. Not that I believed in Sheila or her visions, or second sight, or whatever it was called. But she reinforced my fears; I had to do something. I rushed through the dimly lit halls, inhaling the lingering scent of sage, and took the stairs two at a time up to Madam Juju.

Max was not overjoyed to see me. "What are you doing here?" he asked groggily. "You're supposed to be in bed."

"Max, it's important. I have to tell you what I've found out."

"Does the doctor know you left the hospital?"

"No, of course not. Max, please listen. We have to go look for the Kid."

"What time is it?"

"Around one." He groaned and flopped back down on the bed. "Come here." He held his arm out to me. "Come to bed, as long as you're here."

"No, Max. Get up, get dressed." I threw his clothes at him, putting temptation aside. "Listen to me. We have to go out to the country."

"The country? What are you talking about?" At least he was sitting upright again. He got out of bed and took my face in both of his hands, examining me closely. "Are you sure you're all right?" Concern creased his brow.

I smiled. "I haven't gone off my head, if that's what you're worried about."

He flashed the wonderful smile that I hadn't seen enough of yet. His heavy-lidded eyes drooped a fraction more. His voice turned husky. "Sure you don't want to come to bed with me?" I hugged him, but pushed him away. "No, not now. Go take a shower, or throw some water on your face. We need to talk, but you have to be awake and alert."

Reluctantly, he turned me loose, yawned enormously, and wandered into the bathroom.

I examined the walls of the room closely, with secret compartments in mind, but found nothing. On the other hand, how secret would a hiding place be if you could spot it right away? I'd turned the overhead light on, but true to hotels everywhere, the wattage wasn't great, even with the addition of the bedside lamps and the little fringed monstrosity on the dresser. The closet seemed a more likely prospect.

"Do you have a flashlight?" I called into the bathroom.

"In the pickup," he answered, emerging with a wet face and hair. He pulled on his jeans and toweled his head. "Okay, Sherlock, what cooks?"

I told him about my visit with Kate in the nursing home. "She told me someone's after the Kid, wants to kill him."

"Why?"

"For the jade, Max. All this ancient history has stirred up a case of modern warfare. People are angry, they don't want the Kid benefiting from something that doesn't belong to him. Or," I said wearily, "they're just damned greedy and have their eye on some easy money."

"But killing for it, Thea? That's pretty damn extreme."

"All I know is Kate's truly frightened for the Kid, and if there's a chance he's—"

"And who is Kate?" Max said, building up a head of steam. "Does she really know what she's talking about or is she just rattling on?"

"I believed her completely, Max," I said, not batting an eye. I just hoped Max never had an opportunity to chat with her. "And as for who Kate is, you won't believe it."

"No, don't tell me, the lost princess of Shangri La."

I laughed. "Almost as bizarre. She's Madame Juju."

"You're kidding." He was surprised.

"No." We both turned to the picture on the wall. Now

that I knew, I could see that the hairdo was more of a 'twenties style, and the undies, or whatever they were, rather ageless. She and Mavis might both have been Ladies of the Night, but they weren't contemporaries, by any means. "The Kid told me she's the only person left in town he knows. She doesn't look much like that anymore," I said. In fact, I saw little resemblance to the feeble woman in the home, except, perhaps, for the glimmer of fun that sparkled behind her eyes. "She and the Kid were great friends in those days, when nobody knew he was the Nickel Kid. According to Kate, he frequently hid his loot here until the heat was off. In fact, secreting things seems to be a *modus operandi* with him. Kate suspected he'd hidden something in her room, so she had me look. I found an exquisite jade vase. There was still dirt on it, Max, so it had been buried, too, but it wasn't one of the pieces I dug up. He must have gotten it when Phoebe took him to his place."

I followed Max into the bathroom and while he combed his hair I began to check out the walls and cupboards. "And I'd be willing to bet he hid something in here the night Phoebe was killed." I told Max about waking in the middle of the night, thinking someone was in the room.

"But I was here with you."

"I know you were. You were snoring."

"I don't snore."

"Maybe not, but you were sound asleep," I accused him with a broad smile. "Some protector you are. Most of the sounds seemed to come from in here, but I must admit I wasn't totally awake."

Stained wood narrowly grooved to resemble fitted boards covered the bottom half of the bathroom walls. It looked quite old. I got on my hands and knees and peered under the sink. Max did the same behind the footed tub.

He grunted. "Here's something."

I joined him. A door, giving access to the water pipes, was placed awkwardly in the wall behind the front end of the tub. A small brass catch had to be turned to open it. Max tried, but couldn't get his large hand and arm in the small space.

"Let me. I'm smaller." I wedged myself between the wall and the front of the tub. A repairman's nightmare. The house-cleaning wasn't impeccable, either. Dirt and fuzzy-wuzzies sprinkled the tile. Finally, I got the catch turned and pulled the door open. I couldn't see anything but pipes, and my back blocked most of the light. Max got the ridiculous tas-selled boudoir lamp off the dresser and plugged it into an outlet by the sink, then held the light to shine in the hole.

"There's nothing here," I said, disappointed, and began to scootch out. I banged my sore shoulder on the tub and had to bite my lip to keep from crying out, but the hesitation made me notice something I hadn't before. "Wait a minute. Look at this, Max." I brushed dribbles of dirt off the bottom of the cubbyhole into my hand and held it up for Max to see. He looked at me as if I were insane.

I closed the little door, backed out and stood up, bringing life back to all my cuts and bruises. I opened my hand again to show him the dirt and laughed at his expression. He thought I'd really lost it.

"This isn't the kind of dirt and dust that collects in places like that," I said. "This is soil, Max, like the crumbles of dirt in the newspaper the vase was wrapped in; it dribbled out all over the floor in Kate's room when I found it, too. And there's more dirt just like that behind the tub." Thoughtfully, I dusted my hands off over the wastebasket. "Max, what if instead of hiding something in here last night, the Kid retrieved something? Something he'd hidden earlier, when the room wasn't occupied?"

"Mmmmm," Max mumbled. *"Pure* speculation, Thea." He eyed the hiding place skeptically. "But ... maybe. Let's go sit down a minute." Max sat on the bed, head in hands, pondering, or maybe falling asleep again. He looked up, and said, "The Kid does know someone here besides Kate."

"Who?"

"Tonight after dinner at Racy Ladies some old duffer came in looking for him. Funny name. Sat and talked with Garland, Buster and me for awhile. Deefy Hammersmith. Old blowhard kind of guy. Garland bought him a drink and really set him off."

"Oh, I think that's the man who dresses up like a mountain man for the rodeos and fairs. He has a pet fox and I got to pet him. And you're right: I saw him and the Kid together at the rodeo. But, Max, we can talk in the pickup."

He looked up. "You're serious about wanting to go to the country?"

"What will it hurt to go look for him? If I'm right and he's still out there, maybe injured ... Well, it's already been twelve hours; that's a lot of exposure for an eighty-two-year-old man. And if I'm wrong, there's no harm done. I just feel as if I deserted him, Max. I can't rest until I'm certain he doesn't need help."

"All right, sweetheart," Max said with a sigh of resignation. "I shouldn't do this, you know. I should take you back to the hospital and look for the old duffer myself."

"Not a chance." I gave him a kiss. "You wouldn't know where to look."

I grabbed a sweatshirt out of my suitcase and changed

into heavier running shoes. Max pulled his boots on and picked up a jacket. He had just opened the door when the wail of an emergency siren blasted through the silence of the night.

I jumped. "What's that?"

"Fire." Max stood alert, listening. Three blasts. "Three means a fire out in the country. They're calling the volunteers in town. Must need help." A door slammed downstairs. "Let's go. I've got a two-way radio in the car."

We met Rocky in the front vestibule, hair standing on end, buttoning his shirt. He looked surprised to see us. He held a cordless phone in his hand.

"The brush fire north of Brochecks started up again," he told Max. "Wind's whipping around pretty good and they're wanting to get some fire breaks going before it gets any worse. The warden's out to Buster's place, wants everybody to meet there. He's got equipment he can hand out."

"We'll go help. I keep a couple of Indian packs in the truck. They got a spotter?"

"They're looking for Kendall. Haven't found him yet, but as soon as they do they'll get him in the air."

Florie hustled through the dining room and joined us. She eyed me suspiciously. "I thought you were in the hospital."

"The doctor released me early," I said blithely.

She turned to Rocky. "Sheila's not in her room, but I'll get one of the girls to take over here so I can run some food and coffee out to Brocheck's. They'll need help with sandwiches."

"Okay. I'm going to the city yard to see if they need a blade hauled out there. See you later." He gave her a peck on the cheek and we left.

Max and I took off in his pickup. Lights came on in many of the houses as we drove by and joined the stream of vehicles leading the way out of town.

"What are Indian packs?"

"They're big bags with a hand-held hose attached." Max answered. "You fill it full of water and wear it like a back pack. I'll show you when we get there."

"Are all these people volunteer firemen?" More cars and trucks fell in behind us.

"Could be, but you don't have to be an official volunteer to participate." He fished a cell phone from under the seat. "I'm going to call the rig and make sure everything's all right there."

He spoke briefly, asked a few questions and said he'd keep in touch. "They're not in any danger. Fire's several miles away. Anyway, probably everyone in town who can get away will be out at Brocheck's even at this time of night, or morning." He adjusted the radio under the dash to tune in the fire warden's communications. "Excitement's in short supply around here, and a fire has a certain entertainment value, I guess. People who don't want to actually fight the fire bring out food and keep a steady supply of coffee and sandwiches ready for crew members. Everyone gets their blood pumping."

"Still sounds like scary stuff to me."

"It can be. When the wind gets to dancing around anything can happen. Keeps you on your toes. But these people are old fire hands. Everybody keeps in radio contact and they'll get a spotter in the air who can see exactly where the flames are and tell the fighters how to get there. Sometimes it takes a bit of fancy cross-country driving to get where you need to be."

He turned the radio's volume up, listened intently for a few minutes then turned it back down.

"How can you understand what they're saying?" I asked. "It sounds like gibberish."

"Sometimes one channel is clearer than another. You get

used to it. It doesn't sound like the fire's out of control, the warden's just taking precautions so that it doesn't get that way."

"Is it close to Corcoran's place?

"No, not at all. So we can go to Corcoran's first and set your mind at rest. I think there's a back road we can take to Brocheck's from there. How does that sound?"

"Fine. I do appreciate you doing this for me."

"Do you have a specific spot where you want to look for the Kid? Something the deputies might have missed?"

"I think we should check as much of the dry creek bed as possible. That's where I got dumped, maybe the Kid did too," I said. "Then, the original Corcoran homestead site's not far from the main ranch buildings. A trail leads to it that's not easily seen and could be missed. There's not much there but a small barn in imminent danger of collapsing, and a dugout."

"A dugout?" Max gave me the megawatt smile that lit his somber face with piratical charm. I knew he was thinking of when we first met. "One of your favorite places," he said, teasing. "Did you go in this one?"

"You know I didn't," I said ruefully. "But it did make me think about the time you and I found Minnie Darrow unconscious in the dugout at Halfway Halt. I suppose that's why I'm feeling drawn to the Kid's old homestead site." That and Sheila's vision, of course, but I doubted Max would list psychic revelation as a reason to roust one's self out in the middle of the night to go look for someone. "I know it would be a huge coincidence to find him there, but I need to look, anyway."

He reached over and took my hand. "You have to promise me you'll take it easy, Thea. A concussion, even a light one, can be serious. I should be shot for bringing you out here. Tell me if you're getting tired or sick. I can do the hard work, okay?"

I reassured him on that point. I had no intention of going back to the hospital.

"You know, Max," I said, "I keep thinking about the trips Phoebe and I took to the Kid's place, and wondering what his real agenda was. Certainly, in both cases, more than just a nostalgic look-see at his old home. Do you know how long he's been in Rawhide?"

"Not much more than two weeks, three at the most. He'd just hit town when I called you."

"I'm pretty sure he hadn't been to the country before Phoebe took him. As far as his trip with me, I think he fully intended to get his jade, with or without my help."

"Then maybe the first trip with Phoebe was a reconnaissance," Max offered, "to see if his cache was still in place. He must have been straining at the bit, wondering, after forty years."

"I think he searched the house, too. Must have had stuff there, too."

"Why?"

"Because the door was freshly jimmied."

"Wouldn't he have had a key?"

"Maybe not. Florie probably has the keys. He might not have wanted to ask her for them, or didn't want her to know he was going to the ranch."

He shrugged. "Or maybe he simply forgot he might need a way to get in the house."

"Right. I don't think he'd have any qualms about stealing a key if he knew where it was. I have a hunch that if we ever find him he'll have the missing key to Madam Juju in his pocket. Anyway, he either found or didn't find what he hid in the house. We know he retrieved at least one piece of jade that was buried: the vase. And," I added, "he probably also discov-

ered that digging is a lot of hard work and he didn't have the
strength to do it himself. Which is why he got me to take him
to the country the next day. Grunt labor."

"Okay, but the crucial point is: what happened after the
Kid and Phoebe got back to Racy Ladies?"

"I don't know." I felt certain about the first part of the
scenario, but beyond that there were too many unknowns. "I
think he'd hide the jade, out of habit, if nothing else," I said,
trying to think it through logically. "Madam Juju wasn't occupied, so he stuck the vase in there. But when Phoebe gets
murdered, he figures he'll be the prime suspect and is afraid
the police will find the jade when they search the house. So
he takes the risk of sneaking in our room, gets the vase, planning to hide it Kate's room when he gets a chance."

We turned off the highway onto the county road. Jets of
dust from the vehicles in front of us roiled in the headlights.
Max adjusted his speed slightly. "You know," he said, after a
moment, "it's not a crime to have a piece of jade in your
possession."

"Umm." Even in the closed cab the bite of dust stung my
nostrils. "Unless you have the Kid's reputation, maybe."

"Even so, what could be proved? Who could identify a
piece of rough jade that was stolen forty or more years ago
from someone who is dead now? It's a rock, for God's sake.
Don't they say possession is nine-tenths of the law?"

"Two of the pieces, the vase and Buddha's Fingers, might
be identifiable. The O'Donnals could have photographs if
both pieces belonged to them. That could establish a claim,
couldn't it?"

"I'd think so." Max concentrated on his driving and the
radio, then gave me a long considering look. "I know you've
developed a fondness for the Kid, Thea, but there's another

way to look at what happened between him and Phoebe. Here's my take on it: Whatever the Kid does with the vase when they get back to Racy Ladies, Phoebe decides on a bit of larceny herself; a lot of people think old folks are fair game. But the Kid—a hardened criminal, Thea, regardless of his age and colorful background—is nobody to mess with. The Kid discovers the vase is gone, suspects Phoebe of double-crossing him, or whatever it is that crooks think, and kills her. Then hides the vase in Madame Juju as you said."

"I'm trying to keep an open mind, Max, but I still don't think the Kid could have killed Phoebe. But Phoebe *was* sparkling with excitement about something she wanted to show me. Do you suppose it could have been the vase? Why would she steal it, Max?"

He shrugged. "Giving her the benefit of the doubt, she might not have intended to keep it, just wanted to find out what it was and its worth. Particularly if she knew it was the Kid's long-hidden treasure. You said she was hot after a story."

"I just wish we knew where she went that night and what happened to her before I found her on the porch."

"Did she say anything to anybody?"

Max drove at top speed, sending the pickup flying over the graveled ruts of the road, throwing dust on those who followed behind us. I held my breath as he swung wide around a flat-bed truck carrying a backhoe.

"She might have told Garland Caldwell; she was talking to him before she left Racy Ladies," I said, trying to remember. "She was full of herself, believe me. Flirting and putting the moves on Garland, big time. His wife was furious. Phoebe didn't stay for dinner at Racy Ladies. She had already left when I came back down to the lobby at eight o'clock to wait for Jimmy."

"Chin?" Max asked with a raised eyebrow.

"Yes. He took me to dinner at The Lotus Cafe. That's how I met his aunt and uncle, Patrick and Auntie Lee. Tell me about Jimmy, Max. What does he do? I thought he lived on a ranch, but he said no."

"He's a hell of a steer-roper, I can tell you that. I understand that the Chin, O'Donnal and the other branches of his family are a real close-knit clan. Jimmy's an insurance broker and real estate agent. Handles ranch properties, probably knows all the ranches in the county better than anyone. His family was in business, so he was raised in town, but I know he spends a lot of time out at the ranch helping his cousins, and Buster, too."

"Wait a minute, Max," I broke in. "I know where Phoebe went: the rodeo dance. She told Kendall she'd see him there. He stopped by Racy Ladies to give her a ride, but she'd already gone. We can ask Kendall if he saw her there and who else she might have met."

"The police have probably already asked him, Thea. *We* don't have to figure this out, *they* do."

"I know, but I can't help wondering. Something happened to Phoebe that night other than getting drunk. She could have told someone else about the vase. The wrong person. Maybe that's who murdered her, and was the third person at the Kid's place. He could have gone there the next day to look for more jade, and hidden when the Kid and I got there. After we dug it up he tried to get rid of both the Kid and me, and took off with the jade."

"Possible, possible," Max said considering. "Tell me again why you were so certain the Kid couldn't have killed Phoebe."

"Well, it was this light thing, Max."

Chapter Twenty-Three

Max listened patiently as I told him again about having spoken to the Kid downstairs at about the time when Phoebe was being murdered.

"The killer was still upstairs when I found the body, because between the time I ran downstairs and Rocky ran back up to check on what I'd said—and we're talking about a matter of minutes, maybe even seconds—the light I'd left on in Phoebe's room was turned off."

I'd no sooner spoken the words then my mind began to buzz with reconsiderations. What I'd once thought so sound, now seemed shakier than California. Damn, damn, I thought, I'd even risked my life on my belief of the Kid's innocence. Where had my brain been?

I must have looked like a guppy. "What's the matter?" Max asked.

"I hate to admit it," I said, disgusted with myself, "but my pet theory is unraveling like a poorly knit sweater. It didn't *have* to be the killer who turned the light off, but it still couldn't have been the Kid." A picture of Sheila Rides Horse, gliding swiftly into Phoebe's room to retrieve the Tarot card, popped instantly into my mind. "I didn't think two different people could have been upstairs and not run into each other."

"And now you do?"

"Yes. Chance would have to have had a part in it, but it could have happened." Particularly, I thought, if one of the people involved were Sheila Rides Horse with her psychic impulses.

"So what's your conclusion now?" Max asked.

I sighed. "That you could be right. The Kid could have killed Phoebe. When I met him in the hallway that night, I assumed he was coming back from a last smoke before going to bed, but he could just as easily have been coming from the back staircase, returning from the scene of the crime, as it were. He looked exhausted."

"Then who turned out the light in Phoebe's room?"

"Sheila Rides Horse. I know she took the Tarot card from Phoebe's room, she as much as said so. I just wasn't sure of the timing. She's a psychic, Max. Don't laugh, but I think she sensed something had happened upstairs and went to investigate. She might even have been up there when I discovered Phoebe's body. Anyway, I believe she took the card from Phoebe's room and turned the light off when she left."

"But she didn't kill Phoebe?"

"No."

"Proof?"

I shook my head. "Hunch, instinct."

"Budding psychic?"

"Right." I smiled, glad for his light tone.

"I didn't realize Sheila was involved in this mess, too."

"It's complicated, to say nothing of confusing. I'll tell you all about it, but not now. After we look for the Kid. I guess the truth is that I don't want anyone I know to be a killer. If your speculations were right, Max, and the Kid caught Phoebe stealing from him, he could have been waiting upstairs for her to return, ready to confront her."

"Or ready to kill her. I doubt he'd have gone back downstairs to get a knife from the kitchen. He probably armed himself first."

True, I thought bleakly. I couldn't bear to think about it. Couldn't believe how quickly, how thoughtlessly, I'd let him assume the role of Gramps in my life.

Perceptive as always, Max wrapped his hand over mine and held it. "I'm sorry, Thea. But the Kid is the most likely suspect. I mean, I can see how someone might get steamed because their family got robbed of valuable property forty or fifty years ago, and even want to wreak some revenge on the Kid, but he isn't the one who got hurt. What happened to Phoebe was a vicious, calculated murder by someone who knew exactly where to plunge a knife to cause instant death. The attack on you was no light thing, either. The results could have been just as deadly."

"You think he did that, too."

"I think the chances are likely that he did."

"But what happened to Phoebe at the dance, or afterwards? And where is the Kid now?"

"Lots of unanswered questions." His thumb rubbed the back of my hand tenderly. "But there has to be more to this than just the stolen jade you dug up, Thea. One person killed, another missing, one seriously injured. That's a lot of damage done for—how many pieces did you dig up?"

"Ten, maybe more. Some were quite small. All were top gem quality, according to the Kid."

"Even at that, there doesn't seem to be enough money involved. I don't know anything about the value of rough jade, and I'm sure the market fluctuates with demand, but if each piece were worth a thousand dollars, that would hardly be enough to get the kid set up in the country, if that's what he truly intended to do."

"Oh, Max, I've wondered about that, too. A lot of what he said was his way of manipulating me into doing what he wanted me to do. But poor old Kate has her heart set on 'going home.'"

Max rested his hand against my cheek. "So now you're going to bleed for Madam Juju."

I laughed. "I guess I'm a lost cause."

"I like you that way. Back to the jade. Even if it were worth much more than ten or twelve thousand ..."

"I suspect the real value comes when the stone is turned into a work of art. But I don't think there's a top price for violence, Max. People have been killed for much less."

"Sure, but I don't think we're dealing with stupid kids, here, or crazed drug addicts either. I find it puzzling is all."

The radio crackled, cutting through an excited voice. Max fiddled with the dial and turned the volume up. Even he couldn't understand what was said, but we both picked up on the urgency. He grabbed for the phone, dialed twice unsuccessfully, then finally got through.

"What's going on out there?" He listened for long tense moments. "Damn. This is Max Holman, we're about fifteen miles out, headed your way." He hung up. "That was Brocheck's. Fire's jumped a bunch of breaks. Took them by surprise. They need all the hands they can get."

He contacted the rig again. "You can see it? What in hell

happened? Shut the rig down and get out of there. Don't worry about that. Get the crew out, you don't want to get cut off. We've got a deep enough dirt perimeter; it'll probably burn around us."

Max skidded to a stop and turned the truck around. We had passed the turnoff to Brocheck's ranch and were headed to Corcoran's. "We have to go to Brocheck's first, Thea. I'm sorry. I've never seen anything like this. It's freaky, almost like some goon's out there setting fires."

"I understand, Max. Is the fire closer to Corcoran's now, too?"

"No. It's still north of Buster's place. Look, as soon as we get a chance, we'll go look for the old guy. Okay?"

"I have to, Max, even if he turns out to be a murderer."

Once again we lurched past the flat-bed truck carrying the 'dozer. This time we were going in opposite directions.

"That truck didn't turn in at Brocheck's either," I said.

"They're probably coming at the fire from a different direction. Or they've found a new hot spot."

We went back to the Brocheck turn-off and a few minutes later pulled into the drive in front of Buster's ranch house. It looked like a used car lot. A water tank truck was right behind us. It pulled off to the side and a group of men with two-way radios immediately gathered around the cab.

"Come on," Max said. "Let's see who's inside." He looked longingly at the group around the tanker, but was too polite to turn me loose amongst a group of strangers.

Three women stood at an island in the middle of the kitchen manning a sandwich assembly line. Hildy Gilstrom emptied the contents of a large coffee-maker into an assortment of thermos jugs and prepared to brew another pot.

Hildy looked at me with surprise and suspicion. She

pointed her finger at me and waggled it. "I thought you were in the hospital. You all right?"

"Yes, I'm fine, Hildy."

"Where's Elizabeth?" Max asked.

"In the other room, I believe," Hildy said, prissy with disapproval.

"Someone calling me?" A tall, heavy-set woman bounded energetically into the kitchen. "Max! Good to see you. And is this your sweetheart?" She took my hand, engulfing it between both of hers. "I'm so pleased to meet you."

"Thea, this is Elizabeth Brocheck, Buster's wife."

Elizabeth dropped her voice and turned her back on Hildy. "Have you seen Buster, Max?"

"No, we just got here. Is he out on the fire line?"

"I don't know. I'm worried about him."

"What's going on?"

"I wish I knew." She glanced over her shoulder in the direction of Hildy and drew us farther away. "He's been nervous as a cat, can't sit still. All riled up about Kid Corcoran and this old jade. Lordy, I wish that man had never come back to Rawhide. I'm afraid they're going to do something real stupid."

"They? Who's they?"

"I don't know, but that Hildy Gilstrom is egging Buster on. He's been going to town every night. If he were ten years younger, or twenty," she amended wryly, "I'd think he was having an affair."

The back door swung open again, and more people filed into the kitchen led by the old Chinese couple, Patrick O'Donnal and Auntie Lee. I wondered if Jimmy Chin had come with them.

"Come on in," Elizabeth called, rushing to help the old couple with the load of supplies they carried.

"What's this, Patrick? Are you going to make us some of that marvelous Moo Goo Gai Pan?"

"No. I got the fixin's for Sloppy Joes. These guys are going to need something more than cold sissy sandwiches to tide them over," he said with a cackle, hoping to get a rise from the women slathering mayo on bread, and delighted when he did so.

Elizabeth hooked her arm into Max's and drew us aside again. "I'd appreciate it if you could keep an eye on him, Max. He promised not to go to the fire line, but you know Buster. Thinks he's still a kid."

"I'll do what I can, Elizabeth," Max said. She thanked him and went off to help Patrick get the pots and pans he needed. I noticed that Auntie Lee and Hildy were in a corner talking quietly.

Max turned to me. "I don't know what this is all about, but I'm going outside to see if I can find Buster. Do you want to go with me or stay in here for awhile?"

"I'll stay here and help out for a bit; just keep me posted." Though I didn't say so, there were several things I wanted to pump both Hildy and Auntie Lee about. Max would surely advise keeping my nose out of things, but curiosity is indeed an abiding sin. And incurable.

I wandered over to where Hildy manned the coffeepots. She had to stand on a stool to pour water into the tall pot. "Hi," I said. "Anything I can do to help?"

"Sure. There's two more thermos jugs over there that somebody brought in. Let's get them filled and ready to go."

I squeezed by Auntie Lee, who stood at the counter chopping onions. "Hello," I said. "It's nice to see you again."

She nodded. I grabbed the jugs, and went back to the pots. Auntie Lee eyed the cuts, scrapes and assorted Band-aids on my arms. "Looks like you wrestled a pole cat."

"It felt like it, too," I said with a laugh.

"What happened anyway? Do you remember?"

"I fell into a pile of brush, weeds and stickers," I said, dreading another barrage of questions.

"Before or after the Kid rang your bell and high-tailed it out of town? What were you doing out there with him, anyway?"

I gave her the brief sanitized version without, of course, any mention of jade. I wanted to question her about the price of rough jade, but couldn't think how to do it without rousing her suspicions.

Trying to lead in at a different angle I said, "I was fooled by the jade imitations I saw at the Lotus Café. I thought they were genuine until you told me differently. They're quite beautiful, anyway."

She eyed me with the disdain of a true connoisseur, and made a disparaging noise. "You would not think them beautiful if you had seen the real thing."

"What were the original pieces like?"

"The one called Buddha's Fingers looked much like the replica in the case, but the artistry ..." She shook her head and raised her palms, unable to find the proper words.

"The other piece was a bowl, wasn't it?" I asked.

"I couldn't find anything even close to the original piece," Patrick broke in brusquely, browning chunks of hamburger in a large pot, "so I bought that bowl instead, and the lotus bud. Thought they'd look nice in the restaurant, give it a touch of the old world, but it just made this one"—he jerked his head at his wife—"mad."

"Yes," she said. "Every time I see them I get mad at that Corcoran kid. He stole them right out of my parents' home. Family heirlooms."

"Loot, you mean," Patrick said triumphantly. "You can bet that jade came from the sack of the Imperial Palace."

"You don't know that," Auntie Lee said with a sniff.

"How else would a poor peasant who crossed the ocean to work as a cheap laborer come up with a piece of jade? Ha!" He banged the pot with the wooden spoon he was using.

Hildy rolled her eyes expressively at me and the others and hid a little smile. Evidently the argument was familiar to everyone.

Patrick wasn't finished. "Corcoran stole the jade from us, our relations stole it from the Emperor. What difference does it make? I like my fakes better, anyway."

"What did the other piece look like?" I jumped in again, hoping I wouldn't stir the flames, but needing to know, anyway.

"Ahh," Auntie Lee rhapsodized. "Beautiful, beautiful. A tall green vase with dragon handles. When I was a child I used to stare at the dragons until they seemed to move. I was afraid to touch it. I thought it was alive."

My heart began to thud; the description fit the vase hidden in Kate's room. "It sounds lovely. Do you have pictures of the pieces? I'd love to see them."

She sniffed disdainfully again. "No. Why would you take pictures of jade? You must hold it in your hands, lose yourself in the depths of color, examine the artistry from every angle. The true beauty of jade wouldn't show up in a photograph."

The door opened, accompanied by a burst of wind that riffled everything loose in the room. More people filed in to join us in the crowded kitchen. Florie was among them, lugging another giant coffeepot. She nodded curtly to everyone.

The conversation changed subtly. Hildy and Auntie Lee turned back to their respective jobs. Onions tossed into the old Chinese man's cooking pot sizzled and filled the air with a tantalizing aroma. I wondered where Max was.

"Here," I said to Florie, "let me help you with that." We hefted the coffee-maker onto an open countertop at the far side of the kitchen.

"Thanks," she said, with a timid smile.

"Have you got anything else?"

"A couple of bags by the door." I brought them in. Whether I liked her or not, I thought I owed her some kind of explanation. "I'm sorry about your grandfather, Florie, and if some of the blame for his disappearance rests on me, well, I apologize."

She looked surprised by my words. "Believe me," she said, "I'm sorry if he hurt you. I ... I just haven't handled this situation well. Mom was always so loyal to him, until ... but I hated his guts. I didn't know what to do when he showed up." She began to take sandwich-makings from one of the bags. "Did he go into Mom's old house out there?" she asked, casting a sideways glance at me.

"No, but I had the feeling he'd been in there the day before."

"You think the Zimmerman girl took him to the country, too?"

"I'm pretty sure she did. Why?"

"Did he seem mad about anything?"

"No," I said. At least not until he hit me over the head with a shovel. "Why do you ask?"

For a moment I thought she was going to tell me, then her face closed and she said, "Oh, nothing important. I was just wondering."

The door swung wide again, letting in a group of weary soot-covered fire fighters who collapsed around the large kitchen table. Everyone converged on them, coffee was poured and platters of sandwiches were passed around. Tension tightened every face as talk of the fire bounced around the room.

"It's a bitch. Wind's throwing it across the creeks."

"Took all of Hornby's garden draw."

"Where's the warden?"

"In the air with Kendall Hauser."

"Called in three more counties for help."

The location names meant nothing to me, but the seriousness of the situation couldn't be mistaken. I slipped out the door. I had to find Max.

A powerful yard light softened the black night in a wide area, but cast dark shadows beyond. Car and truck headlights spiked the deeper darkness with moving beacons. The wind whipped my hair, and the acrid smell of smoke stung my nose and eyes. I met Garland and Trish Caldwell a few feet from the door, headed for the house.

"Thea," Garland, said with his usual bonhomie. "What are you doing here? I thought you were in the hospital. We've come to help."

Chapter Twenty-Four

My favorite couple, dressed like Johnny Cash clones in crisp black jeans and dark shirts that probably cost at least sixty dollars apiece.

Trish watched the frenetic activity with sparkling eyes and more enthusiasm than I'd seen in her before. "This is exciting, isn't it? Can you see the fire from here?"

"I hope not," I said, scanning the sky. "That would be too close for me."

Garland said, "When we heard the fire was on Buster Brocheck's land we wanted to help. He's a nice old guy, but I must say I'm surprised to see you here. I heard you had a brush with the ex-con." He shook his head in amazement. "We're not very far from his place, are we? I would have thought you'd want to keep your distance from the old devil."

"He doesn't seem to be much of a threat at this point. He's missing," I said, looking over his shoulder, trying to spot Max.

"Trish, why don't you go along with Thea? I'm going to join the men over there and see what I can do to help."

"I'm sorry," I said quickly. "I have to look for Max. Just

go in the house, Trish, I'm sure they'll have something for you to do."

"I don't want to help in the kitchen. I want to go where the fire is." The perpetual whiner.

And I didn't want to be saddled with either one of them. Rude or not, I turned and left. Let them take care of themselves.

Passing from one knot of people to another, I peered at faces and asked if anyone had seen Max. Trish trailed behind, stopping now and then to talk with people, gathering information much as I was doing. I didn't care what she did as long as I didn't have to babysit her.

Finally I found a woman with a long blond pony tail directing traffic and barking orders into a radio, who pointed me to a barn-sized garage. I found Max there, working with another man on the engine of a tanker truck. "Thanks, Holman," the man said and slammed the hood in place.

Max smiled a welcome and slung his arm across my shoulders while he waited for the man to start the truck. When the engine roared, he gave the guy a high sign and turned to me.

"Hi. You okay? How's the head?"

"I'm fine. Tell me about the fire. I understand it's burning on the Ahchin place."

"It's taking off like sin in a wooded area on the upper end. They're worried about the pastures. Jimmy's sending another crew up there."

"That means the fire's getting closer to Corcoran's too, doesn't it?"

"Closer, yes, but there's no danger. We can still get over to Corcoran's. I offered to take a truckload of guys to the north fire line. It's close to the rig so I'll see if any damage has been done, but I'll be right back. We'll take a quick look for the Kid, then see if Jimmy needs us to pitch in. Okay?"

"How long will it take you?"

"Under an hour."

"Did you find Buster?"

"No, not yet. Nobody seems to know where he is, but I'll keep on checking." We stopped at Max's truck. "Get something to eat and rest for awhile. I'll be back to get you as soon as possible." He gave me a long thorough kiss. "Some vacation this is turning out to be for you."

I watched him drive off to where another crew gathered and begin to load the men and equipment in the back of the truck. I headed to the house.

"Thea," a voice called. Trish. Out of the corner of my eye I saw her standing in the shadows waving. I pretended I didn't hear her and went in the back door.

The kitchen was packed with people. Even more exhausted men and women had returned from a stint on the fire line. Elizabeth Brocheck fussed over them, making sure they got food, directing them to the bathrooms, or a place where they could lie down and rest for awhile. She brightened when she saw me and beckoned me over.

"Did you talk to Max?" she asked. "Has he found Buster?"

"Not yet, but he's got several guys looking for him and they'll let you know as soon as he's located."

"This has been an exhausting day," Elizabeth said, inspecting her crowded kitchen and family room, then gave a little laugh. "I guess it's not even day yet, is it? Grab a cup of coffee, Thea, and a sandwich if you like, and come join me for a minute. I need to put my feet up."

We took our coffee to a large back bedroom kept off-limits by a closed door. She sat on the bed, resting her back against the headboard, and I sat in a small club chair.

"Actually, this has been an exhausting couple of weeks, ever since Kid Corcoran came to town. I don't know when it got out of control." She contemplated her coffee and sipped it slowly. "Buster wasn't at all upset when he first heard the Kid was back. Then all of a sudden jade fever took over, and everybody's out to get revenge for past wrongs."

"I heard stories about the Kid's sins practically the minute I hit town." I said. "I also heard that he might have killed Buster's father. Is that true?"

"Nobody knows. It certainly looked accidental, I know Buster always thought it was, and he's the one who found him. Shortly after Reuben's death the Kid left for California. That was enough to condemn him in a lot of people's eyes. But Buster's a realist. Reuben Brocheck wasn't a very nice man, nothing like Buster, who's a big, kind-hearted, hard-working teddy bear and always has been. Reuben and the Kid grew up together and were partners in a lot of shaky deals, most of them involving jade. Buster's been at peace with his father's death for a long time. Until Hildy got hold of him. I don't know what she's up to, but I wish she'd leave Buster alone."

We drank the rest of our coffee and Elizabeth heaved a big sigh. "Well, she said, "I better get back to work. Thanks for listening to my old-woman's worries."

"My pleasure," I said. "It did feel good to rest a minute."

"I wish you'd lie down here for awhile. I don't know what that doctor was thinking about. He should have at least kept you overnight."

"Thanks, but I feel astonishing well." Which wasn't exactly the truth, but close enough to the mark not to matter.

To my surprise, Trish was hovering close by when we left the bedroom. I introduced her to Elizabeth, saying, "She and her husband are here from Oregon, vacationing." Elizabeth graciously took her under her wing and I slipped away to the kitchen.

"Want to give me a hand?" Hildy asked.

"Sure."

"I've made enough coffee to last me a lifetime, and I'm sick of it. Too damn crowded in here, anyway. A bunch of us are going to take some food to the guys working the Ahchin blaze. We'll take my truck and set up a rest area a ways back from the fire. You can help pack up some food." She handed me a large plastic bag and I began filling it with the sandwiches that two other women handed me.

"I'll go with you," Trish said, appearing beside me again like an evil genie.

"Fine," Hildy said. "Get as many of those spigoted thermos jugs as you can." I could tell Hildy was a born organizer. "Lee can take over the pots here and keep the brew going."

Auntie Lee looked up from where she and her husband were listening to the radio communication. "The fire jumped Blister Creek," she said, a look of shocked disbelief on her face.

"What does that mean?" I asked, alarmed.

"It's jumping around like crazy," Hildy said. "Could be headed this way if they can't get it stopped."

"We'll be burned out," Auntie Lee said.

Patrick O'Donnal clicked his tongue at her reassuringly. "Won't be the first time. The boys are out there, and Jimmy's sending more. They've got Hotshots on their way from Colorado. We'll be all right." He handed me a roasting pan filled with Sloppy Joe filling.

"Let's go," Hildy barked. Everyone pitched in carrying food and boxes of supplies out to Hildy's truck and loading them in the back. I had to admit that Trish did her share of the heavy work and really seemed intent on being helpful. A bunch of men dressed in yellow coveralls jumped in the back of the truck, along with the women balancing the food supplies. Someone else tossed in shovels and a variety of other items.

Jimmy Chin stood by the truck with a radio in each hand. Hildy pulled him aside for a private conversation. Garland Caldwell stood beside him taking it all in with unbridled enthusiasm. Jimmy held the truck's door open for Hildy and gave her directions, listening to the radio at the same time.

"We got a two thousand gallon tanker headed out there," he said, "and some grass units. Be sure everyone has a yellow vest on. Don't get far from your radio."

Garland took the roaster from my hands and passed it to a woman in the truck. Trish and I raced back to the house for another load.

Elizabeth handed me a food carrier and two packages of styrofoam cups. "Tell Max that I've gone with Hildy when he gets here, would you please?" I asked her.

"Oh, dear, do you think you should? Why don't you stay here and help me in the kitchen?"

I was tired of being treated like an invalid. "I'll be fine," I said impatiently. Trish grabbed two loaded food cartons and waited at the door for me. "I'll be with Hildy," I told Elizabeth on my way out.

Elizabeth huffed. "I don't know how safe that will be."

"Thea," Jimmy called, noticing my presence for the first time. I handed the thermos and cups into the truck. "What are you doing out here?"

I went over to speak to him. Garland took Trish's load and handed it to one of the men.

"Max and I came out to help. Is the fire close to where you and I met yesterday?" I asked, still trying to get a fixed idea about its location.

"Not yet, but that's about where Hildy's going to set up. A couple miles west of the old soddy. Don't worry, they'll get the fire under control long before it reaches that spot."

I watched Trish climb into the passenger side of Hildy's truck and nod back to Garland. The truck roared to life.

"I've got to go," I said, turning toward the tail of the truck.

"You going with them?" Jimmy asked. "Where's Max?"

The truck started up.

"Hey, wait for me!" I yelled, jumping for the tailgate, but Garland was in my way. We collided with a thud and he fell to the ground. I swore under my breath and gave him a hand up.

"Sorry," he said. "Did you want to go with them?"

"Yes, that's what I'd planned."

"Well, I'm following in my car. You can go with me."

I felt like Job, and Garland Caldwell was my case of boils. But any ride, I guessed, was better than none.

Jimmy eyed him skeptically. "You're sure you know what you're doing? You got a four-wheel drive?"

Garland said he did, pointing to a Blazer parked a few feet away. I could see fishing gear in the back seat.

Jimmy handed him a small radio. "This is tuned to the fire channel. You can hear and talk to anyone on the frequency. Listen at all times and stick close to Hildy. Stay with her unless a crew leader needs your help."

Elizabeth came out with two more bags of sandwiches, and set them down beside Jimmy. "Send these out with whoever goes next." Jimmy was back on the radio, but pointed to me and Garland, who was backing the Blazer.

She clucked at me with disapproval, but didn't lecture. "If you see Buster, tell him to get his sorry butt back here before he has a heart attack."

She left and I asked Jimmy where the road went that we were going to take.

"It's a private ranch road, but if you follow it long enough it intersects a county road about fifty miles out. You'll take it to the east end of the Ahchin place. There's a left branch that goes to Corcoran's and a right branch that goes to Ahchin's winter pasture. That's where the water trucks are going. Don't take either of the branches, they're rough going and hard to follow at night. Stay on the main track and stop when Hildy stops, and you'll be okay."

Garland opened the Blazer's rear. Two large cartons took up most of the cargo space. I tucked the bags beside them. Jimmy threw in two yellow vests, and we were on our way.

Now that I knew we could get to the Corcoran ranch on this road, I wondered if I could talk Garland into taking me there. All I wanted was a quick chance to look at the dugout and the old barn. If the Kid wasn't there I'd call it quits and leave the search to the sheriff's department.

Garland was quiet, his face dark with concentration as he hurtled ahead trying to catch up with Hildy. Finally, during changes in terrain, we would catch an occasional glimpse of taillights up ahead. I kept my eyes peeled for a left-turning branch, thinking I'd rather misdirect him than ask for a favor. I saw the road just as we were upon it, I opened my mouth to say something when to my surprise the Blazer turned that way. It wasn't a hard left turn, just a veering set of ruts, so it could have been accidental on his part; I said nothing for the moment. The taillights in front of us still popped in and out of view, so we appeared to be going in the right direction. The ruts got deeper and rougher.

Garland grunted. "This road's sure rough."

"Yeah," I agreed, bracing myself against the dash. We careened into a gully, then up over a rise. The lights ahead were closer.

For a moment I thought I was the mistaken one, we must have been on the right road after all. I began to rethink my strategy. The vehicle ahead of us stopped and a few minutes later we pulled into a clearing behind it.

I popped out my door. Garland got out too and approached the truck ahead of us, a flat bed truck with a winch. "I'll get the vests and stuff," I said going around to the back. I opened the hatch and pulled out the yellow vests. One caught on something and I gave it a jerk that brought something else along with it. A small purse of some sort, with a thin strap that looked strangely familiar. I held it up to the hatch light. It was bright purple—Phoebe's purse.

Chapter Twenty-Five

I looked up. Garland Caldwell stood over me, his face grim.

"This is Phoebe's purse," I said, not quite comprehending what it meant.

"Yeah." He snatched it out of my hand and tossed it back among the supplies. "Come on, let's go." He grabbed my arm. I tried to shake off his hold, but his fingers dug in painfully.

"You're hurting me," I yelped indignantly, struggling to pull away from him. "Turn me loose."

"Don't give me trouble and nothing will happen to you." He twisted my arm up behind my back and pushed me forward around the Blazer.

A tall figure stood nervously in the shadows by the truck in front of us, shifting weight from foot to foot. I peered through the darkness and recognized the scraggly hair and missing teeth of the mountain man, Deefy Hammersmith. He fidgeted uncomfortably, not meeting my eyes.

"Get going, Deefy. We've got to move fast, thanks to you, asshole."

"You wanted a diversion, I got you a diversion," he whined like a defiant teenager.

"I wanted the fire north of Brocheck's, you fool, not on this side. Everyone in the damn county is coming here now. We got to be gone before sunrise."

I looked from one to the other, incredulous. "You *set* the fires?"

"Nothing but stupid rubes around here," Garland muttered, pushing me forward again. "Deefy, run that Blazer up the road about half a mile. Blink the lights a couple times, then hot-foot it back as fast as you can. She'll find it; she should be heading this way already. She'll be pissed if she has to walk too far."

Trish, he must be talking about Trish. But my mind whirled with more important questions. "You killed Phoebe?"

"Your little friend lived dangerously. If Corcoran hadn't killed her, I would have." He gave what might have passed for a chuckle at any other time. "In fact, I thought I had. What a surprise you gave me when I saw you hauling her up the stairs." He flashed me the grin that was supposed to make females fall to their knees. "Do you know where that vase is?"

"What vase?"

"The one Phoebe had. She wanted to sell it to me," he said as if it were the most incredulous thing in the world. "It belonged to me in the first place."

"What did you do to her?"

He shrugged. "Flipped a pill in her drink, nudged her with the Blazer. She wanted to meet me at the Legion Hall, so I obliged her."

"But why did you want her dead?"

"Because she was stupid. Don't you be stupid, too."

I stumbled as he propelled me across the uneven ground, but tried to find a landmark of some kind. Anything familiar. How close were we to Corcoran's?

"He didn't know it, but Corcoran did me a favor killing that bitch. Did my work for me. Now you're going to do *his* work for me."

"What are you talking about?

"You're going to show me where his jade is."

"What jade?"

He tightened the twist on my arm. I cried out.

"Remember what I said about being stupid?"

"In the garden," I said, caving instantly, but that stuff was long gone, anyway.

"That's better. Just tell me what you know."

"He had jade buried in the garden at the old house."

"I know about that. I saw you dig it up." He laughed again. "What'd you say to set him off? He sure whacked you a good one. Were you like Phoebe, wanting a piece of the pie?"

"You were in the house," I said, answers and questions bombarding me equally. "What did you do to the Kid? *You* took the jade I dug up."

"Of course I have the jade; do you think I'd let Corcoran con me? We had a deal and he ran out on me. Thought he could cut me out and get off with the whole haul himself. He picked the wrong man. Tell me now, we're running out of time, where's the big stuff? The boulders. The big money items. I've already got a buyer for that five-hundred-pound piece of Imperial."

"I've told you I don't know. Why would he tell me where it is? He tried to kill me. I didn't know he had anything other than what I dug up. Look, Garland," I said, trying for reason, "this is silly. I don't know anything, and what's more, I don't care what you do. You can plow up forty acres for all I care and take everything you find. Just turn me loose."

We both heard someone coming up the trail at the same time. He slapped a hand over my mouth before I could react, but it wasn't a knight in shining armor, just Deefy returned and slightly out of breath.

"About time," Garland growled. "Get me something to tie her hands, and get that 'dozer started up again."

Deefy came back with a roll of duct tape and Garland wrapped my wrists tightly together in front of me. Garland held up a silencing hand, and we heard a car approach. "That'll be Trish," he said. He tossed the tape to Deefy and went to meet the car. "Tape her mouth and feet if she gives you any trouble."

"She tell you where it's at?" Deefy asked.

"Not yet, but she will." His confidence worried me.

"You're wasting your time. How can you be so sure it's on the ranch? I certainly don't know anything about it," I said.

"We know it's out here," Deefy said, "'cause this is where the Kid told me to bring the 'dozer. He hired me, said we'd split everything down the middle if I'd get the equipment and help him get the big stuff out."

Deefy eyed me warily, as if afraid I'd do something—forcing him into action.

"I think you're out of your league, Deefy. How did you get tied up with Caldwell?"

"I was supposed to pick up the Kid at Racy Ladies tonight at eight-thirty. I waited, but he never showed. Me and Caldwell got to talking there, comparing notes, you might say." He scratched his head as if bewildered as to how it had all come about himself. He didn't seem to be too bright. "The Kid screwed us both," he finally said.

"How?" He turned away from me, not wanting to say anything more. But he seemed my best hope. "Come on, tell me. Maybe we can even help each other."

He brightened at that. "He and the Kid were supposed to be partners, but the Kid skipped out on him. Caldwell didn't even know the Kid was an ex-con. Found out by reading a story in a paper."

Phoebe's story. I found some grim humor in the thought of Garland Caldwell intending to do a helpless old man out of everything he had, only to find he'd been out-conned by the granddaddy of them all. What a blow to the ego.

"Took him awhile to track the Kid here, but he did. He's been watching him since. Caldwell told me he seen Corcoran digging up some jade this morning and followed him to an old sod house on the Ahchin place. That was jade he was supposed to share with me, and he was hiding it at the soddy."

"Do you think Caldwell's going to do any better by you?"

He shrugged. "Guys gotta make a living somehow. Money's slim pickin's around here anymore. When we got here tonight with the 'dozer, he took it to the soddy first thing. Thought he'd find the big stuff there, but it wasn't. I didn't do no 'dozing out there myself."

I got the distinct feeling that he was protecting himself from something.

"He killed the Kid, didn't he?" I felt certain there was no chance of finding the Kid alive now.

"I don't know nothing about that."

"Where do you think the Kid is, then?"

"Caldwell said he skipped out again."

"You better start thinking about it. You might be next."

Trish and Garland walked slowly into view, deep in conversation. At sight of them Deefy rushed off in the other direction. I tried to think what my options were, or if I even had any. Most important, I had to find some way to get away.

Deefy still seemed my best bet even if at the moment he was mired in denial. How could anyone with a pet fox not have a soft spot for another helpless creature? Very easily, most likely. Trish didn't bother looking at me. Garland was issuing orders in a low voice, but I caught some of it. "Go straight to Rock Springs. Mail the boxes first thing, don't wait until you get to Denver. I'll meet you as soon as possible." They wandered back toward where the Blazer must have been parked. With Garland's back turned, I moved swiftly in the opposite direction, grabbing a chance to lose myself in the darkness. But Garland was instantly beside me. He punched my injured shoulder with a short, hard jab. I grunted in agony and dropped to my knees.

The 'dozer coughed, sputtered and came to life. Garland jerked me to my feet and pushed me forward.

"I can't help you, Garland," I said through clenched teeth. "You're the one being stupid now." He cracked me across the face with the flat of his hand. I reeled with the blow. Shocking pain raced through my skull.

He grabbed me by the hair, holding my face close to his. "Corcoran's very words were this," he said, giving my head a shake. My eyes went blooey, I couldn't focus. "'She knows; she'll tell the police; finish her off.' But I finished him off instead. He had the nerve to pull a knife on me. When I went back to where I dumped you, you were gone."

He kept shaking my head, emphasizing his words. His contorted face blurred in front of me. All I could think was, the King of Swords, the King of Swords. *Here is the King of Swords. Sheila, I've found him,* I wailed inwardly.

He turned me loose and I dropped to the ground, cradling my head in my bound arms. The pain and dizziness receded, leaving a dull throb. I raised my head carefully, worried about the concussion. I needed all the power my poor brain could summon. My shoulder hurt worse than my head, which seemed like a good sign. I needed to think. I needed time. Max would come looking for me soon; I had to find a way to survive that long.

Garland stood a few feet away watching the approach of the 'dozer. My eyes were so accustomed to the darkness that I could see quite well. We'd moved away from the cluster of trees and suddenly I noticed a rounded hump of ground. The backside of the dugout. We were at the old homestead site. I got to my feet. Garland grabbed my shoulder and pushed me ahead of him into the clearing. Now I could see the faint shadow of the leaning barn, and in a flash of inspiration knew where the Kid had hidden his stash of "big stuff." Or at least, I thought, it made a good enough story to keep Deefy and Garland occupied long enough that I might be able to get away. There was a risk that Garland would kill me as soon as I told him. I had to hope he'd be suspicious enough to wait for proof before getting rid of me. I had no doubt of his ultimate intent.

I would have to run at the first opportunity, I thought, hide in the darkness. I couldn't just tear across the open prairie. If I could I find the soddy, it would offer some protection. I knew the general direction. I could follow the creek bed hidden by the heavy brush. I didn't allow myself to consider how flimsy a plan it was, or how well I could run with my hands tied. No, I thought, pumping myself up, I could do this. He might be the King of Swords, but I was the Queen. His worthy opponent.

The 'dozer lumbered into the clearing. Garland grabbed my shoulder. "Where?"

I didn't want to give in too easily, nor did I want to get hit again. I needed all my faculties. I looked at him sullenly. "Why should I tell you, since you'll just kill me anyway?"

"If you don't tell me, I'll make you wish I had." He raised his fist.

"Wait," I said, swinging my arms up to protect myself. "All right. Don't hit me again." I gave him a dejected slump, hoping he'd think I was completely cowed. I jerked my head toward the old barn, its wooden frame listing nearly to the ground.

He grabbed my chin. "It's empty; I've looked in there, you fool."

"He worked them into the foundation, that's why the damned barn's falling down."

He stared at me. "Shit," he muttered, "I should have thought of that myself." He motioned to Deefy, who got off the 'dozer and followed us to the barn. The boards creaked as Garland pulled at the flopping door.

"To hell with this," Garland said, "just doze this baby over, so we can get to the foundation." Deefy ran back to his machine and roared forward.

I tried to look around without being obvious. Garland still had a grip on my arm. I wanted to pick my spot, position myself for the easiest and most protected getaway. And it had to be soon, before Garland got the idea to bind my feet as well as my hands. The dry creek bed dropped off gradually behind a cluster of small evergreens to one side of the barn. Scraggly, but decently tall scrub and bushes lined both banks. I moved toward it, pretending to get out of the way of the 'dozer. Garland stood close by me watching Deefy position the heavy blade against the boards and put on the power. The boards shimmied. Garland jumped.

"Not that way, you fool," he yelled, dropping my arm, "push them away from the interior." Forgetting me, he ran to the 'dozer, swearing a blue streak. I slipped behind a tree and down into the creek bed, running, scrabbling, bracing myself against the bank with my bound hands to help keep my balance, trying for as much distance as possible while I had the 'dozer covering the noise I made.

I negotiated three bends in the ravine, before silence reigned. I hugged the bank and burrowed into a bunch of scrub, pulling a tumbleweed over me. I couldn't gauge the distance I'd covered, but felt sure I was beyond easy spotting. I buried my head in my arms, gasping for breath, waiting for my racing heart to slow. Silence dropped over me.

I listened intently. In the far distance I could hear a vehicle of some kind. The road and Hildy's rest area crew were tantalizingly close, but could I cross a couple of miles of open prairie without Garland catching me? Other noises, closer, were more disturbing. Garland searching stealthily? Or the wind rattling the weeds? I kept my head down and didn't move.

Then a shout, "It's here!" Deefy, I thought, not too far away. Could I have been right? Was the jade really there? I prayed Garland would be torn between retrieving the jade and his need to find me. The 'dozer started up again. I felt frozen in place, terrified of moving. Where was Garland? Cautiously, I uncovered myself and moved slowly away, expecting to be grabbed instantly. Nothing happened. I moved forward, again sticking close to the bank. If I could just get to the old soddy, I could reconnoiter. Plan what to do next. I moved more slowly now, working my wrists against the tape that bound them as I went, but with no success. Finally I stopped to rest again and chewed on the tape. It was tougher than rawhide and tasted vile. I had to move again. The respite was dandy, but I knew it was only that. Garland was like the duct tape, he wouldn't let me go easily. I'd also reached the point where I had to know where I was. I inched my way up the bank and peered over the top. Nothing looked familiar. I had no idea where in the creek bed I was. I could see a dark blotch up ahead. How far? A football field? I couldn't judge. Could it be the soddy, or just a small rise in the land? Did it matter as long as the direction was right?

Doing nothing seemed like death, so I crawled out. If only I could get my hands undone. There was too much cactus around to try crawling, but I stuck to the shadows and kept low, moving awkwardly toward the dark lump. Fifty yards from whatever it was, I heard a truck start up. Behind me. My heart thumped. Garland. Had he seen me, or was he hunting randomly? I hunched over as far as I could and ran through the darkness.

No lights, just the low rumble of noise coming closer and closer. I dodged behind the mound, stumbled on something and fell flat on my face. My lungs fought for air, every breath burned my throat. I didn't care who was after me. I was done. I couldn't move another inch. My chest heaved, the faint scent of putrescence touched my nostrils. Shakily, I rose to my knees and turned to see what I'd stumbled over.

Chapter Twenty-Six

A body lay sprawled face down a few feet from me. Pale light glimmered off the plastic oxygen hose wrapped tightly around the Kid's neck. I'd stumbled over his oxygen carrier.

I rose with a bone-deep weariness and stood over the body. The Kid had driven his jade here in the Bronco after knocking me out, probably to hide it again, so he wouldn't have to share it with Deefy. Garland had followed him here and killed him. Undoubtedly the jade was in the boxes Trish would mail in Rock Springs.

Garland hadn't even bothered to dispose of the body. One of the Kid's arms stretched out towards me, and at its fingertips lay a knife. The pig-sticker I'd seen the first day I met him. I twisted my bound hands as closely together as possible and clumsily picked the blade up by the handle. "Thank you," I said, refusing to acknowledge the tears that threatened to close my throat.

My sword, I thought triumphantly, wrapping my thumbs and a couple of fingers that reached around the handle as best I could. Not a solid grip, but better than nothing. A sound caught my attention. I froze. It seemed to come from the mound itself. The hair lifted on the back of my neck. I had turned to go inspect what was left of the bulldozed soddy when Garland Caldwell stepped out of the shadows.

Neither of us said anything. The roar of the 'dozer and squeal of the winch rang faintly in the distance. I braced my legs and held my arms low, hoping he couldn't see the knife. The Kid's body was between us. Caldwell would have to step over it to get to me. I backed up a few steps, giving myself plenty of room. Garland might win in the end, but I was prepared to do some damage.

It happened so quickly, I didn't have time to think. He made the step and I raised my arms, swinging them in an arc toward his neck. The knife sliced through the thin shirt at his shoulder, on to his neck and across his cheek and nose. He screamed with surprise and pain, covering his face with his hands. Blood coursed through his fingers. I ran like hell with no idea where I was going.

"Thea," a voice called like a disembodied spirit floating on the wind. "Thea." I glanced around, but could see nothing but an animal of some kind. Terror filled me, but I couldn't stop my forward motion, thinking only of balance, moving my feet across all the hazards. Gradually my pace slowed as my lungs gave out and my legs turned to jelly.

A horse and rider passed by me and pulled to a halt. "Thea." The horse spun and the rider slid off, arms and legs windmilling. "Shit!"

I stopped, panting. Sheila Rides Horse sprawled on the ground. She rolled over and got to her feet. I backed away, looking behind me, skittish as a fawn. Garland was nowhere in sight, but the night was dark and the shadows still deep.

"I heard you call me," Sheila said. Her Indian dress was stained and bedraggled. "I was up at the fire. Nobody would give me a ride so, what the hell, I took this horse. I've fallen off five damn times." She lifted my bound hands and took the knife from my fingers. "What happened?" she asked, slicing carefully through the tape. Tears of relief ran down my face when my hands broke loose. I wiped them away with the back of my hand.

"That's Clover," I said dumbly, staring at the animal.

"You found the King of Swords."

"Yes. We have to get help. Fast."

She seemed to sense I couldn't talk about it yet. "Okay, let's go. Do you know how to ride?"

"No."

"Neither do I. Getting on is the worst part. I have to find a low spot." She led Clover to a washout and he obligingly stood still for her to mount, her leather dress scrunched all the way up her thighs. "Come on, he won't stand still forever. He pretty much does what he wants to do."

I climbed on behind her, holding the awesomely sharp knife carefully out to the side, but unwilling as yet to throw it away.

"Here," Sheila said, taking the knife from my hand. "I guarantee, we will fall off. You'll kill us both with that thing." She sliced a hunk of leather from the bottom of her dress, rolled the blade in it, and gave it back to me. I gripped the leather comfortably. She kicked her heels until the horse moved forward, increasing his pace to a fast, smooth motion that felt like flying. We clung to the horse's rough back with our legs. Sheila had a firm hold on the halter rope and mane, while I clutched her back. We found the road and headed for Brocheck's.

We did well until headlights shone ahead of us. "Hang on," Sheila yelled. "The stops are bad."

She pulled back on the rope and the horse skittered and slowed, tossing his head, twisting. We slid from one side to the other.

"Hang on," She cried again wrapping her arms around the horse's neck. I slid to one side, but saved myself and scootched back on top. Finally, Clover stood still, tossing his head as if it had all been a wonderful game.

Both doors of the pickup burst open. Max jumped from the driver's side and Jimmy Chin from the other.

"Hell, woman," Jimmy bellowed, "what are you doing to my horse?"

Sheila threw her arms up in a victory salute. "I didn't fall off! We're alive!" She turned to me with a big grin. "I guess I'm an Indian after all."

I hugged her, and held out my arms for Max to help me down. His face was dark and dangerous. He set my feet on the ground. But before he could speak I asked, "Did anyone find Buster?"

"No."

"We have to get back to the soddy. Fast. I think he's there."

The four of us climbed into the pickup. Jimmy gave Max directions and we sped through the approaching dawn.

"The Kid's dead," I said, dazed, everything beginning to register into a horrible picture. "Garland Caldwell killed him. They 'dozed the soddy and buried Buster beneath it, but he's alive. I think I killed Garland. I slashed him with my sword."

Chapter Twenty-Seven

We sat around a table in the dining room at Racy Ladies. A closed sign was on the front door. Florie and Rocky, Jimmy Chin, Dwayne, Max and me, and Sheila, or occasionally Sheila. She was serving us dinner, and eating with us as well.

Buster was in the hospital. Garland Caldwell was in jail. Trish was in custody in Rock Springs.

We had reached Buster just in time; exposure and shock were about take their toll. He and Hildy had been dealing with Deefy Hammersmith too, planning and arranging an elaborate search of the countryside—a jade treasure hunt in all the areas the Kid had been known to haunt.

"All legal, Buster assured me," Jimmy said. "They were going to get the proper landowner permits, share the gains, do everything right. They brought Deefy in because he knew the Kid well in the 'fifties and 'sixties, he also knew all the old jade-field stories."

"What Buster didn't know," Dwayne piped in, "was that good old Deefy, always out for a buck, was cutting deals with everybody. Buster caught him and Caldwell 'dozing at the old soddy on the Ahchin place, thinking there might be jade hidden there. When he saw the Kid's body, Caldwell knocked him out and 'dozed the soddy over him, then sent Deefy out to set fires north of Brocheck's, which would draw everyone away from Corcoran's until they were finished. Deefy and the wind screwed that up, too. Let me tell you, old Deefy's singing some pretty songs down to the station, trying to save his butt."

"What saved Buster," Jimmy said, "was the way the sod blocks fell over him, creating lots of air pockets."

"And," Max added, "the fact that Thea heard him moaning."

"I didn't know what it was at the time, or how I made the mental connection." I said. "I'm just glad I did."

"How did Caldwell get involved in all this?" Rocky asked. He shook his head in bewilderment. "He seemed like such a nice guy."

"Yeah, right." Dwayne said with a snort. "Calls himself an import-export dealer. But there's a sheet on him a mile long, every kind of bogus deal you can imagine. Name isn't Caldwell, either. You cut him pretty bad, Thea, but nothing life-threatening."

"I'm glad for that," I said, shuddering at the memory.

"The neck wound was the worst, but all he's moaning about is how you ruined his face. More worried about that than the prospect of spending some years in the pen."

"And you caught him trying to get away with the jade?" Max asked, deftly getting him off the subject.

"They were halfway to Denver. They took what they could get, a six-hundred-pounder and two smaller ones. One of them's the most amazing piece of mutton fat I ever seen. Hildy's out at the old barn now, checking to see if there's any more."

"But who does the jade belong to?" asked Florie, looking nervously around the table.

"I'd think you'd have some kind of claim," Jimmy said. "At least what was found on your land."

Dwayne shoved away from the table and began to pick his teeth. "Yeah, I bet some lawyers will get rich figuring it out."

"But what if it were found in the house?" Florie insisted.

"I'd think it would be yours," Jimmy said. "Why?"

"Go ahead, tell them," Rocky said. "It's been bothering you for years."

"Mother found some rough hidden upstairs in her house, under the floor boards. She sold it and helped Rocky and me buy Racy Ladies. I was scared to death grandpa would find out what we'd done."

"Yeah," Rocky said. "Look what happened to Phoebe Zimmerman."

"I think the Kid thought he had more reason to kill Phoebe than just her stealing the vase from him," I said. I told them about seeing the Kid watching everyone during the cocktail hour at Racy Ladies. "It was the first he knew that Caldwell had tracked him down, and he saw Phoebe talking cozily with him. As paranoid as he was, I'm sure he thought the two were working together against him. That sealed her fate."

I pulled out the box I'd placed beside my chair and put it on the table. "This part," I said to Jimmy Chin, "will give me great pleasure." I took out the green vase with dragon handles and the awesome Fingers of Buddha. I could appreciate the artistry of the piece now, the exquisite detail of the carving, but I'd never look on it again without a chill passing through me.

"Ugh," Sheila said, evidently having a similar reaction. She left the table.

"We've all agreed," I said, indicating the Dunns, and Dwayne, and everyone else involved, "that we had enough verification of ownership to return these pieces to Auntie Lee. Will you do the honors, Jimmy?"

"What? And end the world's longest argument?" But I could tell he was delighted.

"First let me have another look at this beauty," Dwayne said, his hand drawn to the graceful cluster of finger-like fronds. "I've never seen another piece of chicken bone to match this."

"Chicken bone!" I exclaimed.

"Yeah, it's the name of this color of jade. Just like a picked-clean chicken bone. My grandpa found a piece ..."

Max and I lingered over coffee after the others had gone. Sheila came back to refill our cups and sat down with us. She pulled her cards from the pocket of her T-shirt.

"Free reading," she said.

"Oh, Sheila," I said doubtfully. "I not sure that I'll ever want to know what the cards have to say again."

"Shuffle," she said, "and cut."

I did. Max looked on with an amused look of tolerance.

Sheila spread the cards. I was surprised to see as much anxiety on her face as I felt.

"Ah," she said with obvious relief. "The swords are gone. These are happy cards. Love, celebration, renewal." Her voice rose on an exultant note. "A commitment." Even Max leaned forward with interest. "Lots of cups, look at this, and this, and this."

She studied the cards further, then looked at Max sharply. "There are diamonds in your future."

"You bet there are," Max said, squeezing my hand and giving me the full benefit of his smile.

"No," Sheila said. "Not that kind. See, here you are," she pointed quickly. "This is business, money to be made, lots of it. You'll have to proceed with caution. Umm. Some problems, but you'll prevail." She gazed at him wisely. "You like the battles, don't you?"

"Yes," he said. "I guess I do."

"Well, that's in the future. The two of you have some adventures coming, but not for a while." She gathered up the cards. "But now, go have some fun."

"Sheila," I asked before she could leave, "what were the cards telling you?"

"I saw my death. I had a vision warning me to prepare for the journey to the other side. But fate, or whatever it is, intervened; instead of finding the dark-haired man, I took a different path—to help fight the fire. You fought the King instead." She shrugged. "Karma." She tucked the cards into her pocket and went back to the kitchen.

Max pulled me from my chair and into his arms. "I think it's time we started our vacation. What would you like to do first?"

"Can I pick anything I want?"

"Yes, as long as it involves just the two of us, out in the middle of nowhere, without another person in sight."

"Let's go jade-hunting. I read in the book I bought that naked maidens used to walk the streams at moonlight to attract the male nature of jade. And Hildy told me about this spot, way out in the boonies where you can still find ..."